5/22

WITHDRAWN FROM
BROMLEY LIBRARIES

To renew, find us online at:
https://capitadiscovery.co.uk/bromley

Please note: Items from the adult library
may also accrue overdue charges when
borrowed on children's tickets.

About the Author

Jacqueline Roy is a dual-heritage author, born in London to a black Jamaican father and white British mother. After a love of art and stories was passed down to her by her family, she became increasingly aware of the absence of black figures in the books she devoured, and this fuelled her desire to write. In her teenage years she spent time in a psychiatric hospital, where she wrote as much as possible to retain a sense of identity; her novel *The Fat Lady Sings* is inspired by this experience of institutionalization and the treatment of black people with regards to mental illness.

Roy rediscovered a love of learning in her thirties after undertaking a Bachelor's in English and a Master's in Post-colonial Literature. She then became a lecturer in English, specializing in Black Literature and Culture and Creative Writing at Manchester Metropolitan University, where she worked full time for many years, and was a tutor on The Manchester Writing School's MA programme. She has written six books for children and edited her late father's novel *No Black Sparrows*, published posthumously. A second novel for adults will be published in 2022. She now lives in Manchester.

THE FAT LADY SINGS

Jacqueline Roy

With a new introduction by
Bernardine Evaristo

PENGUIN BOOKS

PENGUIN BOOKS

UK | USA | Canada | Ireland | Australia
India | New Zealand | South Africa

Penguin Books is part of the Penguin Random House group of companies
whose addresses can be found at global.penguinrandomhouse.com.

First published by The Women's Press Ltd 2000
First published with a new introduction by Penguin Books 2021

001

Text copyright © Jacqueline Roy, 2000
Introduction copyright © Bernardine Evaristo, 2021

The moral right of the copyright holders has been asserted

Set in 11.6/15pt Fournier MT Std
Typeset by Jouve (UK), Milton Keynes
Printed and bound in Great Britain by Clays Ltd, Elcograf S.p.A.

The authorized representative in the EEA is Penguin Random House Ireland,
Morrison Chambers, 32 Nassau Street, Dublin D02 YH68

A CIP catalogue record for this book is available from the British Library

ISBN: 978-0-241-48269-8

www.greenpenguin.co.uk

In memory of Yasmin Kanji, with love

Introduction

Black Britain: Writing Back is a new series I've curated with my publisher, Hamish Hamilton, at Penguin Random House. Our ambition is to correct historic bias in British publishing and bring a wealth of lost writing back into circulation. While many of us continue to lobby for the publishing industry to become more inclusive and representative of our society, this project looks back to the past in order to resurrect texts that will help reconfigure black British literary history.

The books included in the series are my personal choices, determined by my literary values and how I perceive the cultural context and significance of the books. The series is not to be regarded as an attempt to be definitive or to create a canon. Canons are by their very nature hierarchical and have traditionally been constructed by the prevailing white orthodoxies of academia. Black British writers rarely appear on these reading lists, are rarely taught to new generations of readers and unless they become commercial successes, their legacy very quickly disappears.

My aim is to present a body of work illustrating a variety of preoccupations and genres that offer important and diverse black British perspectives. Good books withstand the test of time, even if they are of their time. I am very excited to introduce these books to new readers who will discover their riches.

The Fat Lady Sings plunges deep inside the hearts and minds of two vulnerable women who have been diagnosed with mental illness. It's the kind of novel where the reader has to relinquish the expectation of a straightforward plot and succumb to the propulsion of its experimentalist, parallel narrative form.

The two women in question are Gloria and Merle, in their fifties and twenties respectively, who are both British with a Caribbean background. It's the nineteen-nineties, they end up in beds next to each other in the ward of a mental hospital and while they get to know each other, we get to know them. Both of them are on medication that numbs their emotions and dulls their minds. We witness their stay in the hospital in real time, present tense, while their back stories emerge in fragments throughout the text. Each woman is afforded her own chapters, alternating, to narrate her story in the first person. We are also introduced to the voices Merle herself hears inside her head. These extra voices provide an externalized running commentary on who she is, what she is doing, what has happened to her, and they increasingly verbally harangue her with huge lashings of vitriolic acid. They tell her she can do nothing right and that everything about her is wrong. Merle is essentially drowning in self-hate. These auditory hallucinations are very real to her although her idea of reality and ours might not correspond.

Gloria's narration is singular and intelligible. She's something of a wisecracker and brings necessary levity to the proceedings.

Her behaviour contravenes the rules of what is considered normal social behaviour, which is why she has been incarcerated. Whether or not a psychiatric ward is the best place for Gloria to be is up to the reader to decide. Notions of rationality and irrationality are always open to interpretation and challenge. What the novel does do is let us in on the causes and manifestations of the women's mental health situations, and we see what happens to people when they find it hard to cope with personal tragedy and grief, when they experience social isolation and unequal relationships, and when past traumas resurface.

Although there are two black women at its core, the novel is not about race or racism, though there are cultural references that make it demographically specific, which is important. There certainly isn't an overt message that they are treated differently on account of their identity, although the novel can be read as an indictment against an ineffective mental health system. The novel exposes the ways the system uses medication to suppress behavioural anomalies enough for them to be released, but the psychiatric care on offer fails to deliver enough useful support to meet the needs of patients grappling with profound issues. That said, there are serious issues in Britain around black people and the mental health system, with high rates of psychosis and detention relative to the size of the demographic. While this is rightly a work of fiction and not a report, it's worth noting this wider context.

Published in 2000 by The Women's Press, this novel passed me by at the time, and I only came across it while researching for this book series. I'm surprised that it didn't come to my attention because I thought I was aware of all the novels being published in the nineties and noughties by black British women, my peers. As with so many books, it seems to have flown under the general radar of the literary world and received little critical attention. Mental health is a less taboo social conversation these days. Its stigma has been reduced and it is more readily and widely acknowledged. Twenty years ago, this was not the case, and I can imagine there would have been some discomfort with reading a novel so overtly and uncompromisingly about black women with mental health issues, and perhaps there was an assumption that it would be a challenging read, rather than enjoyable, surprising, original.

On several levels, this is a novel of daring — thematically, stylistically and, with a lesbian protagonist in one of the women, it breaks with the heteronormative convention of black British writing in the past and even today, with very few exceptions. *The Threshing Floor* (1986) by Barbara Burford was the first collection of short stories published by a black British woman, as far as I know. Its central, eponymous short story, which is actually long enough to be a novella, is also a lesbian story. I used to know Barbara, sadly deceased in 2010, in the nineteen-eighties, when we moved in the same artistic feminist circles. She was a generation older, and certainly much wiser and kinder than my hot-headed self. Originally a poet, *The Threshing Floor*, published by Sheba Feminist Press, was her only sole-authored book. I don't know why she didn't continue to publish because we had lost touch by the end of the eighties, but with so many of my earlier peers producing only one or two books, I am filled with sadness at the thought of all that unfulfilled and, if they did write but didn't or couldn't publish, unshared talent. Fourteen years later, in 1998, Jackie Kay, already well established as a poet and short-story writer, published her first, critically acclaimed novel, *Trumpet* (1998), spanning seventy years of the twentieth century, about the secret life of a woman who lives publicly as a man, and who is in a marriage with another woman.

White British women writers had long written unquestionably queer novels, from Radclyffe Hall's classic *The Well of Loneliness* (1928) onwards. It should be no surprise that both Burford and Roy were published by women's presses in the male-dominated industry of years ago. The Women's Press also published Caeia March's series of lesbian novels, including *The Hide and Seek Files* (1989), an intergenerational and interracial novel with a cross-dressing woman at the heart of it. Even today, there are not many novels that feature lesbian or queer protagonists, of any race.

Most of the black women's novels of the nineties/noughties were bildungsromans. Along with *Trumpet*, Roy's novel is one of the few that stand out in terms of the representation of older female characters.

The title of this novel is taken from the proverb, '*It ain't over till the fat lady sings*', which is understood to mean that we don't know how a situation will resolve itself until it actually does. It is appropriate for a novel that offers no easy resolutions. The reader is taken on a journey and then it's up to them to continue the 'what happens next' in their imagination.

Chapter One

I hear the nurses say they're fetching a new patient so I position myself in the corridor to get the best view. Alex stands beside me and I shoo her away. She wanders to the day room but she soon returns. Don't have the heart to send her off again. Can't see why they let a little girl like her remain on the ward. I ask her age and she tells me she's fifteen. A fifteen-year-old child on a ward full of shouting and swearing and all kinds of sorrow. She's supposed to be on bed rest because she's thin like string and getting thinner all the while. Never seen a black girl have white girl slim disease before. I said it to her once, not right out, and she asked what I meant, but I never told her straight, it seemed too cruel. A nurse sees her standing in the corridor and takes her back to bed. She can't hardly walk from lack of nourishment. It's a shame how this country crushes the youth.

The new patient takes her time to reach the ward. I hear her come long before I see her. She's yelling like a higgler, a whole mix of things, some of it about a baby, some of it about a man named Clyde.

And I tell you this, she is mean like a mongoose with a snake. As she comes through the door, she kicks the male nurse on the shin. I smile at her. Don deserves everything he gets.

They try to calm her. 'Come on love, you're safe here, no one's going to hurt you,' Hilary says, and she tries to sound like she believes it.

She don't behave like she's convinced. She kicks at Don again; as he avoids the blow he's thrown off balance, so he has to let her go. He cusses all the while, even worse than her, fucking this and fucking that, forgetting he should set an example. Before he can catch hold of her, she runs down the corridor. They all chase after her. I put my bet on Hilary, but Louise gets there first. Long-shot Don is miles behind – he needs to give up smoking. But he still has the strength to tackle her when he arrives. Just when Lou and Hilary get it sorted out, he has to play the hero, bring her to her knees. She bites. He bawls. That is the good part.

She is small and thin with hair cropped close to her head. Her dark brown legs are bare even though it's cold like ice and all she has on is a pair of knickers and a grubby vest. I hope it don't shame her later on when she gets back to full consciousness. I look upon her face and for a moment, she looks back at me. I see that she is beautiful.

Don goes to fetch Dr Raines. Three against one but still they have to call up reinforcements. They don't care if she is petrified and in a state of shock. Instead, they get her to the floor and hold her down. Hilary still whispers soothing things but Louise stands over her and waits for Dr Raines to bring the hypodermic needle.

And then he arrives, a big sergeant major, strutting up the corridor like he owns the place. He looks down at the scene and gives his orders out, trying to reach above the sound of the new patient who is wailing fit to bust the walls of Jericho. A diazepam injection, to be followed later by chlorpromazine. No one bothers to be gentle with the needle. There. Now don't you feel a whole lot better dear? Just what the doctor ordered.

'What are you doing, Gloria?'

It's Don. I never saw him sneaking up on me. 'I want to go to the toilet,' I say to him, in my stupid-patient voice.

'Well the toilets aren't round here. You should know that by now.'

'Yes, Buckra,' I reply. Can't help but laugh. He gives this look that says he knows he's missing something but he can't see what it is. All the while, he sucks the bitten finger. He views it as a black thing, a savage thing, I see it in his eye. All the time they just keep on provoking us. Then when we strike back, it proves all the prejudice they carry in their hearts.

'Go on, get off to the toilet then. Or go to the day room. Just don't hang around here. What's going on with another patient is no concern of yours.'

I go a little way up the corridor. Then I turn back to look. Dr Raines disappears into his office at the bottom of the ward. The nurses haul up the new patient and heave her to the dormitory. All attention is on her. The other patients huddle up in rows, scared but excited by the scene.

There is sudden quiet. In the upheaval no one thinks to check on me. I open up the door so soft that no one even turns. In a moment I'm off the ward, in the main building of the hospital. All kinds of patients here, not just the mental ones: legs and arms bandaged up and hands encased in plaster. I start to drag my leg, like it's my hip not my heart that's hurting. And slow, like I have the right to do it, I walk into the open air and through the iron gate.

It's raining outside and I don't have no coat, so I wrap my arms around me to keep warm. Funny thing that – big as I am, I still feel the cold. Everyone in the street is dressed in winter clothes or has umbrellas up, so I stand out. Wish I never worn my red and purple frock.

I am tempted to run, but this will make me stand out more. Maybe Don is coming after me, or Lou. I look around all furtive, but there is no one to be seen. Looks like I'm going to make it after all. But no, I forgot – change of shift. The afternoon crew are walking up the road, not together, no, that would be too easy. In a little line, one by one, so I know I have to dodge each one of them. I think fast, run back through the gate and hide behind the bins. I wrap my dress around me so it don't billow out and give the game away. Can't help but laugh. I can see myself, a fat old black woman, with a bright coloured frock pulled up round her knees, creeping round the bins, ducking and diving like a twelve-year-old about to be caught smoking in the bike shed. I would say how the mighty have fallen, but I never been mighty in my life unless you talk in terms of width. Feeling rather foolish now, so as soon as it seems safe, I emerge, shamefaced, I have to say, but at least I'm off the ward and free.

I go to the bus stop and find my luck is in. As soon as I arrive,

4

the bus pulls up. I pay my fare with the loose change in my pocket and sit on the top deck. Always used to sit upstairs with Josie. As the bus moves slow I watch the passers-by. The world goes on the same, as if Josie's still alive and nothing's changed. Everywhere I look, the future stares me in the face. Billboards. Hoardings. All about tomorrow. But the funny thing is, since I got put in hospital, it's as if time has stopped and the future's been squeezed out of me. It's all past and present now, as if the future don't exist.

I never smoked in the whole of my life, but lately I been thinking I should take it up. The back seat of the bus is just the place, and as far as I can see, no one ever stops you or makes you pay the fine. Getting rebellious in my old age. Shame it took so long.

Seeing as I have no cigarettes to hand, I eat some chocolate. Always keep some in my pocket in case of an emergency. If I was rich, I'd eat twelve bars a day and forget about my teeth.

I'm going home. Just the thought is enough to make me want to sing. But singing is what caused me all this trouble in the first place and got me on the ward, so I suck my lips and try to keep the sound from bursting out. Can't help it though. The sound fills up the bus. Soon I am singing like I never sung before. The other passengers take one look at me and make themselves go thin in their seat, like they don't exist. They don't want me to trouble them. They don't want to talk to some mad old woman with a dark complexion, oh dear no. Eyes down. Lips pursed tight. A few tut-tuts from the front seat. I have to get off before my stop — too much pointing. The conductor threatens to summon the police. If they stop me now, it will be straight back to the hospital. I'm on a section, not allowed to leave the ward. It's a legal thing.

Still cold, even though it's only October and the rain has almost ceased. I hurry past the corner shop and walk across the common by the railway track. It's nearly dinner time now, so the area is deserted; just a few ducks sitting on the pond and a dog or two sniffing through the undergrowth, so I can sing all I want. I raise up my voice and let it ring out. Josie always liked to hear me sing.

Funny to think that singing is the crime that fetched me into hospital. It happened like this: I have trouble getting off to sleep. Been a long time now, since Josie died. In the time between going to bed and getting up again, I get so full of energy that I can't close my eyes. So in the night, when other people sleep, I behave like it is day. And all the songs get sung and all the chores get done and I hoover up the place and tidy it and try to exercise myself, because when it is night and the world is asleep and you is the only one awake, it feels so lonely that you have to fill up time, make it go fast, be on the move so all the sorrow can't catch up with you. And this is what I did. Every night. And eventually, all the people started to complain because they wanted to get off to sleep and they said I was stopping them by playing music loud and singing all my songs. And I don't know how it happened, but one white woman got so vexed that she called the police. And in the middle of my ironing, they came and mashed down the door and turned off the tapes and said I was disturbing up the peace. What peace? I said. The world is not a peaceful place. This is the time of doom and gloom and all kinds of disaster. And the police arrested me and said I had to leave the house and go down to the station and I thought of leaving all of Josie's things and the music that she gave me and I thought of Emilie coming in again and stealing all the ornaments we had and I knew I couldn't go, so I started to shout and say I had to stay and as they pulled me to the door I smacked this policeman on the nose, not because I meant to damage him but because his nose got in the way as I was fighting to remain where I belonged. In my own house. So they got me to a prison cell and somebody recalled I was arrested just the other day in the Arndale Centre for stealing hats and they began to think I was not right in my mind so they called a doctor and he talked to me and I tried to make him understand that there can't be any peace because of all the troubles in this world and all the singing that I do stops the sorrow eating up my heart and the doctor talked a while and then he said I have to have a rest inside a hospital. So that is just to bring you up to date. And now I have to think if I got my front door key, or if I left it in my other frock back on the ward. But no, it's OK, I have it safe.

It's a great relief to see the house just the same as when I left, except the plants have died from lack of water, but I was expecting that. I put on some music, but I play it soft. It's Josie's favourite: Nina Simone and 'I Wish I Knew How it Would Feel to be Free'. I go into the kitchen and open the fridge but there is nothing there to speak of. The cheese has mould and the chocolate's too damp, so it's turned patchy-white and filmy. Just my luck. Still, I find some biscuits in the cupboard and I make myself a cup of strong black coffee. Can't seem to rouse myself to go to the shop and fetch milk.

The main thing I miss through being on the ward is the quiet you have at home. Funny for me to say this when I got put in there because of all the noise I made. But there is no happy sound on Ward C. Keys always jangling about as the nurses open up and close the doors. Young ones crying to go home. This is the kind of sound you try hard to shut out. The sounds I like are the ones you can rejoice in, the sounds that move the soul. That's the difference. And the other thing I miss is a nice clean toilet and a shower you can use without ending up with more dirt on you than you started with. So I go upstairs and decide to have a bath because to sit and wallow in the tub without some nurse banging on the door and asking if you have permission is a very pleasant thing. I put in scented oil, part of a set Josie give me for my fifty-third birthday. It's lasted more than two years now because I always save it up for best.

We done the bathroom up in blue, like the ocean. Josie got posters from the travel agent when we booked the holiday we never got to take. The Blue Mountains and the usual palm tree on the beach. When I was a child and we first arrived, English people always asking why did you come to such a cold, wet place? Don't Jamaica have everything you need?

Hard to explain to people who don't know how it feels to go without. I don't mean not having luxury. I mean not having anything. When my dad came here, he thought he had arrived. He believed the advertisements. *England needs you.* And he had the spirit of adventure. See the mother country, work hard, make a little money. Then go home. Didn't turn out that way, of course.

It feels so good to wash away the dirt of the ward. For the first time in days, it's like I'm in my true body again, even though I'm still feeling the effects of all the medication. The music plays downstairs. I pressed the continue button so the tape will keep on going.

Just as I finish getting dry and putting on the talc, the phone rings. It rings and rings, so in the end, I pick it up.

'Gloria?'

'Yes. Who is calling, please?'

'It's Louise Johnson, from Ward C.'

Lou. Should have let it ring.

'Gloria? Are you still there?'

'Still here.'

'You have to come back to the ward.'

'I'm back home now. Don't have to do nothing I don't want to do.'

'No, Gloria, it doesn't matter where you are, you're still under section and we want you back here. I'm giving you the chance to return under your own steam, but if we don't see you back in half an hour, we'll have to tell the police. They won't take no for an answer.'

'No need to call them.'

'We have called them. We have to let them know whenever a patient on a section absconds. But I've asked them to wait a bit and let you come back on your own. It's up to you.'

'Not hurting anyone for me to be here.'

'You're playing music. I can hear it.'

'Not loud.'

'Loud enough. Your neighbours will be up in arms again.'

'If I was white you'd let me play my music, but if anybody black makes a noise, everyone gets scared there's going to be a riot.'

Louise sighs. 'It's not about anything like that, Gloria. We're

9

concerned about you, that's all. Apart from anything else, you haven't had your medication.'

'Don't need no medication.'

'I don't want to get into that with you now. Just come back right away, OK? Otherwise, I'll have to ask the police to escort you. Is that clear?'

I don't answer her. I just put down the phone. I suppose I'll have to go back. Can't go through all that police stuff again. Feel fit to bawl.

At least I got to see the house again. At least I got to have a bath. I fetch an old bag and put some stuff in it: more underwear, the biscuits from the cupboard, Josie's photograph in a guilt-edge frame. Wonder why they call it guilt? Perhaps it is because you have the most photos of people who have died and guilt is part of grieving, I heard someone say. Might have been that Oprah Winfrey. Or the good-looking one with the bedside manner, forget his name now.

I look around the house one last time. Anything could happen to it while I'm gone. That's the trouble with being on your own.

There is a little welcoming committee of Don and Louise when I return to the ward, but I don't mind them, I just keep on walking to my bed. Alex has a visitor, her father, I would say, and he looks at me like he's picked me up on the sole of his shoe. I'm used to taking this from the white people who come to the ward, but this is a black man and he should know better. I glare at him and start to sing real loud because I know that it will vex him so to hear it.

The new one has been put in next to me. She starts to wake.

She looks so lost, like she's in a daze. I lean across her bed. 'How you doing now?'

She gives some reply but her voice is thick and I can't make it out.

'All right, you'll be OK, it's just the medication. Go back to sleep.' I take her hand. She is afraid, I see it in her eyes. I know her head aches and her limbs feel heavy from the dose of medication she got. Her mouth feels dry like parchment and her whole body shakes, from her tongue to her toes. She is young. And she was brought here on her own. No one to speak for her. 'It's all right,' I say to her again. 'Go to sleep now. You'll feel better if you sleep.'

She starts to shut her eyes but she wakes herself up again with a little jump. She don't dare let go, not even for a moment. I try to tell her she is safe with me, but I don't get through to her. There is a whole mess of confusion in her head and she starts to drift off where no one else can go. 'What happened to you?' I ask, but she can't hear to answer me. The nurses come, and see the state of her. They think she got a bad reaction to the medication. Her body's stiff, and except for the little jumps she gives every now and then, she is still like she can't even breathe. Then all of a sudden she starts to wail again, a terrible kind of wailing and she says I'm an angel come to take her to the Lord. I try to comfort her but she don't seem to feel it, she just sobs from the soul, louder and louder, and there is nothing I can do to stop the sound.

Chapter Two

In the darkness, I hear them talking over me. I try to move, but my body is leaden, it's been that way since the last medication. I'm sleepy but I dare not close my eyes.

'She hasn't moved in hours. We should call Dr Raines.'

'He'll have gone by now. We need the duty doctor. How much chlorpromazine did you give her?'

'Only what was written up. You were with me. Just the normal dose.'

'She must be having a reaction. Get someone here now. Tell them it's urgent.'

There is an angel standing by my bed, a dark angel, full of light. She raises her voice in song. As she touches my arm, I know it's the time of dying. I strive to breathe but I can't take in air. It occurs each time I try to sleep and again as I awake. It's the baby inside me. She's fighting to be born, and in her struggle she kicks up towards my chest, pounding at my lungs, her arms reaching for my throat.

'When did she come in?'

'Last night. Sometime last night, I think. I wasn't here.'

'It's all right, the doctor's coming. Try to breathe. Just breathe.'

The baby stops. I fill the room with wailing, a cacophony of her sounds and mine.

'Stop that. Come on, stop it now. Can you hear me? Do you know where you are?'

She knows. She's hiding inside herself; the way she always does. Screening out the things she doesn't want to see. She let them bring her in. She didn't have to come. All she had to do was behave herself. But she let things slide. She should have known what would happen if she didn't take proper care of herself. She thought that all she had to do was hide and the bad things inside her would start to go away again.

I remain curled up behind the sofa. It seems safer there. A line of light pushes through the gap between the curtains. I lie completely still, scared that if I move, the day will come too fast and everything will slip away from me. I listen for Clyde, but I can tell by the depth of the silence that I am still alone. I need him here to tell me what to do. He's my interpreter. He explains the world to me, gives it shape and definition.

He left because of what she is. She'll always be alone.

I hear the stirrings of the neighbours as they begin to rise. A child screams for its mother and a father's feet thud as he hurries down the hall.

What separates her from them? A door. A wall. Noise knows different boundaries. Noise escapes. Are you listening? I've got inside of you. Look at her now. Trying hard not to hear. She maps their progress through the hours of the morning, tracking them across their floor. She's aware of the sound of running water as they brush their teeth. She hasn't cleaned herself. Not for days. The smell of her. The repeated slamming of the door. Boom bang, boom bang, the sound is inside you now. One by one they leave the house. She wants to absorb the normal things. What is normal then? Does she know? Do you know what normal is?

When the sounds stop, I am afraid again.

She's starting to move. The stiffness of her neck and the dull pain in her back prompt her legs and arms to jerk before she can control them. She wasn't told to move.

I shake my head rapidly, but I can't shut out the words. I become aware of the cold. Since Clyde left, there's been no warmth. When he held me in his arms it hurt, but I want to feel his touch again, the warmth of his breath on my face.

She wants him inside of her, that's all she wants.

I imagine spending forever alone, and I am swallowed by the emptiness. I ease myself out of the space behind the sofa and stumble into the kitchen.

Not in there. You can't go in there. She never listens.

The door of the fridge is open; water pools on the floor.

She is kneeling now. Running her fingers through the water, checking that it's real. Clyde's note has fallen from the magnet holder. It shrivels in the wet.

I remember what it said: 'I need some time to think. I am going away. It's for the best.' I keep going over it, trying to find an explanation in the words. He didn't say forever. He didn't say he wasn't coming back. I try to read the note again but nothing discernible remains, just a blur of squiggles on a sodden page. I want to clear away the mess, but I don't know how; there is a gap between the wish to act and the ability to do so.

Always an excuse. She never gets things done. She sits around for hours, doing nothing.

I sit at the table. The kitchen walls are vivid blue, not the colour I remember. Technicolour walls, like an early colour movie. Ceiling to floor. Hard blue. Where are the edges to things? All the joins have gone to make a seamless space, world without end. The dishes are still piled in the sink. I catch the smell of sour milk. It makes me heave.

Touch your breasts, go on. Feel the softness of them.

My body doesn't belong to me. Hard not soft. No softness here. I need to go to the bathroom.

She mustn't go up there. She's not allowed to go.

I find a silver foil tray. Hunching myself over it, I pee inside, some of the wetness trickling down my thighs.

She's wetting herself. She smells. What a dirty girl. She's crawling towards the kitchen table, crouching beneath it, still trying to make herself safe. No safety any more, not for her. She kneels, one foot trapped inside her jeans. She's pulling them off off off and trying to make the stillness come

but all around me, shapes and sounds are twisting into one another.

She is crossing her arms around her belly, feeling its flatness. Where's the baby now? The phone is ringing. She mustn't pick it up.

It will be Clyde. I want to answer, but I know I have to let it ring. Perhaps it's Mr Bevington, calling to ask me why I haven't been to work. How long have I been away? The oven will be thick with grease. No one but me ever thinks to clean it. It's stopped. I should have answered it. I should have told him I was sick.

She's going over her speech: 'I'm sorry, Mr Bevington, I'm ill, I won't be in today.' What if he'd asked what the illness was? How would she have explained it? They wouldn't have believed her anyway, they never believe anyone, least of all her . . .

even though I've only been off ten days in my whole working life, struggling in through bouts of flu and stomach cramps so bad that I could barely stand. If only Clyde was here. He could have phoned for me. He could have made them believe I wasn't fit enough for work, he can make anyone believe anything. Where is he now?

In the woman's bed, his hand between her thighs, loving her with his mouth.

No.

Yes, oh yes. On the day of his departure, she heard the front door slam and found the note minutes after he'd gone. She ran down the road after him. She caught hold of the back of his jacket, too desperate to care that everyone was watching her.

'Why are you going away?' I whispered to him, tugging at the leather seam.
'You don't know how to behave any more.'
'What do you mean?'
'You know what I'm saying to you.'

There was regret in his voice. She forced him into saying it.

He looked at me for a moment and then he turned, striding off into the distance. I hurried after him.

'What do you mean, Clyde?' I called out.

'You know what I mean,' he said again, without looking back.

She knows.

But I don't know. How do other women behave? What is it that I do that's different?

She is not like other women. She has been marked out. Can you see it now?

I move towards the wall, and slowly I become aware of a single beam of light, shining its way towards me. It circles round me twice, then a third time. The strangeness of it frightens me.

She sits on her heels, trying to pick out a face but all she sees are molecules of light.

They begin to dazzle me.

She has been marked out.

Stained.

Chosen. A black semi-virgin, primed to bear the daughter for the second coming. She'll feel the stirrings of pleasure again, the kind she can only just remember from her teenage fumblings with boys. Oh yes, she let them touch her. Whatever else she tells you.

My body isn't mine. They've taken mine away from me.

It lasts a fleeting moment, the usual way of things. When it's over, the emptiness returns. She crawls back to the living room, behind the sofa once again, knickers to her ankles, stinging round her inner thighs, the badness oozing out of her. How much time has passed? She has no sense of time, no rhythm in her.

Time isn't going forwards in a line, it's moving round in circles and all the time I was living in my future and the child's already born, she's somewhere in the house, safely hidden where she won't be found.

She thinks she hears it cry. Watch her kick her knickers from her ankles and run to the bottom of the stairs. She stands and listens but she never hears.

The sound stops. I feel the strangeness of noise replaced by eerie silence. I go through each room, but all's returned to nothingness.

The door bell rings. Ringing and knocking, knocking and ringing over and over again. The flap of the letter box goes up. Someone peers through.

'Hello. Are you all right?'
I don't recognize the eyes. They are a dull shade of blue. I go up close, trying to figure out if the Devil's here again, or an Angel of God. 'Where's the baby?' someone says. The words don't

sound like mine, they seem to come from somewhere in my belly, guttural and round.

'Are you all right?' the voice repeats. It says my name. I know the name is mine, but it doesn't belong to me any more. Who knows it? Who knows to ask if everything is still all right? Not the Devil, no. 'Have you brought the baby back?'

'I'm from the health centre. Are you going to let me in?'

A bargain is being struck. If I let her in, the child will be returned to me.

'Please, just open up the door. I only want to see if you're all right. We have an appointment, remember?'

She'll have to tidy up before she lets her in. The whole house smells. They'll think there's something wrong with her.

I gather up the cups and dump them in the sink. I stuff a pile of papers behind the armchair. The house is stale. I should have got a freshener.

She must push her fingers through her hair and pat it down. She's running out of time.

I open the door slowly, just enough to let the woman in.
'Hello, I'm Aileen Rose.'

Say nothing. Don't tell her who you are.

The woman looks me up and down. I realize that I haven't

dressed. I have my T-shirt on, but nothing else. My knickers are by the kitchen door where I discarded them. I face the wall and put them on, trying not to let her see that I'm embarrassed. 'I'm OK,' I keep on saying to her, 'I'm just a bit run down.'

Shut your mouth.

'Why don't I go and make us both a cup of tea?' the woman says. 'Have you eaten yet?'

I don't answer her.

The woman finds the kitchen and begins to make some tea.

'Doesn't the kettle work?' she calls.

'You have to use the gas.' I can hear her light it from the living room. It pops. I remember the stack of washing up (and other dirty things besides)

dirty, dirty girl

but everything's unfolding like a dream and I can't make it matter like it should.

She says we should sit down together in the living room and drink the tea. I don't mind. I prefer it here. I like to see the sunshine sparkle through the glass. The light of other worlds shimmers by my head, making me pure again.

The woman says, 'You seem to be in some distress at the moment. Can you tell me what's going on for you right now?'

'No.'

'No?'

'Not distress.'

'How would you describe it then?'

'I don't know.'

The face of an angel is peering through the window. Coloured light.
Distended shapes melded into sound

like nothing I've ever seen before. So I stand up and say 'I have
to let it in.'

'Let what in?'

I stretch across and fling the window up but it has disappeared
again.

The woman shivers. 'It's very cold in here. It's dark too. Don't
you want to switch on the light?'

I sit on the floor and say 'We got cut off. He didn't pay the bill.
He always used to pay them before. He always said that it was
what men do.'

'Your husband? Where is he at the moment?'

'I don't know.'

'All right, don't worry, I'll ring the electricity people, try to get
it sorted out.'

She starts to drink her tea. I can feel her watching all the time,
trying to see if I am made of glass. I stand up. 'I have to go upstairs.'

'What is it that you want to do? Can I come with you?'

I run out of the room. I wait on the landing, listening to see
what she will do, if she will follow me, but there is no sound at all.
I open the bedroom door. It's tidier than the rest of the house
because I've hardly been here since Clyde went, but the bed is

unmade and his jeans are still on the floor where I left them. I've been wearing his things. I like them better than my own. I like the feel of them. The smell. Maybe he'll be back when he has no more clean clothes. He'll want to use the washing machine. He always looks so neat, never scruffy, not like some men are. I open the wardrobe. If I wash his clothes and iron them for his return, when he comes to fetch them, he'll see how much I want him back.

Stupid bitch.

The sound pushes its way in through the top of my head and out again, thinning into air.

A knock. At the bedroom door. The visitor opens it without waiting for an answer. 'I'd like to talk to you about what's happening just now. Shall we go downstairs again?'

I don't want to talk, but I need to know what's going on. Perhaps this woman's part of it, or maybe she's just there to watch. I follow her downstairs and into the living room. She sits in the big armchair, so I place myself on the floor by the door, just outside her line of sight.

'You don't look very comfortable there. Why don't you come and sit on the sofa?'

'I don't want to.'

'OK. Can I sit on the floor with you then?'

'No.'

The woman sighs. Then she says, 'Do you remember the tablets the doctor gave you?'

'Yes.'

'Have you been taking them?'

The tablets are small and blue. Stella something. When I took them, I got the shakes and my tongue felt thick and furry in my mouth. 'I took some of them,' I tell her.

'But you're not taking them now, are you?'

'I took one yesterday.'

'But you haven't had any today. Why don't you go and fetch them? I'll get you a glass of water and you can take one.'

'I don't know where they are.'

Liar. Liar. Liar. Liar,

the words volley back endlessly.

'Is there anyone you could stay with for a while, or someone who could come here to look after you?'

No.

The voice is getting louder now, swallowing my thoughts. I stand up for a moment; being still seems to make it worse. I start walking up and down the room, but the sound still follows me.

'Are you listening?'

'Yes.' How does she know I have to listen to it?

'I'd like him to see you, come and have a talk with you. Is that all right?'

'I don't know.' See who? What does she mean? It's hard to concentrate. 'It's noisy,' I say to her.

'What kind of noise?'

'Too many things are happening. There's too much noise.'

'Tell me about the noise. What is it that you're hearing?'

I want to say it

but she mustn't tell.

'Why don't you tell me?'

I shake my head.

'Why do you keep looking over there, love? Is something happening?'

I can't answer her. I have to concentrate or I won't see where the Devil is.

'What is it, love?'

'Have you got the baby?'

'What baby? Are you thinking about what the doctor told you recently, about not having children? It's all right, it was in your notes.'

'It's here.'

'A baby?'

'It's here.'

Suddenly she's beside me, holding my head. 'No, come on, you'll hurt yourself. Come on. Don't bang yourself.' She sits with me, and makes me very still. I'm not allowed to move.

'I'm just going to make a call, OK?'

The visitor gets out her mobile phone. She begins to speak to somebody.

Stupid bitch. They're putting you in hospital.

'No,' I say out loud, but the woman isn't listening, she's telling them where to come and find me. 'No,' I say again.

The woman puts away the phone. 'We just want to help you, that's all. I think you need a rest, to come into hospital for a little while.'

'No.'

'You don't want to go on being as scared and as upset as this, do you? And I can't let you keep on hurting yourself, it wouldn't be responsible.'

'I'm not.'

'You're banging your head, and your face is scratched.'

'The scratches happened while I was asleep.'

'Well OK, but I think it's a sign that you're not very well at present. We can take away some of the strange things you've been experiencing. They're making you very confused. Think how much better you'd feel if all the noises went away and your thoughts were clear again.'

I am tempted. Part of me wants to let them soothe away the sounds.

No.

The word bangs inside my head. I go behind the sofa again. I sit with my hands covering my ears, my eyes tightly shut. I can feel the presence of the devil-woman but I won't let her in, no, and all the while the child is growing big inside of me, waiting to be born.

Chapter Three

More than an hour goes past before the duty doctor comes to see the new patient. He has to give her an injection to sort out the side effects of the last injection they gave her. She's quiet again now. She's lying on her side, and she stares, but her eyes don't see.

Wish I had my music on the ward to shut out all the sound. I only have a little radio. Don't like to hear the wailing that goes on. Shouldn't have to hear it. Got enough wailing of my own to get done.

Visiting time, so everything is busy. Friends and relatives come in and out of the ward with a nervous look in case the mad axe woman is lurking nearby. Sometimes, out of devilment, I screw up my face until I have pop eyes, a deep frown and a slow, stupid grin that scares everyone like hell. Don wanders past and says, 'Behave yourself, Gloria,' but I don't change the face I have on. Two elderly aunts who approach Mrs Isaac do a double take and decide to pass the new patient's bed instead of mine. Adds at least five seconds to the distance.

It's boring, sitting here on my bed doing nothing but observing all the non-events that happen on the ward. Could be at home in front of my fire, with the telly on. I'd be watching *EastEnders* now with a little drink of rum to get me through the evening.

Wish I had a visitor. No one's come, you know. That is the problem with having only one person in your life. When she goes away from you, it changes everything.

Hilary comes up to me like she smells the isolation I am feeling. 'Why don't you get in touch with your family?' she says. 'Let them know where you are?'

'Don't have no family,' I answer her.

'There must be somebody,' she replies.

This is because she's young and has four brothers and sisters. She can't understand that it's not like this for everyone. So I say to her, 'I had a sister, but she died when I was seven. My mother died before I reached the age of five. My father got ill in 1973 and he's dead and gone now too.'

This is before she was even born but she looks down and says, 'I'm sorry.'

'Thought it would be in my notes.'

Hilary sits beside me. 'I expect it is, but I don't usually read them. It seems best to get to know people first.'

I smile at her because it makes a nice change to be treated like a human being but she's embarrassed by her mistake about my family, so she goes into the kitchen to sort out the drink she has to fix for Alex.

Sometimes I forget I ever had a sister. Her name was Denise and she was two years older than me. When I remember her, I think of the games we used to play. She could skip faster than any other child in the school. She was always picking on me because I was the slow one in the family. She would have got a scholarship, my father used to say, to some big school in England where they wear panama hats and white gloves all year round and speak in a soft voice without moving the lips. She took sick back home so she never got to see the mother country. Funny phrase, that. Britain gives the kind of mothering that would fetch the social workers in.

Sometimes, just before I fall asleep, I remember walking through the streets to school, holding my father's hand as tight as tight can be and jumping over the pavement cracks in case I saw a bear. They had few single mothers at that time, and never single fathers. He was not like other people. He never bothered following the crowd. He was a clever man who never got to use the gifts he had. I was never clever like him or Denise. I was in the remedial class. They couldn't understand the way I talked so I had to learn proper English but I never bothered learning right. You have to hold on to your true-true self in this country, no matter what they do to you. But I lost most of my Jamaica talk, you know, and picked up the English way with words. Couldn't help myself. This is what happens when you live in a place too long.

My father learnt to speak the best English he could get because he thought that speaking Patwah held us back, but even when his words sounded better than a BBC announcer, he still couldn't get no decent job, he still had to work in a factory making brillo pads. So I think education is not for black people. Don't matter how we try. And I don't care about 1066 or the Great Fire of London, or dancing daffodils, so I never applied myself to learning. All my school reports said the same thing. *Gloria does not apply herself.* Never forgotten that.

It depressed my father, but he never said much. He was always patient with me, even when I brought such disappointment to him. When I met Josie and everybody said it was a sin, he stood by me and told everyone it's not important who you love it's the loving itself that counts. We went away when he died because it got too hard to stay. He'd be disappointed now, that I finished up in a place like this. You have to fight, he always said, but not with fists, with your attitude to life. Rise above it, that was my father's favourite saying. He believed that one day we'll be important in this world, as a people, because we are so strong. We've got through all the different trials and tribulations we had to face and still we survived. But I'm not so sure. And I am tired of rising above all the rubbish that we have to deal with. Don't have the strength to do it no more.

The new patient is still sleeping on her bed. Sometimes, when I look at her, it's as if I'm a young girl again. She looks like me, you know. Wasn't always fat. Had a slim figure once, but I done a lot of eating since. Nothing wrong with that. Pity this don't get through to Alex.

Hilary comes back in again and she talks to the new patient. 'Do you remember I told you that you have to have a medical? It's been really hectic today and we couldn't fit it in but we'll make sure it gets done tomorrow.'

The new patient don't say a word. Don't know if she even hears. 'Keep an eye on her, will you, Gloria?' Hilary says to me, and she leaves the dormitory. What do they think? That I'm an unpaid nurse now? That I have to do their job for them? All I know is, I am tired of taking care of things. Sick to death of it and that is the truth. The energy I have goes in all the wrong directions. Got none to spare. Can't even take care of myself these days, let alone another body. They should realize that. But as she lies there on the bed, so still and sad, I know I have to stay with her and watch and keep her company, because feeling alone in this bad world eats into your bones.

Chapter Four

'We have to give you a medical examination on admission. It's nothing to be frightened of. It's just routine.'

Fingers probing her. Feeling out the things she tries to hide. She makes her body small, forcing it into the space between the bedstead and the bedside cabinet. She thinks she can disguise herself. The doctor's face contorts. He should not have touched her, not even with his glove. Her dirtiness contaminates. When can she go home? When she's clean enough. They look inside her head but they find

nothing inside of me.

She's crying again. Look at her. Crying for attention like a baby girl. He scrapes dirt out of her. Examines her. Probes and scrutinizes with his silver speculum. Look at her now, she's lying with her legs in stirrups, spread apart. See the care the doctor takes not to catch her diseases. Gloves. A coat. His face is masked.

Just his eyes are visible. He looks at me, but he doesn't seem to see.

He can see her. Lying there. She no longer knows how to tell the truth.

They remove her from me.

She would have been a bad mother.

Scrape her out.

She was never fit to have a child.

When the test is positive, I'm scared. He won't believe it's his.

She'd sleep around if she could. If anyone would have her.

I want to disappear again, but I'm tired of trying to hide myself. I'm sick most mornings, and I'm constantly afraid.

Clyde works it out for himself in the end. And pretends that he believes her.

'It's OK,' he says, 'we'll get married. You worry too much.'
I hope that we will go away and marry by ourselves. I don't want him to see how few friends I have and that there's no one I call family. But the arrangements seem to spiral and soon there

are a hundred guests, and only three of them are mine. We go to a register office. They say my name but they don't mean me, they mean someone else. 'You are joined . . .'

They are joined. Welded. Fixed.

I love Clyde.

She doesn't understand the meaning of the word.

I want to spend my life with him.

Not joined.

Yet when it's over, I don't feel married after all.

She isn't really married. They didn't marry in a church. She's his second wife.

I'd always imagined a Catholic wedding, even though I don't believe in God. Sometimes I think of my parents. There's been no further contact. I couldn't contact them.

All her sentiment is sham. She's only worried Clyde will see she's not the person he thinks she is.

Winifred is there on my behalf, and Kay and Nyala. I tell myself that once the baby's born, I will never want for family.

Clyde expects another boy. She'd prefer a girl. She makes endless plans for her. She thinks that she deserves a child. She thinks it is her right. But the baby can't survive. Inside of <u>her</u>.

When the baby dies, I sever hope. Inside myself.

He tries to be kind, that husband of hers. In his own little way. 'We'll try again soon,' he tells her. He wouldn't have married her without the prospect of a child. She conned him. Always a deceiver.

Joined. Unjoined again.

She mustn't eat. How can she nourish a body so incapable of giving nourishment?

'You can't go on like this forever,' Clyde tells me, once six weeks have passed. 'We have to move forward, get on with our lives.'

Clyde talks in slogans. 'We should put it all behind us.' That's what he says. Her loving husband. Father of her child. And what does she do? She does what he tells her. She obeys. Pushes out the baby. Expels her. Like she did before

as if we are ashamed of her. As if she never lived.

Chapter Five

They put a screen round the new patient's bed and give her a medical. I can hear the terror that she feels. They decide to sedate her again. At this rate she's going to spend more time asleep than she is awake. My mood is lower than it was. Think all this stuff with the new patient is getting to me now, so I decide to take it slow and sit in an armchair in the day room. This don't please the nurses, who decide to make me fit in my old age. They keep coming up to me with ping pong bats and telling me I have to get up off my arse (only Don says this actual word) and throw my carcass into action. The idea of movement don't appeal. Feeling deadness and the pointlessness of life. But every now and then I feel a little sorry for the young nurse who tries to get me better even though it is a thankless task. So when she comes and pleads with me to play with her, I say yes, OK, and take up my bat and walk.

Ping pong is a foolish game. The proportion is wrong. And playing ball games on a table don't make no sense to me. But Hilary stands opposite, all eagerness, so I pretend that I enjoy it too.

The first few times I miss. My coordination is a little rusted up. But after that I get the hang of it and whack the ball clean off the table. Hilary has a lot of running to do but it don't seem to bother her. We hit it up good and soon I am out of breath and perspiring.

'Gloria,' she says to me, 'how are you getting on with the new patient?'

They try to get us to discuss how we are with one another so they can write it down in the files they keep and say things like 'Gloria is socially adept and mixes well with the other patients.'

So I smile and say, 'Fine, just fine,' though she's hardly said a word to me.

'She needs a lot of care right now.'

I nod and try to look wise. I find that people like to see a little wisdom when you reach late middle age. It seems to reassure them.

The ball drops to the floor and I try to bend down to fetch it but I got a little problem with my knee these days and I can't bend down so agile any more. I slip and fall on top of the ball and mash it up good.

Hilary comes running round the table. 'Are you all right, Gloria?'

'Fine,' I answer, trying to retain my pride.

One of the things you lose quickest when you get put in hospital is pride. Hilary tries to help me up and all the while she says that I am getting too energetic and have to take it easy, forgetting it's because of her I have to play this stupid game at all.

I sit down in the armchair again and rub my leg a bit. Hilary keeps on at me. 'Are you sure you are all right?' she says.

'Fine,' I answer her.

'How have you been feeling these last few days?'

'Not so good.'

'Well, it seems to me that you're a lot better, Gloria. Less excitable. The medication's started to kick in, I think.'

She is my key nurse. It's her job to tell me where my life's gone wrong and what I have to do to make it right. She is twenty-four years old, with blue eyes and a fair pink skin. What has she seen of life? What can she understand of me? 'Still feel low. I prefer high, you know? Even when it's hard to control it.'

'Well that's what it's all about, really, finding ways of controlling your reactions. Not getting so that you don't really know what you're doing any more.'

'I always know what I am doing,' I say to her.

'Well yes, in a way, but when you were high, you couldn't really stop. That's what I mean. Everything was running away with you. It's not surprising really. When someone you're close to dies . . .'

Can't let her continue with the conversation. I go to the corner of the room and gaze out of the window on the scrubby little patch they call a garden. Josie liked to do the garden. She planted all sorts of things, sunflowers that grew tall in summer like beanstalks. And sweet-smelling plants like lavender and marjoram. Some thyme too, and a little bit of sage. She told me that her grandmother on her father's side could heal with herbs. Lots of woman healers, you know. They were healers long before doctors came along with their big fancy books and know-it-all ways.

How do you learn the ins and outs of human beings from a book? You have to be in life, not just read about it. This is the problem with young Hilary. Too many books, not enough life.

Hilary stands behind me and she says, 'I have to take Jim to the dentist now. I'm sorry if I upset you.'

I shrug. No point in trying to explain.

'Why don't you have another game of ping pong? It might help to take your mind off things. But take it slow, OK? Mr Lemmington will play with you, won't you, Mr Lemmington?'

'What?' he says.

'I was just saying to Gloria that you'd like a game of ping pong. Take my bat. And I've got a new ball here. That's it, Mr Lemmington. See you later, Gloria.'

Don't have a lot of contact with the men on the ward. Only in the group meeting and at meal time. I do most of my talking in the dormitory and they are not allowed in there. Mr Lemmington is the kind of man that fills a room. Don't just mean big. I mean he has a presence. You always notice him, even though his new occupation is a mental patient. Some people disappear when they get put in hospital. Not Mr Lemmington. He seems bigger than ever.

But I have to say he don't have no coordination. He holds the bat up like a flag, as if the ball somehow going to leap up and meet it. Get a little bored of this after a while, so we sit down in the day room and turn on the television.

Nothing much on. Just golf. Little balls again. Mr Lemmington don't seem to mind. 'I used to play a great deal of golf,' he says to me. 'Of course, that was when I was younger and fitter than I am now. I lived in America, you know. Lived there for years, until it all went wrong.'

'What happened?' I say. I can see that he is dying to tell me the story of his life.

He shakes his head slow-slow for a minute and then he says, 'Well, Gloria . . . I can call you Gloria, can't I?'

Seeing how we all have to call him Mr Lemmington, I'm not so sure about this, but when people call me Miss Parrish I have to think a while before I know they actually refer to me, so I give a nod.

'Well, Gloria, I had a business, quite a successful business, good life style, beautiful house, swimming pool, big car. We wanted for nothing. But then we hit some difficulties. You remember when there were all the economic crises in Southeast Asia? Well, I had a lot of investment there and we hit hard times. The stress of it all told on me and I had a heart attack, a massive coronary. And I was rushed into hospital. I'd been trying to save some money so I hadn't kept up with full health cover. You know that in America, you have to pay for hospital treatment? The bills were phenomenal. I didn't know how I was going to cover them.'

He removes his spectacles and gazes into the distance with water in his eyes. 'When I returned home and saw that because of my hospitalization I was in an even deeper financial mess than I'd been in before, I got desperate. I tried to take my own life. Well, as you can see, I didn't actually succeed. I ended up in hospital. More treatment bills. So many more bills that I had to go into receivership. And I was still sick, so the costs kept on mounting. In the end, they shipped me back to Britain. And so here I am. At least the treatment's free.'

I can't help myself. I burst out laughing at this sorry tale. Poor old devil, seems like nothing gone right for him. I laugh and laugh. And although it is a sad reflection on myself, I have to admit, from time to time, the misfortune of others is just what I need to get me through the day.

Chapter Six

Gloria pads across the floor. Gloria in excelsis Deo. She puts her arms beneath me and raises me up. She makes me take a sip of water.

She is like a doll; passive and blank, she allows everything to be done to her.

I can't make my body do the things I want. Gloria sits beside me and says, 'You need some nourishment. Come, let's get some milkshake.'

She opens her mouth but the words have been battened down inside her. She must not speak. If her words get out, the darkness will descend.

Gloria takes my hand and guides me through the ward. She glides. The light shimmers round her. We pass the day room and the duty room where the nurses work. The lights are too bright.

She stands too visible beneath them.

I try to hide my face. Gloria doesn't notice. She just keeps tugging me along in semi-flight. She is singing again.

Hosanna in the highest. She opens the kitchen door and seats me at the table. 'I don't want to sit here,' I tell her.

She should not have spoken. Her stomach knots and the sound reverberates around her head, squeezing her until she barely breathes.

'Give it a chance,' Gloria replies. 'You need to see more than just the dormitory. Come and help me get the drink.'

I follow her across the kitchen. She opens a cupboard and places a tin on the worktop. She hands me a spoon. I measure the pink powder carefully. It is hard to focus. I put it into mugs. Gloria nods. 'A bit more in mine,' she says, 'I like it strong.' She starts to giggle, as if she's made a joke. Do angels laugh?

She spills the powder on the table top. She's always been the clumsy one. She can't hold on to things.

'I'm sorry,' I tell Gloria. The noise is shrieking to the edges of my head.

'It's all right, no harm done,' Gloria replies.

Sometimes it's impossible to work out the chain of things. I know there's a meaning in the way the powder spilled, but it always slips away from me, just as I reach the point of understanding. Gloria smiles at me.

Angel smiles. They have a meaning too.

All the meanings jamming up together, all there, for me to figure out.

She won't get it. She is incapable of understanding anything.

One of the nurses comes in. He says we shouldn't be in the kitchen.

She takes up too much space.

Gloria talks. She is angry. Cast out of heaven. They exchange words sharply, too many words. I try to move away, but Gloria won't let me, she holds my hand.

She wants to hide.

The lights are too bright and I don't want to be here any more, in the shouting. All the white men come and shout things about my father. I want them to be quiet.

She is fused to sound.

Gloria takes me into another room and we sit in a magic circle. I am starting to understand the meaning of it.

Chapter Seven

The nurses can't coax the new patient to eat so I take her in hand and make sure she gets something nourishing inside her. No flesh on her bones. She has a hollow look, like Alex. She still don't say much but at least it seems like she is more connected now. Can't say how I know this, it's just a feeling I have.

Don comes in the kitchen and look us up and down like we trespassed on his property. 'What are you two doing here?' he says.

The new patient looks scared and starts to move away but I take her by the hand and squeeze it so she knows she don't need to be afraid.

'She don't eat,' I say to Don.

'She can go to the dining room like everybody else.'

'Not much point if she don't eat when she gets there.'

'What she does or doesn't eat is no concern of yours. Leave her to the nursing staff. We've been trained to deal with her.'

Don makes her sound like a wild animal. Need special training to get her fed. 'Don't make no difference who gets her to eat so long as someone does it,' I answer him. I raise my voice because he makes me vexed. Just a stupid jackass. I would say more but it don't seem right to talk about her like she isn't even here. I feel her twitch beside me like she's going to panic any minute now so I go quiet and let Don think I ran out of steam.

'Wash those cups up, Gloria. The group meeting's about to start.'

The new patient carries her cup to the sink like she's scared it's going to slip out of her hand. Then she follows me into the day room.

Everyone's surprised to see her there. They tried to get her in the group before but she never paid attention. Hilary tells us to carry the chairs to form a little circle. She's going to conduct the group today, along with Don.

We all sit like we're waiting for some big event. No one wants to be the first to speak. Usually, I break the silence. Find it hard to keep my mouth shut. But today, I don't feel up to yakking. It's a waste of time. No one listens anyhow. You say one thing and the nurses turn round and claim you said another, some deep thing that wasn't even in your mind.

One of the male patients puts up his hand like he's back at school. He looks furtive, like he don't have no right to be sitting in the room. Don says, 'You don't have to raise your hand, Jim. Just say whatever's on your mind.'

Jim still sits there with his hand in the air. Don starts to shift in his seat and I can tell his patience is starting to run thin, but Hilary gives this look which means he should let Jim take his time. We have a long wait, but eventually Jim asks, 'What I would like to know is, are we all going to be allowed home for Christmas?'

Hilary says, 'There are a few weeks to go yet, Jim. A lot can change in that time. Wait and see.'

'I need to know now. We all do. My wife's been making plans and all the relatives are coming. I have to know what's what.'

Everyone starts to nod and to say it is the kind of thing you have to plan ahead.

Hilary looks perplexed. 'Most of you will be allowed to go home, although your consultant will let each of you know for sure nearer the time. Any of you that have to stay here needn't worry. There will be lots of fun. You really won't miss out.'

Jim starts to speak again. 'And what about New Year? I don't want to be in here at the start of a new year. I want to be outside so I can begin afresh.'

Everybody murmurs in agreement but I say, 'Why all this fussing about the New Year? You think it's going to be any different? What you think is going to change?'

Mr Lemmington pipes up, 'My dear, just because you're not interested in having a good time, don't deprive the rest of us.'

Everybody laughs. It's as if Mr Lemmington and me swapped places for a moment and he is me and I am him. He's usually the miserable old sod and I am usually the cheerful one.

Jim says, 'Some of us want to be at home with our families.'

'Some of us don't have no family,' I answer him.

'Some of us don't want to be with our family.' This is from

Alex. She can see herself having to stuff three days' worth of turkey and roast beef and cake and chocolate in her mouth. She has more chance of managing to starve if she stays on the ward.

The new patient don't say nothing. She just sits in her seat, rocking back and forth like some crazy person. I nudge her to let her know she shouldn't act more crazy than she is, but she don't take no notice. It's always hard to tell if she is here with us or in some other place.

Charlie lifts his head and says, 'Does anyone even remember what it is we're going to celebrate? It's the birth of Our Lord Jesus Christ.' Charlie has religion so bad he thinks he's the Angel Gabriel and Lucifer both at once. That way he gets the best of both worlds. This is the kind of madness that makes sense to me.

Mrs Isaac looks at him and says, almost in a whisper, 'I'm Jewish.' She don't add nothing else.

Hilary crosses her legs and after another long silence she says, 'There is obviously a lot of anxiety about Christmas and the start of another year. Perhaps we should each take it in turn to say what it means to us, what our hopes are for it, and our fears.'

Everyone gives everybody else a sideways look, the kind which means this is a damn fool thing for us to be doing and I don't intend to be the one to start. The new patient don't follow the intricacy of the group, so she don't catch the look that pass around. Instead, she says, 'The baby will be born.'

'What baby?' Hilary asks, in a tone of encouragement.

She don't go on. She just starts to rock the imaginary baby.

Hilary looks at me and says, 'What about you, Gloria? What

would you like to gain from the Christmas celebrations, and in the future?'

Like I say, normally, it's hard to shut me up once the group gets started. I got a lot of complaining to do and the meeting only lasts for forty minutes. But lately I been stuck in a low, and for a while now, I barely open up my mouth. Dr Raines says this up and down feeling is a symptom of the illness I have, like it's the flu I got. By the time this place is through with me, I'll be nothing but a page from a psychiatric book. This is such a bad thought that I decide to make the effort and say something about this Christmas business, but as soon as I start to speak all I can think about is Josie and the plans we had. Never imagined being in the future on my own. See it as a void, a deep hole which nothing is ever going to fill. I don't say this though. I just say, 'I don't have no plan, I just expect to be on my own.'

'Is that what you want, Gloria, to spend Christmas and New Year alone?'

I shrug. I don't want to go into what I feel right now. It is nobody's business but mine.

'Won't you be lonely?' Hilary says.

If there is one thing I really hate about this place it is the bawling they expect us all to do. Got more important things to think about than how bad it is to be alive. I look at Don. He has that concerned expression on his face, the one he has to practise in the bathroom mirror for at least ten minutes every day. And it is as if the new patient understands that I don't want to give an answer to the question because she says, 'The baby and me . . .'

49

'Go on,' Hilary says, with encouragement still in her voice. 'The baby and you what?'

'It got inside me and made me ready. There has to be a birth before the death of space. We're running out of space and time. Time goes backwards and forwards at the same time when the future comes. I don't want to be caught up in the backwardness of space. When a person dies, another waits ready to be born.'

Hilary nods as if she understands what all this means. I nudge the new patient again. They are going to keep her here forever if she carries on this kind of talk. 'We can't be saved,' she adds.

Charlie seems to know exactly what she means. 'The sins of the world!' he says, jumping up and down in his seat, unable to contain the excitement he feels at the thought of all that sin.

'Good won't take away the evil,' the new patient says.

Don rolls his eyes. He don't need to speak. For once, I take his point.

Hilary says, 'Everybody seems to be getting rather excited. Can we get back to the question of Christmas and your feelings about the future?'

'What makes you think we have a future? We're coming up to the apocalypse. We're all going to die,' Charlie says, satisfaction in his voice.

'I'm not going to die,' Mr Lemmington says mournfully. 'Nothing kills me.'

'We could try a stake through the heart.' I don't mean to say it, it just slips out. Don starts to laugh. Then Mrs Isaac. Soon everyone is doubled up with laughter. Mr Lemmington looks pained.

'What I'm getting,' Hilary interrupts, 'is a sense that people are more scared than anything else at the thought of the future. Is this what you're feeling?'

'Christmas, New Year, it's just a date on the calendar,' I say to them again. 'That's all it is.'

Don sighs and stretches out each foot slow-slow. He contemplates them for a moment. Then he says, 'We just keep going round in circles.'

'Magic circles,' the new patient adds, staring at Don as if he has discovered some great truth. She even stops rocking the invisible baby.

Hilary says, 'There seems to be a great need in all of us to attribute some kind of magic to the ending of one year and the beginning of another. And it is a chance to start afresh, I guess, like Jim has said. But there is some truth in what Gloria's saying too, isn't there? It is just a date.'

I smile at Hilary. She is the only one who is talking any sense right now.

'Several days of public holiday,' says Mr Lemmington, 'which suggests that the powers that be attribute it with some significance. What I want to know is, will the hospital even be open?'

'We never close,' Don says in a weary tone. 'And as Hilary told you at the start of the meeting, there will be things laid on for those of you who aren't allowed to go home.'

Everyone starts muttering about how they do or do not want to be in hospital for Christmas.

Hilary leans forward and she says, 'You know, something's just occurred to me.'

Her words hang in the air. Everybody loves to have fat thoughts in this damn place.

Hilary goes on, 'I think everyone should keep a diary, a record of their thoughts and feelings about the future. It would be a way of clarifying things, perhaps, recognizing what we want out of life and how we might go about making the changes we have to make in order to look forward with a bit of optimism.'

We. Bet the nurses won't be writing no diary.

I fish in my pocket for my radio and put the headphones on. Blast from the past. A little lovers' rock.

Don leans over and pulls the headphones off my ears. 'Come on Gloria, pay attention, listen to what Hilary is saying.'

'. . . So I want each of you to begin a Life Book. That is, a record of your lives, where you come from, what your families are like and how that's made you the people you are now. You should also record your feelings about the future and answer some of the questions I was asking earlier about what your hopes and fears are for it. OK? I think you'll find that it's good therapy, a way of focusing on all the things that are most important to you. I want you all to start as soon as possible and be ready to read some of the things you've written in the next group meeting.'

The meeting ends. Everyone puts back the chairs. I look around the room. Not much enthusiasm for The Book of Life. Mr Lemmington says he don't have time to write that kind of stuff, which makes me laugh because I never seen him do a thing on the ward except play ping pong and fetch himself a cup of tea from time to time.

Hilary comes up to me and says, 'How did you get the new patient to come today?'

'Just asked her if she wanted to,' I answer. This is not strictly true, but I'm trying to get the nurses to see they get a better result from asking than any other way. They're hard to train though. Think I got my work cut out.

Always find the time drags between supper and going to bed. Sometimes I watch a little television, but the men always hog the set and we have to put up with football or snooker most of the time. Some of the patients read a book but my concentration's not so good, and anyway, I'm not a great one for reading. I play a game of patience if I get too bored but generally, I just sit in the day room and chat to the other patients when they are feeling up to it. Trouble is, most of them have given up on conversation.

Think I might take up a little needlework. Used to do a bit of crochet when I was a girl. I could make a doily so delicate and neat that you would swear it was fashioned by machine. My father used to put them on the arm of the chair in the front room and all the friends who stopped by would say how fine it looked.

Hilary comes into the day room and she sits beside me. 'All right, Gloria?' she says.

'Can't complain,' I answer her.

She laughs and says, 'That'll be a first if I know you, Gloria.'

She is tall, and she always wears a skirt to work, which I like because if you look scruffy and put on jeans with holes in them, it looks as if the work you do don't have no proper value to it. But

I don't see she has the right to behave like I'm just a naughty child she has to get under her control. So I sit, and feel vexed.

After a time she notices this and she says, 'I know you don't really complain a lot Gloria. It's more that you assert yourself.'

We talk then, for a while, about this and that. Nothing very important. Then she says to me, 'If you're bored, why don't you start on that project I was talking about this morning? It would be so interesting, like that Windrush thing they did some time ago on television, about the first immigrants to this country. I'm sure you must have a story to tell. Why not start to get it down? I've just spoken to Dr Raines and also to Rhoda from occupational therapy and they think it's a great idea. Rhoda's volunteered to help you all get it going.'

Not sure if I want my life looked into like a Third World museum piece. 'Everyone going to read it then?'

'Not if you don't want them to. But I'd like to see it, as your key nurse.'

'People's lives are a very private thing.'

'But it will help you if you write something down. Go on, give it a try, Gloria.'

So I write about my mother and my father. My mother died before I reached five years old. She walked out to Chin Loy's shop and had a heart attack. She never regained consciousness. You should have seen the people who flocked to the funeral. Such a fine thing, my father said, everyone was there. He was proud as he could be to see how many paid their last respects. She never had an easy life but she always did her best for us, I do remember that. A lot of closeness in the family. A lot of laughter too, like I had with Josie. Don't see why the laughter always has to stop. When my sister died as well, my father wanted to go away. He said Jamaica made him think of all the sadness in his life and he wanted a fresh start, and to make something of himself. He went on ahead, and left me with my auntie until he got the money for my fare. It took a long time, but eventually, he saved enough. I was sent on the boat with my uncle John who took good care of me but all the time I felt afraid of living in the mother country, away from everyone I knew.

It was strange at first to see my father after all those months, almost like I didn't really know him any more. Never thought I could settle here. My father worked his fingers to the bone, all the overtime available. He knew that to be successful in this country, you have to be twice as good. All the older generation tell this to the youth. And it's true, you know. But sometimes I think it's too much pressure. No wonder all the youth drop out of school and lose their motivation. I think this is what is happening to Alex. She's sitting by the window tonight, staring out into the dark like she is thinking a whole lot of thoughts she don't want to think. She is fatter now, but still very thin, and I wonder if she will ever learn to eat enough. All her energy is going into starvation and there is nothing left over for survival. We are a people of survival, like my father used to say. You have to learn to push yourself against the odds. It seems like the survival instinct's missing in the patients here. The new one, and Alex, they seem bent on self-destruction. That's how I know that I should not be here. I thought survival had gone from me, but now it seems as if I still have it in my bones, and even Josie's death never knocked it out of me completely.

This is what I want to say when I start to write. But it don't turn out so good. The words don't string together and it don't come across that clear. I shut the notebook they gave me. Stupid thing, writing down your thoughts. Always prying in this place. The other day, Don tried to ask what me and Josie done in bed. He never asked straight out, but this is what was on his mind. Never answered him. Don't have to say nothing to him about the life we had. It's no business of his, no business whatsoever. Dr Raines says I have to tell everything to him and to the nurses if I want to be well. It's part of the treatment and the cure. But I will only say the things I choose to say. And if keeping some things to yourself is a form of madness, then so be it. I will be madder than a hurricane.

Chapter Eight

The nurse says, 'Begin with your father and your mother. That's where Gloria started. It seems like a good place.'

She picks up her pen but she struggles with the words. She can't say the things she wants to say because of the blankness inside her.

I am a blank page. It is white. Why is there no black paper? The lined pages in the notebook crackle as I turn them. Words spring into my head but they won't land on the page. I want to write, but there's so much that I mustn't say.

I am inside everything and outside of it at the same time. If I write things down, the bad things will start to happen. Penetrate. Deep inside of me. Between my parted thighs. Words spread diseases. I try to keep my words inside me but they keep getting out. My father was a good man but bad things happened to him. This is the way of the word.

She must begin with her father and her mother.

My father died. I am dying too. Inside and outside at the same time.

The sun was shining

This is a house and a tree and a girl and a mummy and a daddy and the sun is shining.

She has to concentrate. A few short lines are all she's written down in more than an hour. She tries to think but catching thoughts before they slip away again seems to be beyond her. What a stupid girl. No wonder he had to go away from her.

My father went away. The men came and took him.

They are playing in the backyard. He's teaching her to catch a big red ball. Dolly is sitting on the grass. She is watching them. Dolly can't catch. Dolly will never learn. She will learn. She's a clever little girl. He tosses the ball to her open hands but time after time it falls between them.

It smells of grass and mud.

As it bounces away, she trundles after it impatiently.

'Time to stop now,' her father says, but she shakes her head so hard that the world around her starts to spin.

'No, again, Daddy. Throw again.' She has to get it right. She wants to be able to catch and throw the way her father does. She wants to show him what a clever girl she is.

'Time to stop,' he repeats. 'It's getting cold.' He starts to walk away from her.

'No!' she shouts.

He picks up the ball. He is carrying it indoors.

'No!' She starts to scream. He is taking her ball away. She runs after him and holds his leg. The sky is turning purple, angry marks across it. She hits his leg. She is screaming still, the sound echoing, inside and outside at the same time. It is loud. It is louder than the loudest noise in all the world. She tries to snatch the ball but it is too high, he is holding it above her head and she can't reach however high she jumps. She wants the ball. She wants it. She hates him for taking it away from her. And now her mother is coming. She is running across the grass. Her face is angry and frightened at the same time. She wants to stop screaming but she can't, the sound is somewhere above her head and she can't reach it any more. The sound has brought the running men. They are following her mother across the fresh-mown grass. Her father is shocked into stillness for a moment. Her sound makes him run. He breaks away and runs towards the wall, scrambling over it. The men grab him from behind and pull him back again.

'Get the child inside!'

Her mother tries to drag her in, but she stands firm and makes her body stiff. Her mother picks her up; she rests on her mother's hip held tight, unable to struggle. As they go inside the house, she begins to wail. She tries to hit out but her mother grabs her hands and pushes her into the living room. 'Stay there,' she says, 'just stay, OK?' and she shuts the door.

There's something in her mother's voice that quietens her. She wipes her eyes with the back of her hand. Then she goes and sits under the table. It seems safer there. A miniature rocking horse lies on its side. She reaches out and pulls it towards her. As she pushes, it begins to rock. The movement is hypnotic. It starts to soothe. She hears voices from the back of the house. Her father and the men. Shouting. She made it come. She tries to make it go away again. Her father says bad words. She made him say them. Scuffling. The sound of crashing ornaments. Pounding feet shuddering through the hall. The front door slams. She scrambles to the window. Her father's hands are pinned behind his back. One of the men pushes his head down as they force him into the car. Her mother is standing on the street. She's crying now. Her father twists his body in order to look back at her.

'I'll get help,' she says. 'Don't worry, Sam, you'll soon be home.'

Then he's gone.

Her screams have torn the air in two, and the drumming of her feet. She opens the door and runs back into the garden to find the red ball. She holds it to her tight. Her doll is beside it. Someone broke Dolly. Her head is smashed in pieces. Dolly can't be mended.

The baby's face is crushed. The house is smashed. The windows cracked. I mustn't touch the door or the dirt will get inside me.

60

She can't sleep any more because she's always scared. She doesn't know what will happen when she starts to close her eyes. It's noisy all the time and she wants it to be quiet again. She wets the bed. The windows break and dirty things are smeared around their door and pushed through the letter box. Then she is sent away. Maybe now she's gone the bad things in the world will stop.

She stays with a family of boys who tease her and take away her doll, the new doll, not the same as Dolly. She is called Francine. They tell her it's a silly name. Thomas is thirteen. He plays with her. Her mother said her father sent the doll to her. Where has he gone? He should have given her the doll himself. She can't help crying when she thinks of him. They slap her when she cries, so she tries to stop remembering. Thomas makes her play rude games. She is sore inside but she mustn't tell. Her father will never come back if she tells. She wants to go home all the time. It hurts inside. Sometimes her mother phones but she doesn't tell her when she's going home. She is five when her mother finally comes for her. They don't live at the old house any more, they're moving far away. 'When will Daddy be coming back?' she asks her mother endlessly.

When will I be going home? It hurts inside.

See the dirty little girl lying on the bed. She is writing words. See the clever girl writing words in the bed. She will split the sky.

Chapter Nine

You say I have to write a notebook telling what I think about being here and what put me here and how I'm going to get better. I'm not sick, but I know you're going to say if you think you're not sick, you must be sick, because normal people don't behave the way you do and you have to see that, but if I tell you I know I'm sick, then you think I'm agreeing with it and I'm still sick, OK? You tell me I have problems writing clear and I should talk instead but maybe it's your reading, not my writing needs attention. This tape recorder thing you give me, it's old as the hills, and what if someone pinches it? Can't take no responsibility to keep it safe, you know. Expensive equipment this tape recorder stuff. And who's going to pay for the tape?

It's hard to tell your thoughts for all and sundry to have a listen to. Don't see how this is going to make me any better . . . talking to a machine don't make a whole lot of sense, so I started to imagine I'm talking to an actual person, but it still feels strange. What good can it do to say your thoughts?

My first thought is this: I want to be discharged real soon, so I'm putting this down for you all to listen to and I hope you listen good. And hear this: my second thought is, if you want sick people to get well, you have to build them up with decent food like you get in good hotels, not all this stuff that tastes like chicken shit. The ones that can't eat are not going to get started on their eating with rubbish like this. You have to give them decent food . . . shrimp, jerk pork and proper home food you would want to eat in your own house, not all this spotted dick and thing. You don't get an appetite thinking about a thing called spotted dick. You hear what I'm saying?

Lots of dicks in this place. No, not for true. Dr Raines is 'a brilliant physician'.

'Can I say something now?'

That's the new patient just come in the room. She wants to talk to the tape.

'What should I say?'

'Say what you want.'

'I don't know what to say.'

'Say anything you want.'

'One, two, three.'

'You can say more than that. If you take the . . . wait up . . . you can get . . . Don't leave the door . . .'

She left the door wide open. No one thinks about the cold. You know it's cold in here? This dormitory is always cold. You get stiff if you sit in the cold too long and the drugs make you cold, cold like ice. You could warm it up for me, you know. And what you said about fixing up my leg, you not forgotten yet? And you said that social worker woman was going to call. She don't call yet. Takes her time, for true.

When we going to do that visit home you promised? I only have one pair of pyjamas left and I put them in the wash. If you don't have a nurse to spare, one of the patients could take me there, one with a free pass to leave the ward. We could go straight there on a forty-seven bus — it stops right on my doorstep.

I miss my things around me. There's another picture of Josie we could fetch from the bedroom table. When you have your own things round you, everything makes more sense than if you just have all this hospital stuff. I can get well quick and be out of here real soon if things get more familiar. One small bag of clothes is all I have and they never even packed my dressing gown. I got it in the sale at Selfridges . . . oh, must be fifteen years ago at least. Josie helped me choose it. My waist was thinner then, and my figure not so full, so it don't fit all across, the way it did, but it don't look shabby yet, and the colour's still nice . . . green it is, a beautiful lime green, makes me think of grass and trees. Josie said green suits me to the ground.

So why you make me say this stuff on tape? Who is going to listen? What's it all for anyhow?

Chapter Ten

'It would help us to understand more about your situation if you could write something else for us in the notebook you've been given. Perhaps you could let us know more about your husband, where he is at the moment. Do you have a number or some way we can get in touch with him?'

She can't believe he's gone, yet she's always known he'd leave her. Go back to his wife, and Marcus. He missed his son. She's crying now, as if tears will bring him back, her face puckered, stained, her lips curled upwards in despair. Stupid enough to have imagined that he loved her. Stupid enough to have imagined a future for them both. With the obligatory boy and girl in their own image. A nice little nuclear family.

Not a world for children, she tells herself. If she repeats it often enough, she may come to think that being childless is her choice. She has little trouble deceiving herself. Got it to an art. She told herself that she loved Clyde and now she believes it.

You should have seen her on the day he left, running through the house, trying to find a way of being close to him even in his absence. Rummaging through his clothes, sniffing them, fingering the books he's read, dabbing herself with after-shave. And when she's done with that, she goes to the window, thinking that perhaps he's changed his mind and is hurrying back along the street to be with her again. She stands there for an hour, straining to see him, thinking that if she looks away, she'll destroy the possibility of his return and he'll be gone forever. Panic's setting in. He doesn't love her any more, yes he does no he doesn't yes he does.

Has she remembered the note? The note he left for her, held to the fridge with the pineapple magnet. She's gone to read it again, in case there's something in the words she didn't notice last time round. She's got no pride. She should hold her head up and just get on with things. She's always been weak. No wonder he left her. She isn't even attractive any more. The other day Clyde told her she looked like the victim of a famine.

Why does she want him back?

He's been hell to live with.

She's had to put up with having him round the house all day, under her feet, sitting in the big armchair (the one the bailiffs didn't take), feeling sorry for himself as if he's the first black man to be unemployed. He thought he was immune. He thought that if he worked hard enough and took pride in himself, all good things would come to him. He thought that others failed because they did a sloppy job or they didn't take the risks or the opportunities that came along so when the restaurant folded, he took it hard. Blamed himself. Blamed her.

And she was to blame. Look at the facts. She's never been a proper wife. Didn't give enough support. Too busy with her own concerns.

Only thinking of the emptiness inside of her. Not aware of the empti-
ness inside of him. She's remembering the day they stripped the
restaurant. Took out everything that could be sold to pay off all the
debts. The stock first: crates of beer and wine returned to the brewery.
Tables and chairs, piled into vans, pictures removed from the walls.
The African hangings auctioned off. She liked the one with the sunset
in it. Where is it now? On someone else's wall, in someone else's res-
taurant. Clyde's face was expressionless. He stood in the corner,
watching as they took away everything he'd built. All his confidence.
He used to be so strong but he hasn't been the same since then. She
should have noticed what was happening, but she's never been percep-
tive. Insufficient caring. Not much warmth. She isn't good at warmth.
Something missing in her. Hole where her heart should be. Not the
right anatomy.

She's trying to make a coffee for herself. She's forgotten the order of
things. She's standing there, empty, unable to think what she should
do. Water. Coffee granules. Sugar. Milk. She isn't listening. Put them
in the cup. She can't do it. Something missing in her brain. Stupid as
they come. That's why he left her. He saw what she was becoming.

She tries to figure out what's happening. All the words, tangled in
her brain. Looking to work out what everything means. All the words,
every word in her vocabulary, sorted through for clues. And still she
doesn't understand.

She turns on the radio.

Words.

The voice inside my head slips into the radio, and broadcasts out again.

She doesn't understand. She picks it up and rattles it, as if the voice can be shaken out. Every movement that she makes is seen, broadcast to the world.

Everything I am and everything I do. Observed.

She doesn't have the sense to be afraid. It puzzles her too much.

It entrances me too.

To entrance, to mesmerize. Entrance, to come in. The words are the same. I've never noticed that before.

Why are the words the same? It doesn't make sense.

She is discovering new ways of seeing. New ways of hearing, too.

The changes are confusing me. If Clyde was here, he'd tell me what this means. He'd explain what's happening.

Clyde didn't understand, any more than she does. Why does she think he's gone? He couldn't take it any more, her strange moods, the way she never seemed to hear when he was talking to her. She dives, suddenly, beneath the kitchen table. She's starting to be frightened now. Perhaps there's an angel beside her, relaying messages from God. Or maybe it's an alien. She's sifting through the possibilities, trying to make sense of it. She's settled on God, the obvious choice for a lapsed Catholic. Now she'll have to think about evil, consider the possibility of sin. Aliens would have been a cleaner prospect. Less inclined to judge.

She's becoming aware of the dirt within herself. Stains. Sin. The stain of sin. Born with it. So this must be a punishment: Clyde's departure. The noises in her head. It makes a certain kind of sense and she needs sense now. How long will she sit beneath the table? Too many words are chasing round her head, each sound rising and falling, until she hears only the noise and can't pick out the meaning. In the absence of meaning, there comes a kind of quiet.

What will she do? She will sit here motionless, listening to the noisy silence. Wondering when Clyde will come. Fearful that he won't. Time will pass the way it does in dreams, with the sudden awareness of an hour gone. Or minutes. She won't know which. She will feel totally alone, yet she will also feel invaded. Occupied. Unable to distinguish the chaos inside herself from the world outside. Boundaries broken. She's fallen outside everything, dropping endlessly.

Chapter Eleven

Time passes slow on the ward. Sometimes it feels as if I only dream I'm here. It's hard to catch reality. Half the time, I lose count of the days. So when Hilary scampers in the dormitory and says, 'Anyone for chapel this morning?' I know it's Sunday and a day of rest.

The funny thing about being stuck in hospital is I used to be a nurse. Not a proper one. The kind that cleans and cooks and does the donkey work. Maybe I still have a job. Don't know for sure. A little after Josie died, I never bothered going into work. Couldn't see the point. But I never got round to handing in my resignation. This social worker says she'll try to sort it out for me. That's all they ever do. *Try* to sort things out. No harm in trying, but a little success from time to time don't come amiss. She says the manager don't return her calls. Could have told her that.

Fifteen years I worked there, in the old people's home. One thing that gets me down about this country is the way the old ones find themselves locked up as soon as they give any trouble. This is when I feel most glad I never brought a child into the world. A thankless serpent is sharper than a child's tooth, as my father used to say. He could always make me laugh. Miss him now, you know. Miss him deep.

Should have kept my faith. Don't know exactly when I lost it, it just crept away. Yet on Sunday morning, when I was at work and had the early shift, I used to take a little group of residents to church. They waited in the hall and put on gloves and hats and we walked up the street in a slow, shuffling procession.

The church was on the corner, but it was not my kind of church. Not a lot of singing there and the worshippers were white. We stumbled into a pew, and Mr Tatton dropped his prayer book same as always, every week. The pages hung loose, so they scattered. Mrs Harrison began to pick them up. Think she had a thing for him. She looked at him all soft from time to time, and kept straightening his tie. Sometimes I saw the loneliness in the people I looked after and it got inside my bones.

Mr Tatton started to sing, even though no music was playing in the church. 'Onward Christian Soldiers'. Me and Mrs Wilson began to laugh, but no one else seemed to see the funny side. The thing with Mrs Wilson was, once she got started on the laughing, she never seemed to stop. She just went on and on, her shoulders heaved and a trickle of saliva slid down her mouth. And all the while, Mr Tatton kept on with his singing, 'With the cross of Jesus going on before.'

I had to take Mrs Wilson from the church. She was almost in hysterics. Mr Stevens hobbled out behind shouting, 'Who's got my money? I can't find any change for the collection box.' I pulled out fifty pence and put it in his hand. 'A pound. I want a pound. You can't give fifty pence to God, he'll strike you down!'

'It's OK, Mr Stevens, the Lord is just. Fifty pence, a pound, it's all the same to him.'

But Mr Stevens had no faith in a just and gentle God. The God he worshipped was the kind that turned you to a pillar of salt just for looking back.

I was still laughing as I reached the porch. Just after Josie died, my body behaved like life was still a joke though my mind was full of sadness. Mrs Wilson's body and her mind long since parted company as well. I struggled to make her stand up straight, but for some reason she kept folding in the middle. We carried on laughing and tears filled up my eyes.

Hilary interrupts my thoughts and says, 'Come on Gloria, we're ready to go to chapel now. Get your cardigan, or you'll be cold.'

I decide not to move. Get fed up with being told do this, do that. Never seem to get a choice. At least when I worked in the old people's home, I got to do the telling. Never thought I'd miss my work. But now, stuck here, I wish I could go back. Except I'd still have to deal with all the shit. And I don't mean just the problem with their bowels. It's other things I mean, like the way they treat you when your skin is black . . .

'Don't let her touch me,' the old woman screams, and she flinches as if my fingers burn. 'Don't let her touch me! I don't want no darkie touching me, you understand?'

Kelly, the other care assistant, concentrates hard on the pillow she's plumping up, but eventually she says, 'Don't be silly Dorothy. You know Gloria. She gets you ready every other morning.'

'You do it, Nurse. You know what they're like. She'll make me ill again.'

Day after day I bathe her and I get her dressed. From time to time we chat about her son, who is sixty-five himself, and the four grandchildren who live by the sea with children of their own. Her body's stiff with rheumatism and she can't raise her arm. I learn to handle her so the pain is never more than she can stand but it takes a lot of practice. You get close to someone when you have to clean their teeth and wash their feet. When I was young, the stale, musty smell of age made me turn aside sometimes. And it was hard too, long ago, to see old people's nakedness and not show fear. Had to teach myself not to laugh at the foolishness I saw in an old person's body. When you are young, you never think upon the time when you'll grow old yourself. But worse than a body in decay is when the mind is wandering. At least when you're in a proper mental state, you can still fight back. At least you're not defeated yet. So when Mrs Carrington says that stuff to me, I remember she has to count on us for every little thing and what a trial it is for her. I remember too that in all likelihood she has me confused with someone else. I say this in my mind, but it still don't take away the hurt. Years now I lived here in this country, but I still feel the abuse I have to suffer. I pause, and wipe the dust from the headboard with my handkerchief.

Kelly says, 'I'll get her ready, Gloria. Why don't you see to Angela? Her daughter's coming to visit her this afternoon.'

I hesitate. Don't want to wash Mrs Carrington no more but it seems wrong to walk away. I want to show her that her attitude is bad, as if I have a way to prove we're not a people that contaminate. *Foolishness*. I go to Mrs Harrison. I never call her Angela. I never speak to them on first name terms. The other staff assume I have a grovelling mentality. They think it is because the residents are white. No. It's because I know how it feels to suffer disrespect. There's enough disrespect in this sad, sad world without me adding more.

I start to brush her hair until it falls round her face just right. Then I take out her good dress, the one her daughter sent. I know Mrs Cox will let me have the time to see she's dressed up neat. She likes us to get them looking nice when visitors come. Wish I was allowed to give her such attention every morning. She needs to know that someone cares.

She is one of the easy ones. She don't shout at us or get upset but it never seems like a good sign to me. I like to see a bit of life in people, not this deadness all the time.

As I help Mrs Harrison put on her shoe, she keeps on asking when her daughter will be coming home from school. Every once in a while, the thought of getting old like this scares me so deep that it's hard to keep my hand from shaking. Always thought that Josie would grow old with me, keep my mind on track, and keep the loneliness at bay. Nothing is certain in this life. Nothing except death and dying.

I breathe in deep and take in the smell of urine, which disinfectant never seems to cover up. When I finish washing Mrs Harrison, I have to wipe her bedside cabinet. Don't know how it

74

keeps on happening, but every other day it stinks to high heaven. It's a constant battle to keep the home nice.

'Why do you bother?' Kelly always says. 'They only foul things up again.'

Mrs Harrison asks if she can smell fish cooking in the kitchen.

Some of the residents only know what day it is because of the activities we do. Tuesday night is bingo. Thursday is keep fit in the afternoon. Friday dinner time is fish and chips.

'But you always come to chapel with us on Sunday mornings,' Hilary says. 'Are you sure you don't want to?'

I shake my head. It's funny being stuck here in hospital after all the work I done with people suffering confusion. Seems like everything is turning upside down.

Chapter Twelve

The sound of laughter reverberates around me interspersed with song. I don't know where it's coming from. I look round, trying to locate it. Dr Raines points towards the window and he says, 'It's only Gloria, one of the other patients, it's nothing to worry about. I think it's coming from the dormitory.'

We are walking round the garden. Dr Raines said that if we went outside, I might relax a little more. His stride is bigger than mine; it's hard to keep up. He smokes a cigarette.

He'll be dead soon. Lung cancer or thrombosis.

Between drags, he's asking endless questions. I don't know how to answer them. He seems to be frustrated by my silence. 'What about the voices?' he says as we pass the statue of the founder of the hospital. 'Can you tell me when you first remember hearing them?'

It is a trick question. I slow my pace almost to a stop.

Don't answer him.

I wasn't going to.

That was the day her head broke in two. Split. Each half like the open shell of a pistachio. She tries to pull back the sounds, but they float through the gap like a speech bubble, words suspended in the air. There is nothing left inside her now. Everything is outside, clamouring noisily for her attention.

The voice begins inside. Then it's out again. For a moment, I think the sound has sprung from Clyde, but then I see that he is still asleep. My fingers move once more, circling my own softness, probing the moistness, and again the voice screams

Don't touch it!

a strange distortion of a male voice, inside and outside at the same time. I lie still, too afraid to move. Perhaps I have imagined it. Sometimes, in the seconds before drifting into sleep, strange things happen; it's the same for everyone, nothing to be scared of. I nudge Clyde, wanting reassurance, but his breathing is heavy and deep and he doesn't stir.

I sit up and stare at the shadows. Clyde's shadow is large and round, humped under the bedclothes. His smell is still on my body, the taste of him still in my mouth. I want to feel something when he touches me but there is nothing. When we were first together, I began to think that he was part of me; even though his closeness scared me, it soon came to feel so sweet. No sweetness now. Nothing. He knows that there is nothing too, so he probes to hurt, leaving a soreness inside me that I think will never heal. I can feel his roughness and the endless exploration of my body that makes me cry out, not in pleasure, no, I am afraid, the salty sweat trickling down my thighs, his body taut on mine, making me his, a statement of possession, not of love

and now she is possessed, a God-Devil in her, good devil in and out, traces on her breasts, her lips, his mark.

The figure beside me turns. Still asleep. So still, yet the room is full of sound, whispers, barely audible, voices multiplying. I strain to hear, but they are always out of range. Maybe I can see the voices, make them look at me. I climb out of bed and stand in the line of light that penetrates half-open curtains. Look at me, I ask them silently, knowing they can hear. Look at me, then. I pull my nightshirt over my head, wanting to be seen. Are they watching now? I can't tell.

She can't tell anyone. She must keep her silence.

When morning comes, I am still standing there. Clyde wakes up; his eyes scan my body, but there is no sign of recognition. He's forgotten who I am. 'What are you doing?' he asks.
'Watching,' I reply.
'Watching what?'

'I wanted to see something.'

'What did you want to see?'

'Nothing,' I answer.

He sucks his teeth. 'Are you going to get dressed? You look indecent, standing at the window like that. The whole neighbourhood can see you.'

'No one can see me,' I say to him.

He gets up and pulls the curtains together. 'What's the matter with you? You're behaving like you're ill or something.'

'Nothing's the matter.'

'Get dressed, will you?'

I walk slowly to the wardrobe.

Are these her clothes? They belong to someone else; Clyde's other wife has been here while she was asleep and brought all her things: skirts and blouses, jeans and shoes, installed herself; become part of the house in a way that she has never been. She pulls them out and throws them on the bed. Then she notices a dress Clyde bought for her when they had the restaurant. It is black and purple, tight around the waist and hips. He said it suited her, brought out her curves, made her look feminine. She sniffs it. It doesn't smell like hers; someone else has worn it.

'Is she still here?'

'What?' asks Clyde.

'Is she still here?'

'What are you talking about?'

'Tell me.'

'Look, just get dressed. I don't know what you're talking about.'

He always denies everything, pretends she's stupid. Does he think she can't see? Then she sees a pair of jeans she knows are hers. She pulls them out from the pile on the bed.

'What are you doing today? Will you be signing on?' I say to Clyde.

'Not until tomorrow,' he answers gruffly.

I shouldn't have mentioned the signing on. He wants us to pretend it isn't happening. He'll be here all morning then. I should try to tidy up the house before I go to work, but it's hard to do it when he's watching me. The order of things becomes confused.

'Don't go in today.'

'I have to go in.'

'You should rest, you're not yourself.'

What is me, this self that he's referring to?

'I have to go in or I'll get the sack,' I say.

'Don't worry about that. We'll manage somehow.'

'I'm going in, Clyde. We really need the money.'

He sucks his teeth. I wish I hadn't said that. He doesn't like to be reminded that I'm the one who's earning now, even though it's only a few pounds. It undermines him, makes him think of all the things we've lost. We used to work together, in his restaurant. He hates to think that I now have to work for someone else, serving all-day breakfasts in a greasy spoon. I look at the clock. It's getting late. I must get dressed. I get a bra out of the drawer and start to put it on.

'Aren't you going to wash yourself?' asks Clyde.

Dirty, dirty girl.

'I wasn't thinking,' I reply.

Suddenly he's beside me. 'What's happening?' he asks. He sounds kind.

'Nothing,' I tell him.

'I can't help you if you won't tell me what's going on. You've been like this since . . .'

He can't say it. I want him to. We need to talk about the child we'll never have.

'Do you think you should go back and see the doctor? He could give you something, help calm you down. It's hard when . . . Look, I know it's hard for you. I'd help if I could. We could fix this. I want to help you, but I don't know how.'

Why doesn't he know? He used to know everything. I hate this new Clyde, his uncertainty. He was always so sure of himself before we lost the restaurant. Yet as he holds me, I feel soothed, and I put my head against his chest. 'I don't know what's wrong.' I know there must be words to describe it, but I don't know how to find them. 'Everything's wrong. It's all wrong. It doesn't feel right.'

Clyde sighs, but he rubs my shoulder. 'Maybe the doctor could help.'

'I'm not sick. I'm just . . . tired.' The tiredness is overwhelming. If I sleep forever, it still won't be enough.

Clyde sits in the armchair. I manage to vacuum round him. The familiar, routine tasks are the ones I enjoy the most. I can order the house: shiny surfaces, clean, white clothes, these are the things I recognize. My body moves briskly, seeming to belong to me again. I listen for unfamiliar sounds, but there are none. I take pleasure in the silence.

Clyde leaves the house just after twelve. He'll be going for a drink with some of his friends. He thinks I mind this so he never tells me. Or perhaps he is afraid that I'll want to come too. His men friends don't matter but the women do. If I'd been able to have a child, it would have been an extra bond between us. What else do I have to offer him? A tired, thin body and a mind that I can't seem to hold together any more.

Fucking whore.

I start at the sound, though the words are spoken softly. The volume grows inside my head while the voice simmers with a cold, hard anger, the kind I fear the most.

She goes into the kitchen and finds a cigarette. Her hand shakes as she tries to light it. She gave up years ago when she was pregnant and she only took it up again last month when the doctor said she'd never carry a child to term. She can see the baby's face whenever she closes her eyes; sometimes she is newly born, sometimes she is three or four years old. More recently, she's turned into an adult; tall and strong and beautiful.

82

No sense in hungering for the things you can no longer have. She learnt that years ago. The most painful things can best be borne once you've buried them. But the daughter keeps on surfacing. She's there in her head and in her soul.

Her alarm clock begins to beep to tell her that she has to leave for work. She's starting to lose track of time. Sometimes she thinks she's been through a day or more and then she finds that only an hour has passed. So she sets alarms around the house to ensure that the minutes of her life are accurately measured.

She remembers to close the windows and to lock the front door as she leaves. Some actions are almost automatic and she is glad of those.

But all the while the voice remains, speaking slowly to me, crowding out all other thoughts.

Chapter Thirteen

Louise comes through the ward and says I'm making too much noise again with all my laughter and excitement. She says we're going for a walk to use up some of the excess energy I seem to have. Don't know what she's talking about. I'm not excited, still feeling low.

Normally, I like the break from the usual routine but not with Lou. She treats us like we are only here for her inconvenience. But I have nothing else to do so I go fetch my coat and hat like she ordered. The new patient has come back from seeing the doctor now, so they get her to join in, which takes me by surprise. I thought she'd be too wrapped up in all the demons lurking in her head. But she walks slow-slow down the corridor like she's in a dream, and her fingers brush along the top of the radiator as if she has to touch it to be sure that it is real.

It's quite a little party Lou and Hilary take out today. Jim says he wants to come. Charlie too. Mrs Isaac and Mr Lemmington decide a walk is better than the boredom of the unit. Alex also says she wants to join us, though she complains all the while about the cold. I'm not surprised she has trouble keeping warm. She has no fat on her. Find it hard to understand this starvation thing. Show me a plate of bun and it's all I can do to keep from cramming the whole lot in my mouth. She must have more strength than I give her credit for. Pity she can't use it for a useful thing, like getting out of this damn place.

One thing I find now I'm not so high is I mind foolish things a whole lot more. Like now, when I look at myself standing by the door, waiting on Hilary to let me out like I'm the household cat.

'I don't want to go,' Alex says in a whiny voice.

Hilary hears and she replies, 'What's the matter?'

Alex speaks in a whisper that the whole world can hear, 'Tell him to put his shoes on.'

Hilary looks at Jim. 'He'll be OK with what he's wearing. It's a dry day, he won't get wet.'

'No, you don't understand,' Alex says, and she pulls on Hilary's sleeve. 'He's got his slippers on.'

'It doesn't matter, Alex.'

'Everyone will know where we're from.'

Think there may be other clues, like the fact that Alex don't have an ounce of flesh upon her bones and Charlie's shuffling walk, and the way the new patient mutters to herself at intervals. But Hilary just says, 'Oh, I see. Well, if that's all that's bothering you, why don't you wear my name badge?' and she takes it off and pins it on Alex's coat. *Staff Nurse Hilary Gibson*. She will have to remember not to answer when they call her Alex. I smile at Hilary. You never catch Don or Lou or Dr Raines giving up their names for us. They keep separate in every respect, in case somebody mistakes them for the mental ones. Different toilets. Different meals. And a wide, invisible line between them and us.

We set off. Alex looks like she don't have no energy to go more than a few feet, but she walks brisk, like the nurses do. 'I have to burn off the calories,' she says to me, when Louise is out of ear-shot. Fat and calories is all she ever thinks about.

The new patient's still in a daze. Hilary takes her arm and steers her along so she stays in a straight line. Louise brings up the rear and hurries on the ones that drag behind, saying we must be back in time for lunch. Alex makes her steps slow again. She wants to avoid eating more than anything.

We troop downstairs, along the corridor, past reception and through the main gate. It seems strange to be out in the fresh air after so long on the ward. Up ahead, a group of schoolboys pelt each other with half-empty cans of drink. One comes hurtling towards Alex and she ducks. Even though she starves herself, her reflexes stay as sharp as ever. 'Keep together,' Louise says as we try to cross the road. A car comes straight for Mr Lemmington but I know it's going to miss – he is one of the immortal ones. And sure enough, it screeches to a halt a foot away. Mr Lemmington goes rigid with fear. The driver gets out and starts to swear and cuss. Louise marches up and tells him Mr Lemmington is a psychiatric patient. So much for everything being confidential. Alex looks as if she wishes the ground would swallow her but the driver backs off quick – he don't want to catch a dose of mental illness.

Being out lifts my spirits. The relief is so great I can't hardly keep the spring out of my step.

'She's skipping,' Alex says in an outraged tone, and she points at me.

'Nothing wrong with a little happiness,' I say to her. 'Trouble with you is you so fucking miserable.'

She looks shocked that someone old enough to be her gran can use a word like fuck. Alex was born and raised in the nice-nice area of London. Her doctor father keeps her away from other black people in case they hold her back. No hard-edged thing ever entered her existence, no reality. She is too white for half the world and too black for the rest. There's no place on this planet she is going to fit. This is why she opts for starvation. Life is just too tough.

I continue to skip, even though it marks me out as a mental patient. It's not a bad label. It gives you room to do the things you were never brave enough to do before.

Wish I had been braver when Josie was alive, but I'm not the only one to blame. After my father died, the pastor said what me and Josie had was wickedness. And when a Caribbean writer came to the community centre and read from his book, everybody said homosexuality never happened to black people, only to white, and his book was a lie. And Josie got disowned by her own family and told by her sister Emilie she was the devil in disguise. So how could we remain in the neighbourhood and live true to ourselves when the people we loved were so ready to turn their backs? After Emilie found out, we knew we had to go away. We kept it hidden after that. And as the years went by, everyone decided we were sisters. Once you are fat and past forty, they think you don't have intimacy any more. But when I look back, I feel such shame. Not shame for how we were, shame for all the hiding.

Alex is still glaring at me. The girl is so thin her skin looks like paper and fine, downy hair has started growing on her body. She thinks she is different from the rest of us. She thinks a name badge will fool the world. She can't see how she looks to everybody else. Funny how it is so hard to recognize yourself.

We go in the post office to cash our giro cheques. They pay you to be a mental patient now. Spend mine as soon as it appears. The new patient slips as we come out and falls in the gutter. She's on too much medication. She has started getting fits, I seen it happen to her. Told the nurses but they don't do nothing, just keep on shovelling tablets inside her. Don't matter how she feels so long as she don't give any trouble. That's the only thing they care about.

Louise picks her up and dusts her off. We go into Boots. I see Alex buying laxatives. Louise sees it too but waits for her to pay before she takes them off her. I buy perfumed soap. It's an uphill struggle to keep nice on Ward C. I'd like someone to come and fix my hair. Used to take such pride in my appearance.

We go to Woolworths after this. Mrs Isaac buys herself a pair of shades. Then she gets a denim hat. She puts them on right away, as if she needs to be disguised. Don't see why we have to hide ourselves.

There's a little gift shop on the corner of the street. I follow the new patient through the door. She picks up a bunch of red roses, artificial, but they look so good they could be real. She also buys two packs of incense sticks. The woman behind the counter tries to wrap them in white tissue paper, but the new patient starts to shake and yells she wants them wrapped in orange or a little blue. The woman looks at her and decides she must be from the hospital. Never seen a package finished off so quick. Louise comes in and bundles us out of there again. She tells the new patient off for making such a spectacle.

We stop in the park before we go back to the ward. This is Hilary's idea. She thinks we need the calm of flowering plants. Still a lot of brightness for the end of October. Blue sky coming through the grey and a lot of autumn colour. It makes me think of a poem we had to learn at school: '*Season of mists and mellow fruitiness*'. Mellow is a word I like. It rolls off the tongue. Thought I never got nothing from my education, but some things stick, even if you try to shut them out.

Mr Lemmington wants to feed the ducks. He has a wad of stale bread he's been keeping in his pocket. One piece goes in and every duck for miles around flocks to get another. They fight for it, and then the gulls come and snatch it away. There is a life motto here but I get enough of this from the group meeting so I don't tax myself thinking what it is. Wish I could stay here in the park where everything is lively and colours fight with one another to get your attention. Wish I'd brought a picnic. Could have had it on the grass. Wish I didn't feel so full up with feeling, every feeling in the world, all tossing round my body in a rage.

The new patient don't keep up with the rest of us as we start to walk back to the ward. She gazes round her in a state of wonder. Think she must be seeing more than just the park.

Jim sidles up to her and puts his hand on her hip as she walks. She tries to shake him off but his hand remains. Even though she looks drawn and has exhaustion in her step, all the men look at her with admiration and think she is a piece of property for them to touch. Hilary has to tell him to let go of her.

Alex is leaving me alone again now. Can tell she's wrapped up with her laxatives and how she got caught before she could put them to good use. Her body must be one big mess by now, like it's not her own. Or maybe she feels closer to her true self like this. This is one of the worries I have about being a mental patient. When I'm in this state, I feel more like my true self than I ever felt, even when Josie was alive. That's the thing that scares me most about this being crazy stuff. If you don't watch out you start to like the feeling.

Chapter Fourteen

I hide the flowers and the incense in the bottom of my wardrobe when we get back from the walk. I notice my notebook again, the one the nurses gave me. I read it through. The words are broken, letters scattered on the page. I lie on the bed face down. The notebook rests beside my chin. I'm thinking what to write. After a while I sit up and scribble some more words. One of the nurses comes into the dormitory and sits beside me. 'Let me see,' she says. I stop writing and hand the notebook to her. She scans the page. 'You haven't written very much. It seems a little muddled. Is that how you feel at present?'

Endless chaos, she creates. Her head won't stay on straight.

I nod my head. It leans at an angle.
'Once the medication really starts to kick in, you'll be less confused. Why don't you write some more? Try to tell us what you feel.'

I feel. I don't feel. I have become a stone. There is nothing to separate me from things. I am all things and everything.

The nurse will read the words and think she's crazy but she doesn't care, she writes the words down anyway.

The nurse picks up my notebook again. 'It must be frightening to think you are so powerful,' she says. She's getting in my head.

The x-ray vision of the world shines on me again. Everything I am is known to everyone.

'I don't suppose you'll believe it when I say that no one knows what's going on inside your head unless you tell them.'

'Everyone can see.'

'No, that isn't true. No one can see anything that you don't show them,' says the nurse.

'I am transparent.'

'You feel transparent.'

'I am transparent. Everyone can see inside of me.'

Her mother takes her hand. She walks beside her mother to the prison gate. The building is high and the windows are like slits. She thinks of castles and kings and queens. Doors are opened and closed with keys in locks. Sometimes a button is pushed and a glass partition slides open and then slides shut again almost silently. She is caught in the glass. She didn't pull her hand away in time. She is trapped in its transparency.

Everyone can see her. Silly girl. Her hand is swelling and it hurts. She holds it up for everyone to see but she doesn't scream. She is too scared of the sound she makes.

Her mother rubs her hand to make it better but the soreness doesn't go away. 'You have to keep your mind on things,' her mother says. 'Pay attention more. You're always dreaming.'

Always dreaming. Her mother sees the dreams. Her mother tells her she is such a naughty girl. She wets the bed in her dreams and when she wakes she finds the sheets are cold and damp. She closes her eyes. She keeps them closed to send away the badness. She doesn't want to see the dark. If she shuts her eyes she thinks she can imagine she is in the light but it never seems to work and before she can stop it, the darkness floods the world.

The darkness is inside of me, glowing darkness and transparent. Lies to see through. When the light comes and I am visible again, the earth will crack.

'What a pretty girl,' the big man says. He kneels and brushes her face with his hand. He smells of disinfectant and tobacco. 'Does your hand still hurt?' he asks. 'Naughty door to hurt your hand.'

He turns to her mother. 'We have to check your bag.' He escorts them to a desk. Her mother shows him what is in her bag. A purse. A comb for their hair. A packet of crisps that they will share on the journey home. Tissues. Lipstick. Two elastoplasts. The intimate details of their lives. Her mother has to turn her pockets out and take off her shoes and hand them over for inspection. She stands in stockinged feet, toe-nails painted.

We are probed, every part of us. Between my legs. Francine watches as he strokes. Nothing is private any more. Everything I am is known to everyone.

'I have to take the teddy bear.'

The tobacco-disinfectant man prises her bear from her. They put it on the desk. Someone cuts, snip-snip along the seam. She stays silent when her teddy screams. She takes him in her arms again. His stuffing starts to float down to the floor. 'It's all right, I'll mend him,' her mother says.

Body split. Nothing mends. Everything in pieces on the floor.

'It will mend,' the nurse says to me. 'Things do mend.'

She doesn't remember many other visits. It's easier to write to him but he never sends a letter back.

Sometimes I can write the things I want to say but sometimes it is hard. If you take my words away from me, I will not exist but there are too many words in my head, they keep spilling over the sides and into the outside where they are swallowed up into the air. When the air has too many words in it, people choke on their words.

This is why I have to be so careful what I write and sometimes stay silent. My words are the most choking words of all. They ooze out of me.

The nurse says, 'It's as if words are things to you.'

Words are things. They shape the world. When she writes to her father, she sends herself to him. She posts him drawings of their new house. It isn't as big as the old one but it's quiet. No one throws stones any more or posts dirt through their letter box. There isn't any writing on the walls. She has to sleep in her mother's room but she doesn't mind. Each night she prays that God will let her dad come home again. Her mother says God listens to good children. When he doesn't come, she knows that it's because she isn't good enough.

The nurse sighs and gives my book back to me. It is quiet on the ward, quiet and still. Why is it so quiet? In the quiet, I am constantly afraid.

Chapter Fifteen

Don't like the quiet. When it goes quiet, I have to make a noise, to liven up the place and stop myself from thinking. They say I am acting up and must see Dr Raines. He's the headmaster in this place, so I expect him to give me a detention. Never been in his room before and I don't want to go now, but I get pushed in by Don and find myself in front of him.

'Have a seat, Miss Parrish,' he says.

My chair is fixed to the floor but his rotates with an irritating spin. He don't bother facing me, he just keeps scribbling down words in his book. 'Just a few notes,' he says to me.

'You can't ignore me, you know.'

'No one's ignoring you. I just want to refer to your case notes.'

The notes look like a book. All them things written about me but I never get to read them. Alex says I can make Dr Raines show me. Some kind of information act, legal and everything. 'What you writing?' I say to him. I have to repeat the words over and over because the first few times he behaves like I'm not even here in this room. He don't care. He don't expect no sense from me.

I'm getting bored now, so I go to the window. Alex says the curtains make her want to puke, but I like them. Strong colours. Everything in Britain's so anaemic. I start to pull at them. He tells me to stop misbehaving. He thinks I'm a child, eight years old. In hospital, you lose your age. My eye falls on the pictures on his wall. Women in African dress with picknies strapped upon their back. An old black man with rheumy eyes, leaning on a stick. Very liberal, very nice. What was that phrase I saw printed in the magazine? *Ethnic chic*.

'Would you like to come and sit down again now?'

'No.'

'You seem hostile.'

'I just don't want to sit in a nailed-down chair while you get to sit in one that spins.'

'You wish to be treated as an equal?'

'That would make a nice change, Mister Doctor Sir.'

'I'm willing to swap chairs with you if you'd prefer it.'

He is clever, this one, in a cunning kind of way. Brer Anansi, always has to get one up on you. So I say to him, 'It won't make no difference. You still going to behave like you know everything and I know nothing whichever chair you sit in.'

'It sounds as if you see me as some sort of father figure.'

I start to laugh, I just can't help myself. As if a man like this could be a father to me.

He picks up my scorn of him so he says, 'It was just an observation. Perhaps we could spend this time thinking about the kind of relationship you had with the other members of your family.'

'Why?'

'Because you haven't really told us very much about yourself.'

'I could have been anything. I could have been a brain surgeon.' I heard the line somewhere once. I say it to bamboozle him. Then I picture myself slicing off the top of Raines' bald head. I dig inside his skull, trying to find some throbbing grey cells. No luck whatsoever. I probe him like he is always probing me. The thought makes me laugh like a hyena. Got him puzzled now, he don't know what to make of me, the man has fewer brains than a jackass. I climb on to the desk. He can't think what to do. He starts to speak, then seems to change his mind. I stand up and look down on his bald head. It shines. The desk is like a stage. I strut my stuff. Then, I start to sing. I have a good voice, lots of power. Could have been Aretha Franklin. *Chain chain chain, chain chain chain, chain of fools.* I take a bow. Then I slide down on top of a paper mountain and sit, cross-legged. Never used to be so agile. The case notes slip to the floor, all his words about me floating down. I lean forward and pat him on the knee. It throws him like mad. He thinks a fat, middle-aged black lesbian has the hots for him – a white, skinny blob of slime with a grey moustache. That is the glory of being a mental patient. Nothing is impossible.

I talk on. Nowadays, I do a lot of things at once. Before he knows it, I'm off the desk again. I run to the window and start to bang the glass, still talking loud. I force him to listen, even though he never seems to understand a thing I say. He don't like my loudness. I see his face reflected in the glass. He screws up his mouth.

'Please sit down, Miss Parrish.'

He calls me Miss, but it's no mark of respect. No. It's because he has contempt for me, like I have for him, but because he has to pretend to be sane, he can't show it – it goes against his hypo-critic oath.

'You still seem rather excitable. Perhaps we should increase your medication.'

He don't really talk to me. He thinks out loud. If I was to say no thank you very much I don't want your fucking medication, he would not hear a word. Selective deafness. Only I say it for true. Don't mean to. It just comes out.

You know how normally when you speak, there's this thing in your head like a censor that tells you what you're not allowed to say? Well I don't have that any more. If I had to name one thing that is different about me now, it would be that. The barriers have gone. They don't work, not even if I want them to. The way I feel is like a runaway robot. A runaway robot on speed. I'm pro-grammed to do things, silly things sometimes, like the day I went to the shopping centre and pulled all the tea cosy hats off little old ladies and ran away with them. It just happened. Never planned it. Suddenly the thought was there and instead of thinking this is a bad idea, it seemed fine at the time. Don't know how else to explain it. So there I was, running round the Wandsworth Arn-dale snatching hats. Mugging, the police called it. Seven counts. But when I got put in here because of the loud music and all the singing I done, the charges got dropped. If I had not come in here, they would have put me in a court and sentenced me, Dr Raines said. He thinks I'm better off in a place like this. And I'm sup-posed to be the mental one.

'We need to give you a greater degree of control over your actions, Miss Parrish.' He's referring to the medication again. He

99

thinks chemical control is the same as me controlling things. I try to tell him that it isn't, but he don't understand. It's that selective deafness again.

The curtains are purple and lime. I start to wrap one round my waist. He tries to stop me doing it. We fight. He thinks I fight for real, but this is not the case. If I was, he would be on the floor by now. He yells for the nurses. They all come running and pull me off like I'm really hurting him. Going to give me an injection now, like they are always giving the new patient, but it just slows me down, don't knock me out, and still I keep on going all the time no matter what they do to me, everything bubbling to the surface, all these words that came to me when Josie died: fuck and shit and dyke and queer. Words I never used to say.

They take me back to the ward. I get in bed, but I can't stay still, it's like I suffocate. The new patient shuffles round the dormitory. Then she sits herself down in the centre of the room, as if she has to be in the heart of things to feel alive but she stays still, like all the life's been knocked out of her. The nurses like it when we're still: they see it as a sign we're getting better, but to me it always means we got a whole lot worse. They try to move her back to bed but she just goes on sitting like a piece of furniture, and we all have to walk around her.

Chapter Sixteen

She sits on the floor in the centre of the room, her notebook laid out in front of her. She always used to write things down; in the past it enabled her to see the patterns of her life. She could read her own words and see her existence plotted out before her, neatly packaged, so much less chaotic in the writing than in reality. But now the reverse is true; the writing seems to tangle her. It is as if it comes from somewhere else; she sees chaos in every sentence that she writes. When did words start to muddle her? She tries to think back, but answers are beyond her.

See her writing now, trying to draw the pieces of herself into something whole for the nursing staff to scrutinize. Why does she bother? One crazy woman is much like another to them.

Why do you want me to write things down? Words can't explain the things that are going on inside my head. You want to see me, but I am invisible, I have no feeling that anyone can see. If you look you will see a blank space. My body disappears from me, it is not my world. There is no way of writing down the important things. Words aren't enough. Every time I write, I build another me that is not the same as this one. There are too many versions. Each version puts me in a different space until I am endlessly outside myself. I am in a hall of mirrors. I look at myself and then I disappear in all the other images that are me and not me. I have no face. When I smile it's an illusion. I am always the reflection.

She is wearing her new school uniform. She looks smart, her mother says. She tries to put on her tie but as she faces the mirror, her hands become confused. She doesn't seem to know her left from her right. What a silly child. Now she's made the end too long, it hangs below the fattest part and flops against the waistband of her skirt. She has to start again. She'll miss the nine o'clock bell if she doesn't get a move on. Slow. She is incapable of hurrying. Sister Mary will call it West Indian time. She will say that she doesn't want West Indian time in her classroom, only Greenwich Mean Time.

There are two kinds of time, the real time and the time that I am in now. Something shifted and put me in a different phase. I am in a parallel universe. Most things are the same but strange, not real. Or more real. Sometimes reality has too much intensity. When I get back in real time again I will understand what my life is. All my thinking is about undoing the timeslip I have fallen into. Time slips away from me. Real time and unreal time. No one can connect with me in unreal time. I escape from them. This is why I can't be loved. You can't love the thing that isn't there.

Sister Mary will try her best to like her, but it won't be easy; she never understands what is required of her. But she will always work hard and she'll try to behave herself.

There she goes, trotting off to school, attempting to match the big steps of her mother. This is the fifth first day in just two years. She's tired of all the changes. She doesn't want to be new. She wants to be in places that feel familiar. She stays by her mother's side. Her mother is brisk even though she's always tired. Worn down, she calls it, by all that life has thrown at her. When she tells her mother that she is worn down too, her mother laughs and says, 'You're too young for that. When you're my age and have had my trials in life, then you can claim that living's worn you down.' She laughs again. 'Seven years old and she thinks she's had it hard.' Her mother barely notices the things her daughter does. Not the crying in the night, nor that she barely eats. Her mother is so tired that nothing seems to register. Tired of running. Tired of hoping for her husband's release. 'She campaigns tirelessly', the newspaper says but it isn't true. She is full of tiredness. Nothing left inside her. Nothing for the child that trots by her side. How many letters has she written? How many times has she seen her MP? Someone must soon see that he is innocent. She seldom has the energy to play with her daughter. They hardly talk. The daughter knows it is because she split the sky. They arrive at the school gate. Her mother doesn't wait. She nudges her through.

She joins the line of other children. No one else is new. They all came a long time ago. When they reach the classroom, she stands in front of the other children. Sister Mary asks her name. She doesn't want to tell. She shakes her head and buttons her lips. She's not allowed to say her name, her mother says, not the real one, only the pretend one. 'What's your last name, dear?' Sister Mary says. She's starting to sound cross.

She forgets. Her mum said it wasn't Jordan any more, but she can't remember what it is.

Sister Mary tuts. 'All the other children here can tell me their last name.' She looks in the register. 'James. Your last name is James.'

Everybody laughs. Someone says, 'That's a boy's name.' She starts to get hot. She wishes she was still called Jordan. She doesn't want to be called James. She wants to tell them that it's not her proper name, her mother made it up, but she's been warned that if she tells, the shouting people will come after them again.

Reality is locked in names. If you can name something, it has a reality. When you don't have a name you are invisible. If my name was known to me, I could be seen, but they took my name away and if it gets spoken, the world will end.

Sister Mary tells the class that James can be a last name too. Then she tells her she has to sit beside a boy called John. There are two other children at her table: Geraldine and Christopher. Geraldine is from Barbados. They smile at one another. Each table has a name. Theirs is the Dolphin table. John says he chose to be called a dolphin because they're the cleverest animals on the earth. Soon he is her friend. At playtime, he shares his Milky Way with her, two bites each.

Once, I could be seen and I ate and drank with other people who could be seen too but not with my real name.

One morning when her mother brings her into school, everyone begins to stare. She looks at her mother, who says she thinks they know about her father. Her mother purses her lips and holds her head high. She is trying not to cry. Perhaps they'll have to move again. Her mother hurries from the playground, the folds of her dark brown coat wrapped round her tight to ward off the cold that she now feels. The daughter watches her go. Why does her mother never seem to stay? She goes to find John but he says he doesn't want to sit with her. His mother says he can't. He says that she is not allowed to be a dolphin any more. She tells him that it's up to Sister Mary, it isn't up to him.

If I was a dolphin, I would be different and feel things in a different way but other people can't accept this and they make me into a different thing from the person I should be. Dolphins swim. Dolphins are fish but they are called mammals. Nothing is the way you think it is. When something is one thing it is really another. This is the illusion. If I was a dolphin, I could be

warm—blooded and swim too, a fish that isn't called
a fish.

She doesn't get moved off the dolphin table, but John becomes a bear
instead and he sits on the other side of the room. At playtime he shares
his Milky Way with Christopher. Geraldine still lets her play with her
tennis ball. She likes the furry feel of it. At the end of playtime, John
comes running up to her. 'Your Dad's in prison, he's a very bad man,'
he says excitedly.

'He isn't,' she answers.

'He is, he's in prison. My Dad says.'

'But he isn't bad. He didn't do what they said he did.'

'He killed a child with a knife. And a woman too. Cut them up in
pieces so they looked like dog meat out of a tin. She's got blood on her.
Look at the dog meat girl. She's got blood.'

'I haven't.'

'She has. Look, she's got a knife. She'll stick it into everyone.'

They surround her. She tries to run, but the ring closes and she can't
get through. Sister Mary comes. 'Go inside, everyone,' she says. 'Go
in at once.'

Sister Mary tries to be kind. She tells the class that it doesn't matter
what her father did, it wasn't her fault, we are not responsible for the
things our parents do. She says that everyone should just work hard and
play hard and not put their noses into things that don't concern them.

'But he didn't do anything,' she says to Sister Mary, but she isn't
listening.

Her mother fetches her. She comes in a taxi. Usually, she enjoys
riding in a car, it's a special treat, but she knows they will soon be going

to another house to live and she'll be starting at another school. All the way home, she sits close to her mother and she tries not to cry.

The badness wasn't his but it escaped into me. When I kill, I leave no trace, just silence and the reality of evil living in a soul.

She starts to close her eyes but she knows she mustn't sleep. She has to stay awake to stop the bad things getting in and out of her.

There is a sudden noise. It makes her jump. Gloria is laughing, getting tangled up inside her thoughts. She wants her father to laugh with her again. She has to catch the ball. It flies towards her up so high . . . She stretches out her arms, holding up her hands she waits and waits but as it lands, it falls between them. See her smile. She is always the reflection.

Chapter Seventeen

Don comes in first thing and flings the curtains open. Then he says, 'Come on, let's see some smiling faces. All except you, Gloria. You smile too much already.' This is because it's Founder's Day and we're all supposed to give thanks and celebration to the man who made this unit possible. In the nineteenth century, a doctor decided that people afflicted with mental illness should be treated kind with unlocked doors and proper food and no more padded cells. So he put his money into a new hospital and all the insane got treated nice and lived happy ever after.

The old hospital's long since been demolished and a general hospital with a psychiatric unit put up in its place. But since it is two hundred years almost to the day that this man founded nice and caring psychiatric treatment, the hospital have decided to use the occasion to raise some funds and to show the public what a good thing it is a place like this exists.

All week, we've been having guests shown round the ward. They come in groups of three or four from every place you can think of. Some have American accents and some flew in from

Scandinavia. They troop through the dormitory and look around and see how happy we all are from the tender loving care we get.

A little party comes through now, led by Lou. They smile at us. The new patient rocks herself and chants a bit. Lou looks pleased as punch because it proves the need for all the nursing skill she has to offer.

'It is a little cramped,' one of the guests mutters in his beard.

Louise pretends not to hear.

'There isn't a great deal of room,' he repeats, sounding critical.

Lou has to notice now. She says, 'Well of course, inner city hospitals don't have a lot of space, but siting such a unit here has been very important. It's to do with ensuring that patients remain part of the community. Their visitors have easy access to the unit and our very flexible visiting times are part of that. We don't believe in moving people with mental health problems out into the sticks where they will remain forgotten. That was the old way.'

The bearded man falls silent, but a woman with red hair and long nails painted black turns to Louise and says, 'Surely real community care means looking after people in their own home environments?'

'Of course, that is the preferred option, but patients who might be a danger to themselves or others need more intensive care in a safe environment which can protect them. And I'm sure you're aware that care in the community hasn't been a great success. Mentally ill patients have been involved in some serious crime, and the incidence of murder has alarmed the public. The suicide risk shouldn't be ignored either.'

I contemplate serious crime right now as Lou tries to pass us off as murderers and cut-throats. I put on a little show for them. In my best pink pyjamas, I run up and down the ward singing praise songs for the founder of the hospital. The sound ripples round the place, and Lou holds back the rage she feels and smiles at me real nice. Then she says, 'Come on Gloria, get yourself dressed. Aren't you feeling so good today? Never mind, we'll soon have you feeling better.'

I laugh even louder now. Who does she think she's fooling?

'If you don't feel well enough, you don't have to come to the sale this afternoon, or to this evening's show. It's up to you.'

I take the hint. It's not that I want to mingle with the public and rummage through the bring-and-buy they have. But there will be a special meal laid on, with sausage rolls and crisps and a big pork pie and it will make a nice change from the rice and kidney they tried to feed us the other day. So I quieten myself down and go and get dressed.

Think I'll wear my orange dress. It's my favourite one. I comb my hair and get it looking nice. And then I find the new patient and put her in good clothes too so she can come and celebrate. She looks like she needs pork pie. I try to get Alex to come with us, but she shakes her head so fast and fierce I have a sudden vision of it breaking loose and flying up through space until it lands full speed on Louise's stomach. It is a happy thought.

'You don't have to eat,' I say to Alex. 'The nurses are so busy trying to make a good impression they will never notice what you put upon your plate.'

'You don't understand. If I come, I'll be tempted. I have to stay here.'

I shrug and content myself with the company of the new patient and Mr Lemmington. No one notices as we leave the ward. They're all too busy with boxes and books for the bring-and-buy. The nurses have collected for weeks for this event. They ransacked their attics and their cellars in the hunt for cast-offs they could sell to raise money for the hospital. We are a worthy cause.

I stand between the new patient and Mr Lemmington and take each by the arm. I put my right foot forward and I chant, 'We're off to see the Wizard, the wonderful Wizard of Oz' and we skip and jump along the corridor in perfect rhythm. Lucky I put on my red shoes. Mr Lemmington needs a new heart, that's for sure. His own heart is buggered up good and the bypass never helped that much. The new patient seems to think she's made of straw. The least thing frightens her, but I hold her tight and tell her everything's OK each time I take a breath from singing.

We quieten down again once we reach the gym. Nothing much happening as yet. The stalls have been set up and the goods are being carried in and laid out for display. Got my eye on a red bag with a silver clasp and a velvet lining. I pick it up and examine it. 'How much is this?' I say to the woman behind the table.

'Two pounds, dear,' she replies.

I thrust the money in her hand and move away before she can change her mind. It's a lovely bag. It's nearly new and the leather's still supple and soft to the touch. I let the new patient hold it and she seems pleased. She carries it so careful, like she's scared she's going to spoil it.

Louise spots us then and comes hurrying over. 'You shouldn't have left the ward without permission.' She looks at the new patient and says, 'She isn't even well enough to be here. And as for you, Mr Lemmington, you should know better.'

I can tell she sees me as the ringleader which is not far off the truth. But she don't tell me off. Think she's afraid I'm going to cause a scene. She looks at the other two like she expects them to walk meekly back to the ward but they don't move. 'Well?' she says to Mr Lemmington.

'If it's all the same to you, Nurse, I'd rather stay here. There's a buffet in the next room and later there'll be dancing and the show. I think I'll stay and take a look.'

It is obviously not all the same to Louise but she never says a word. She just takes the new patient by the arm and starts to steer her back.

'She don't want to go,' I say to her.

'Be quiet, Gloria.'

'She don't want to go. Let her stay with me. Going to take good care of her.'

Lots of heads turn to see what all the noise is about. Just what Louise fears. She lets go of the new patient and says in a tight voice, 'All right Gloria, if you promise not to do anything silly and to come back to the ward at the end of the afternoon. I'm trusting you, you understand?'

I nod slow. I take the new patient by the hand again and lead her to the book stall. She lights up when she see the books laid out and tries to inspect them all. I take the red bag from her for a moment while she looks. She starts to read there and then, turning the pages of a paperback so fast it almost tears in two.

'Slow down,' I say to her. 'You can stay here all afternoon if you want.'

She nods and starts to take her time. She repeats lots of sentences out loud, as if she's testing the kind of sense they make. Never heard her say so much before.

Mr Lemmington joins the crowd who gather to hear the speech some hospital manager starts to make. They put him on a PA system and his voice echoes round. 'Patient care . . . safe environment . . . nurturing . . . moving back in the community . . . excellent results . . . necessary for their safety and that of those around them . . . mental illness is a fact of our society . . . we have to protect everyone involved . . .' The same old stuff. I tune him in and out. The man likes the sound of his own voice.

The new patient's still engrossed in all them books. She don't have no money with her, she left it on the ward. I offer to lend her some so she can buy but she shakes her head and says, 'It's all right, I just like to look.'

This is the first time I have ever heard a whole sentence from her that makes sense. I try not to look surprised. She smiles and goes back to digging through the books.

Not much else of interest as far as I can see. They start to sell raffle tickets and I buy one or two – my luck has to change one of these days. Might win a bottle of champagne. And before I can stop myself I imagine giving it to Josie and the look upon her face and the fun we have as we drink in front of the fire, watching television.

And then it is a funny thing, I see Josie come towards me from the corner of the room and I know she can't be there but suddenly anything is possible. I try to concentrate on what is happening around me but I find it hard. My mind keeps wandering. For a while, I forget about Mr Lemmington. I forget to keep an eye on the new patient. Everything seems so busy and I must be busy with it, it's like I have no choice, I just get pulled along. Find myself running round the room, snatching things off all the table tops and throwing them in the air so high they spin and I catch them as they land. Don't see no faces, just see colour spinning round, and the light of the sun shining down on me through the high window of the gym. I feel so warm and full of life, but I feel I cross a line and then I start to fall, down, then up, then down again; I'm flying now, faster than the sounds around me, faster than the light, and I am happy-scared, and it's like the best ride in the world, and I'm still in my own body, I can feel my arms and legs, yet I am weightless too, nothing holds me down, and everything is right and wrong at the same time. The new patient rapidly comes into view. She looks at me like she is seeing something new. 'Gloria,' she says to me, and she tugs on my hand and tries to bring me back to earth, but I'm not ready to return just yet, still flying off the edges of the world.

Chapter Eighteen

They make us leave the gym. Gloria is different. I take her hand again. I want to talk to her, but it is hard to break the silence. Don leads us back to the ward. He is angry – I can tell by the stomping way he walks and how he pulls the keys that are fastened to his belt with a piece of string. Gloria will be disappointed that we missed the pork pie. I take the bag and hold it tight. I want to keep it safe for her. It is a beautiful colour. She is a red person. Sometimes when I look, I don't really see. Today, I'm seeing lots of things. For the first time, I become aware that she is large, with warm brown eyes. Her smile is not a reflection. I put the bag in her wardrobe. We sit on our beds. After a while, she comes over and sits next to me. 'You writing in your notebook again?' she asks. She leans over my shoulder and adds, 'They make me do it on a tape.'

'Why?'

'Can't read my writing. Can't understand the things I write.'

I nod. They can't understand what I write either, but it doesn't seem to bother them. They impose their own meanings on it.

Gloria gets up again and walks awkwardly to her own bed. She sits on it and looks at me, but I don't mind her looking – she is a watcher, she is allowed to look. I pick up my pen and try to write. Hilary said I have to get more done. They want to see everything. 'Tell us more about your parents,' she said, 'the kind of family you came from.' It's not that I've forgotten. It's just that I don't want to tell.

Some things are private, they are not for seeing or being seen.

She won't tell the truth. She doesn't know what the truth is any more. She sits on her bed and fabricates. You can't believe a word she writes.

I loved my father.

And hated him too. She was ashamed of him, but she buried that. Now she must resurrect him.

When he came back, it wasn't really him.

He sits in a worn armchair in the centre of the room. It is their one good piece of furniture. Like a cherished ornament, he's been given pride of place. She and her mother walk around him and admire. He sits there passively, unable to decide what is expected of him. Every now and then, her mother fetches him a cup of tea and a plate of bourbon biscuits on a tray. 'The comforts of home,' she keeps repeating, with a nervous smile.

She smiles too. She wants him to like her. She's fourteen, and for the past ten years, her sparse contact with her father has been conducted in public, across a table, not touching, speaking low, trying to remain unheard. They still speak to one another as if they have no privacy, and they haven't hugged yet either. To be in such close proximity, unwatched, is unnerving for all three of them.

'What would you like to do?' her mother says to him.

'Can I have a bath?' he asks.

'Yes of course, Sam, you know you can. You can do whatever you want.'

It's hard to get this through to him. He asks for everything and waits for it to come to him. When they walk to the shops at the end of their street, he remains at his daughter's side, as if they have been welded to one another. As they buy a paper and a few bags of crisps, he shakes his head in disbelief at the price of things. 'It's changed,' he mutters. 'Everything has changed.' She sees that her mother was right to move them back to Hackney in time for his return. Even the familiar is strange to him.

When the familiar becomes strange, reality gets lost. I waited for him to come home but when he arrived it was someone else.

She's been waiting ten whole years for his arrival. She planned celebrations that were full of happiness. They laughed and held one another, the lost years forgotten. But his return is joyless. Her father doesn't want to celebrate. He seems lost. She doesn't know why. She doesn't understand.

When you get looked at it hurts so you learn to hide from the looking and disguise yourself. Then when you try to return you can't be found again.

On the day he is freed by the Court of Appeal, they are besieged by cameramen. Journalists leap out at them in anticipation of a juicy soundbite. But her father barely speaks.

'What does it feel like to be free, Mr Jordan?'

'Great,' he mutters. It sounds like a grunt.

'Were you expecting the court to vindicate you today?'

'I knew that one day I would be free. I knew that God was with me.'

'Can you stand with your wife and daughter on the steps of the court?'

They jostle for a moment, trying to get into position.

'Put your arms around your wife and daughter, Mr Jordan.'

He raises his arms momentarily, but they flop down again, as if all movement is outside his own volition.

If I get touched, I will turn to stone.

'What action do you expect to be taken against the officers who fabricated evidence against you?'

'We're expecting a full investigation,' the solicitor says.

'Do you feel bitter at all, Sam?'

'If you're black you don't expect to get a fair trial in this country,' her mother interjects, but it is as if she hasn't spoken.

'How does it feel, Mr Jordan, to know that the real killer of your first wife and her son is still walking free?'

Her father grunts again.

'What kind of compensation do you expect to get from this miscarriage of justice? How will you be spending your money?'

Her father still doesn't reply. He is nervous and awkward. She is embarrassed for him. The solicitor steps in and says that no amount of money can make up for the ten-year devastation of their lives. Cameras click and whirr. 'I understand that you've been ill,' a woman reporter says.

The solicitor intervenes once more. 'My client's health has been damaged irreparably by the indignities he's suffered at the hands of the prison system. We expect this to be fully reflected in the compensation offered.'

'Do you have a figure for us?' someone else jumps in.

'Negotiations will be conducted through the appropriate channels.'

'Mr Jordan, is it true that you've sold your story to The News of the World?'

'No comment,' the solicitor says. 'Now if you don't mind, ladies and gentlemen, my client is exhausted. He needs to go home.'

Home. Her father sits in the armchair, turning the pages of his Bible and he barely stirs. He seldom talks to his wife and daughter, though when the journalist arrives for the exclusive interview, he seems, for a while, to find a voice.

She sits in the kitchen. The walls are thin. She can hear their voices. But whatever her father is asked, he only talks about his faith and how it's seen him through. He sees his imprisonment as a test from God. She's heard it so many times. She opens her book again and starts to read. At least the truth will come out now, she tells herself.

When the interview appears, they buy thirty copies. It is only as she starts to read that she becomes aware of their naivety. No smoke without *fire — it's there in every word. The picture of her father doesn't look like him. It shows a scowling man, savagery evident in his unkempt hair and the wildness of his eyes. His first wife, Maxine, had lovers by the dozen, some of whom were black.*

They tell themselves that it doesn't really matter. Nobody believes the things they read. The pile of newspapers slowly diminishes. They clean their shoes on them. They are used to line the floor when the new carpet is laid down. They come in handy on the day that they discover her mother's forgotten to buy toilet rolls.

She expects her father's confidence to grow as he gets used to being home. She believes that soon he'll stop behaving like a guest and learn to help himself to things instead of being waited on.

'He's been institutionalized,' her mother says.

'What do you mean?'

'He got used to being told what to do.'

'Well, he'll have to learn,' her daughter says.

'Give him time, it's hard for him.'

'It's hard for us too.'

She'd never imagined her father's presence would feel like an intrusion. He prays and reads the Bible constantly. When she tries to talk to him, he shoos her away impatiently and turns his attention back to the building of the Tower of Babel. Sometimes friends from before he went to prison come to visit, but he seldom welcomes them. When her mother asks why he doesn't want to see them, he says, 'Too much time's gone by, Cecile. We don't know each other any more.'

He's a stranger to everyone, and they to him. His daughter's eventual withdrawal centres not on prayer but on books. She reads at least one a day, preferring the spaces of fiction to the skewed reality of family life.

Chapter Nineteen

He was born again.

The words are always in her head, so she writes them. She is always writing now. She thinks it will protect her, she doesn't know what from. Her whole body aches. It is a punishment. She can't control her limbs; they twitch and tremble, jerking even when she sleeps. Thirst fires her throat and makes her lips crack but she doesn't want to drink; it hurts to swallow. When they bring more tablets, she refuses them. She thinks she has the right.

'You have to take these, you're on a section. We'll inject you again if we have to.'

She pushes them inside her mouth, then cups her hand and spits them out again. 'I can't,' she says. 'They're too big.' Incapable. Even simple tasks are beyond her now.

'It's all right, it's one of the side effects,' the nurse tells her and gets her to break the tablets in two. 'We'll get some syrup for your next dose. Try to keep drinking lots of water, you'll have a dry mouth as well,' she says, before moving on.

She can hear her own thoughts; they reverberate around her. She no

longer has control, the inside of herself is outside now. She covers her-
self with the counterpane

but still it hurts. Dr Raines comes into the dormitory. He sits
in the chair beside me. 'How are you feeling today?' he says.

The question is too large. I don't know how to answer him.

'Have you written anything more in your journal?'

I reach across and hand my notebook to him. He scans the
pages. Then he nods. 'Can I take this away with me?' he asks.

'Why?'

'I'd like to look at it properly. It might help me to get to know
you better.'

She doesn't want to be known. She values the private spaces she's
created for herself.

'OK, if you want to.'

He gets up to go, tucking the notebook under his arm. I try to
remember what I wrote. How much will he glean from it?

Not much. She's better at concealing than revealing.

I slip down underneath the bedclothes again. What did I write?
Sometimes I can see the words, but at other times, they slip away
from me.

In order to exist, you have to be reborn.

122

I remember writing that. What will he make of it? Sometimes, I scramble things on purpose.

Her father wants her to be a good girl but he is saddened by her inability to pray. Why can't she believe? He believes implicitly.

because when you lose everything, you have to find something to believe in.

Her father speaks like a preacher, of sin and redemption and ever-lasting fire. He believes his life has been a test, a set of divine obstacles which he has overcome to survive and prosper. He's one of the chosen now.

I was chosen, then I was forsaken. If you listen to the devil you become his child.

He hears the Word of God. Born a Catholic, he lapsed for a while but in prison his faith grew to mighty proportions. Every sentence in the Bible has a meaning just for him. He has been saved.

She is glad for him. His faith slowly seems to give him strength. He gets out of the armchair at last and goes to the shops alone. He begins to plan for the future.

I have no future any more. With the second coming, the faithless will be abandoned and exist in nothingness.

The church welcomes him at first, but he is too loud in the professing of his faith. He tries to tell the congregation about his love of God and the manner of his salvation, but this is not the Catholic way. He should have been a Jehovah's Witness, or a born-again Christian, perhaps. The priest glares at him, embarrassed and discomforted. He doesn't know his place. Who is he to think he has been chosen? His fervour has its roots in Africa, it belongs outside Catholicism, with its sweeping white vestments, its resistance to song. Yet he doesn't seem to notice their rejection of him. He is still slow and hesitant but there is a glow about him now. He says he understands. He knows what life is, the meaning of it. He no longer hurries past the people on the street, head bowed, eyes to the pavement. He holds his head high and tells anyone who'll listen (and even those who won't), that God loves them and they must take him to their hearts. Soon he is standing on street corners with a megaphone, all hesitation gone. Her mother says that it's a miracle. She watches her father and tries to understand, but the change in him bewilders her.

He takes her to church. They have a pew to themselves even though others are standing. She sits through the sermon, the Consecration and the Blessing but nothing seems to reach her. She tries to believe, for her father's sake, but she can't be good, it isn't in her. She listens to the priest and wants to think that they are loved by God but doubts keep creeping in. They show in her face. She walks with doubt. She holds doubt to her. Doubt is evident in everything she is, even though she never allows it to be present in her words.

Sometimes you have to be silent, it's a question of survival, but your words show even when you do not speak them.

Her father sees and he doesn't understand. He's forgotten the details of his struggle and now he thinks that faith is easy, there for the taking. He thinks she's being obstinate, obstructive, closing her heart and mind to God. Her redemption becomes his priority. Perhaps her faithlessness is bound up in the books she reads.

You have to be careful what words you ingest. Sometimes the badness gets in through the pages.

He comes into her room late one night. He doesn't knock on her door any more. It is as if he is trying to trap her.

'What are you reading?' he says to her.

'Beloved.'

He hasn't heard of it. He takes it out of her hands and studies the early chapters. He only sees the surface. Perverted sexual acts. Sin and corruption. He turns to her in fury. 'How can you read something like this? You're only fourteen years old. No wonder you're the way you are.'

'What do you mean? What way?' she asks.

'You know what I'm talking about.' He goes to the shelf that he's only just put up for her. He knocks the books to the floor. He gathers them in his arms and removes them from her.

She kneels on the bed. 'There's nothing wrong in them. I wouldn't read anything that was wrong, honestly I wouldn't.'

He doesn't listen to her.

He knows what she is. He's seen it in her.

'Read the Bible. The only word you need is the Word of God.'

When there are too many words you lose the sense of things.

The light on the wall above her bed is buzzing. A low, prickly hum that whooshes inside her body through her mouth. She has to make it stop. She stands on the bed and smashes the oval nightlight with her fist; long slivers of glass become embedded in her knuckles, causing them to bleed. Someone comes running. Feet and voices, thrusting their way through. She wants to go home. The shout is welling up inside her but she can't make it leave. *I want to go home.* Which of the voices is hers? She hates the muddle of things, the endless confusion of it. She is fused to sound.

Her arms are pinned. Someone pulls her down on to the bed. Her skirt is lifted. Punctured skin. Sticky fluid running down her leg.

'The needle's broken. You'll have to get another one.'

'Hold her still, she's biting me.'

'She's too strong.'

'Keep her head back then. I don't want fucking rabies.'

'She don't know what's happening. She's scared.'

'Get out of here, Gloria. Just keep her still, Don, OK?'

'She's still under section, isn't she?'

'What do you think? Just get the bloody needle in again before I lose my hand.'

She feels the sharpness of it. Sticky liquid floating through. She remembers from before that she will sleep very soon, and awaken with a foul taste in her mouth and a stuffed-up feeling in her head. She wants Clyde. When will he come? She needs him. From the far end of the room, her father turns towards her.

She tries to run, but her legs won't move. They've put something inside her, it holds her down with invisible weights. Someone is clutching her hand. A woman's voice. A back-home voice that sounds like her mum. She wants to go home. She stands by the door, watching, waiting for her mum to come. She doesn't like this place. There's no ice cream, and her doll's been put in a cupboard until she's good again. 'Come on, come and sit down.'

'I want to go home.'

'You live here now.'

'I want to go home. I'm waiting.'

'Well you can't wait here.'

'I'm waiting for my mum to come.'

She has to get to the baby. She throws off the bedclothes and tries to run to the door. Someone blocks her path. She pushes past and turns the handle but the door is locked. She hammers it with her fists, trying to force the wood and the glass but her hands are sore and bleeding and she can't break through.

'Jesus, not again. We need a bloody elephant gun.'

'We can't give her any more chlorpromazine. She's already had the dose that Dr Raines prescribed. Get her into a side room. Someone will have to sit with her until he comes to stitch her hand.'

'Count me out.'

'Hilary can do it. Go and get her, Don. You should be in the day room, Gloria.'

'I want to stay here.'

'Well you can't. We've got enough to do with this one. It's OK, just leave us for a while until we get her sorted out. You can come back later on.'

'He didn't have to pull her. It's like you said, she's scared. She don't understand what's going on.'

'Just get out of the way please Gloria and let us deal with it.'

The room is small, little bigger than a cupboard. Room for a bed and a chair. Someone is watching her. Whenever she stands up and tries to get out, someone pulls her down again. Why can't she go home? Her mother will be wondering where she is. They get the doll out of the cupboard and lay it in her arms. She's sleeping. She hugs the baby to her.

'What's your baby's name?'

'Francine.'

'Why don't you put her back to bed and come downstairs for tea?'

'You can't leave babies on their own. You have to get a babysitter.'

'She'll be all right, I promise you. Come on, no crying now, you're far too big for that. Come downstairs with me and eat your tea. It's fish fingers, your favourite. Come on, don't make a fuss. If you eat something, you'll start to feel better.'

They try to make her drink from a blue plastic cup but it tastes sickly and sweet.

'This will make you feel better, you're very dehydrated. Dr Raines will be here to do your hand in a minute. Swallow this before he comes.'

She feels the liquid bubble in her mouth. She spits it out. She's left Francine upstairs.

'Lie still, it's all right.'

A man comes in. He has a tin. He probes the sore parts of her hand, picking out the fragments. He gets a needle out and pricks her finger with it. Sleeping Beauty. A hundred years she'll sleep. She closes her eyes, then opens them again. He's sewing her skin as if she's made of cloth, seaming all the gaps. It hurts.

She's sleepy again. Her eyelids flutter down. She has to stay awake, how else can she work out what they are doing to her? But her eyes stay shut. She begins to drift. No, she has to be awake, she has to know what's going on.

The counterpane is blue. It feels rough against her skin. He is sewing her hands together. She can't pull them apart.

'Stop struggling. If you don't lie still, the sutures will be a mess. Can't you keep her still, Nurse? Did you give her the full dose of chlorpromazine? We'll have to increase it, I think. She's a tough little creature, isn't she?'

She isn't tougher than Thomas or Brian, but sometimes she is louder than them. When she shouts they lock her upstairs until she's calm again. Francine stays in the cupboard then, sometimes for days.

'There, it's done. Keep a better eye on her Nurse, I've got enough on as it is without something like this to deal with.'

'It happened very suddenly, there was nothing we could do.'

'I want her specialled for the time being.'

'We haven't got the staff, there are two off sick this afternoon.'

'This is a priority. And you'd better keep her in this room.'

She makes her eyes come open again. She wants to see. The ceiling is white. She is always being watched. God and his angels see everything she does, her mother says. In the name of the Father. The father is dead. He died when she was four. And of the Son. No sons. She can't give birth to sons. She has a baby daughter. And of the Holy Ghost. She feels his presence penetrating deep inside her, a strange kind of ecstasy. Where is the child? She has to draw the strength to find her. Amen. She remembers the words. Her father says them with her. The Lord is with you. All the time. No private spaces. She wishes it could be quieter

129

in her head. There is too much noise. No peace in prayer and praising. Loud enough to wake the dead.

She opens her eyes and rises from her bed. She is standing in the corridor, walking out towards the light, hearing the voice calling her, the voice of God, she knows it now, a back-home voice yet pure. Not God, no, the voice of her mother. No, not her mother, nor her mother's mother. The voice of her mother's mother's mother. The spirit of all the ancestors gathered into one large body who leans over her and says, 'No need to be afraid. Try to go to sleep.'

She is awake and asleep at the same time. She tries to get the bed-clothes off. The room is warm, she can no longer breathe.

'Time for your medication. Come on, sit up. Put these in your mouth. Come on.'

She raises her head. 'I don't want it,' she says.

'You have to take them, you're on a section. We'll inject you again if we have to.'

The nurse holds out the little cup. She takes it and puts the tablets on her tongue. She tries but she can't swallow them.

'Get them down you.'

She can't swallow them. 'They're too big,' she says.

'Is she too groggy or is this a side effect, do you think?'

'Don't know. You've told Raines. Let him deal with it.'

'Do you know what he said? He thought we should have kept a better eye on her.'

'They get paid for sitting on their arses, these registrars.'

'He's useless anyway. He should have given that injection. They bleeped him but he wasn't answering. He only bothered to turn up when it was all over bar the shouting. I suppose I'd better get the syrup.'

They make her drink a thick foul-tasting liquid. She can feel it trickling through her throat and into her oesophagus. It heats up in her belly like a fire.

She needs the fire. She needs to be cleansed, made pure again. Soul white as ivory.

And all the while, the voices echo through her head, spinning her name across the air and back again. She covers herself with the counterpane, but still it hurts . . .

Chapter Twenty

The new patient been put in a side room now so I use her locker to store some of the things I have — not enough room in mine. I fill it with shampoo and baby oil. And then I get the news that Dr Daley wants to see me in the ward round. Knew it was about to happen when I ran out of hair sheen. Every end of hair sheen I get a summons. Feel a little nervous. At least fifteen people will be there and all of them will be allowed to make decisions about my case. Most of them I don't even know, like the one with the short spiky hair and the gravel voice who always wears the miniskirt. She looks me up and down like I'm from another planet and she says, 'I would like to know what kind of progress Gloria thinks she's made since she came to the unit.' Every time is the same. And I don't even know who she is or what she has to do with me. After I answer, she says, 'Gloria doesn't seem to have any real wish to get better,' and she shakes her head real slow and sad, like I am a bitter disappointment to her.

It's nearly lunchtime now. The morning goes so slow when you wait for something. They always see us after two o'clock in the television room. Everyone gets sick of this because they want to watch the afternoon film on Channel Four. It's usually one of them black and white comedy films that everyone has seen at least fifty times – a *Carry On* show or something with Alec Guinness in it. But it passes the time, and it don't make much demand on the concentration, so when we can't watch because all the high and mighty doctors have to occupy the room, we get fed up and remember what a boring thing it is to be in hospital.

'Come on, it's time for lunch. Everybody in the dining room.'

I put away my crocheting. These days, I have no trouble getting started on a thing, but I never seem to finish. This spider web's been going on for weeks and it don't get no bigger. My heart's not in it, I suppose. What is the point of trying to brighten up my house if I don't even know when or if I will be going back? Besides, whichever way you look at it, a doily is a foolish thing. What purpose does it have? And I am tired of staring at the colour. Pink seemed nice and bright when I saw it in the shop, but it is getting stale now. Makes me think of Turkish delight. I have a sweet tooth but I never cared too much for that. Sticks to your gums and has a sickly taste.

I always like to be first in line when them serving dinner. I like a good size portion with a lot of sauce. They never have hot pepper sauce in here you know. And most of the time we get a cabbage leaf floating round in gravy with a slice of Bernard Matthew chicken breast. English food don't have a lot of flavour. Josie used to make dumplings so light they melt in the mouth. And jerk chicken with a tenderness that made you think you gone to heaven. I used to do the sweet things. And I baked my own bread, you know. None of that polystyrene stuff you get in the supermarket.

Today we have sausage, chips and beans, or salad if you're feeling desperate. Hilary is doing the serving so she slips in some extra beans for me. She knows how much I appreciate my food. I sit down at a table with Mrs Isaac and Mr Lemmington. He picks away at a salad leaf on account of his heart. Mrs Isaac gets kosher food in a special foil container with a label on. It looks so much nicer than what I have on my plate that I think of turning Jewish. Not such a funny thing as you might think, to have a black Jew. Sammy Davis Junior for one. And the Ethiopians that got an air-lift to Israel in the famine on account of being the lost tribe – wouldn't mind a visit there some day. Lots of sights to see like the Dead Sea and the Wailing Wall. Wish me and Josie had gone back to Jamaica for a holiday the way we planned.

We went to Brighton once. Not a lot of interest there. Just a stony beach and a run-down fair that had the tiredest old ghost train you ever did see. Bits of string that smacked you in the face as you trundled through, supposed to be the Hand of Evil. And cardboard cut-out figures with glow in the dark paint. Eerie as nothing. Could have done a better job myself. Josie laughed though. She thought it was the funniest thing. I miss Josie's laughter. She always saw the funny side of life though she got downhearted too. She was not a straightforward person. I was always the straightforward one. Sometimes now it seems as if I behave more like her than me, but it's just a way to remember and to keep her close.

'Could you pass the water, please?'

Mrs Isaac is always so polite. I thought at first that she looked down on me, but it's just a distance that she keeps with everyone. She has depression. Her face is like a mask, still and empty, and she never smiles. She always does everything the nurses tell her, but she still don't seem to be getting any better. They've got her lined up for ECT, as a last resort. I tell her not to let them do it but she don't seem to care what happens to her. She eats up all her food and I think she could have done with more. Although it always looks so nice in its little foil tray, the portion would barely feed a chicken. She don't say a word, but I can see the lack of it makes her even sadder. She stares at that foil, willing it to multiply. She has had to suffer – there was lots of deprivation in her family. Her mother and father came to England in the 1940s. They were in a concentration camp. She told us in the group last week. And I sat and listened to the story and it was so hard to hear even though she only told the tip of it. Had to force myself to listen, force myself to think about the hurt in her and the other people in her family. It festers in the soul. Why do we let it happen? Why is it we still allow the hatred to survive? How can we stand aside when Pakistani homes get petrol bombed and gays get beat up in the street and the youth put in jail for crimes they don't commit and the graves of Jews defiled with obscenity and foulness? We're in the twenty-first century and still things don't change.

Alex is sitting at the end of the table. They let her eat without a nurse now because she put on some weight. She come up to me last night and said, 'Look my legs. Look at them. They're thick as tree trunks.'

Made me smile. She has the skinniest little legs that ever did exist and her thighs are the same size as my arms. She has a special diet. She can get bun if she wants it, and biscuits, any time of day or night. Funny thing, that. I want to eat, so they say I should be on a diet. They plan on making me cut down. She don't want to eat, so they are stuffing her like turkey bred for Christmas.

The new patient just come in. Louise is leading her like the blind leading the blind. She is put in a seat and then Hilary fetches her meal to the table. This is a new step. They been feeding her in the side room up until today. Her eyes dart around like she is scared of what she is going to see. She picks up a sausage and takes a bite. Her body is tense, like she is all wound up inside. Suddenly she jumps and throws the plate; gravy and beans spatter over Louise. She starts to yabber something. Think she is seeing devils now. Don't have no problem with that. Louise is easily mistaken for the spawn of Satan.

Don comes in and asks Lou if she's OK. Then he tells the new patient to clear up the mess. It's obvious she don't even hear but he goes on and on, and in the end, something must get through because she runs off down the corridor. Don goes after her and yanks her back but then Louise says just leave her and starts to clean the mess herself. The new patient's screaming now so they haul her off to the side room again. Perhaps they will give her stuff to calm her down, I don't know, all I can think about is this ward round thing this afternoon. Sometimes you can get discharged there and then, straight off the ward and home. So I decide to make myself look so nice that everyone will see how fit and well I am and what a credit I will be to the community, if they decide to care.

Takes me quite a time to choose what dress to wear. It's not like I have a fabulous selection, just that you have to match things up and not a lot goes with the red shoes — the only decent pair I have. Josie said red shoes are just a luxury. Think she disapproved. She liked to have fun, but she also liked to pay the bills on time. Sometimes I used to think that having fun was more important. We never got into a big lot of debt, we just fell behind a bit. Never had the bailiffs in — had more pride than that. Just cut things fine, so sometimes we lived on egg and gave jerk chicken a miss for a time.

And I was right, it's very plain to see. We could have saved all our money for retirement and Josie never would have gone to Spain or got that dress that suited her to the ground or eaten lobster on her birthday at the fancy restaurant. What use is money in the bank if you're too dead to spend it? That's what I ask myself.

I have some mascara in my make-up bag and a little bit of lip gloss. It is a pity that I only have a plum colour as it don't go so well with my orange dress but I'm in a hospital, what do you expect? Don't have no L'Oréal cosmetics hidden in the bottom of my locker. I look in the mirror and sigh a bit. Never imagined living on past thirty-five. Funny to think how long I survive. When I was a little girl we had to write a composition called 'The Twenty-First Century'. I tried to imagine being more than fifty years of age but it was way outside my comprehension. I figured if I lived that long, I'd be rich, with my own car and a husband

and at least six children. Not a lot of that come true, I have to say. Would have liked the car.

I sit on my bed and try not to crease my clothes before they call me in. I notice the new patient leave her money on her bedside cabinet, so I hide it in her drawer for safe keeping. Things sometimes go missing here. Hard to tell if it is theft or just confusion. I lost my watch the other day. The nurses had to fill out a report. Don't mind losing my sense of time. Seems OK to me. The nurses tell me when I have to do every little thing and it goes so slow in any case, it's better not to notice what the hour is. But right now, I could do with seeing how long the ward round has been going on. They say I'm number three. Normally, they give us twenty minutes each and talk to one another in between. Think I'm due in after four. That's a long time to wait when you're hoping to go home. I spray a little perfume on my wrist and hope the scent is not too pungent. Acting sensible is important here.

At last they say they're ready for me now. The television been pushed back so maybe they're not looking at the film between seeing patients. Dr Daley is a very important man, or so his flunkies tell me. Written books. He has a beard like a proper psychiatrist and he uses fancy words which the other people in the team translate. He does this now. 'Well, Gloria, it seems that your sartorial elegance has surpassed itself today.' I look at Hilary and she says, 'You're looking very smart today, Gloria.'

'Yes,' I answer them, 'but I don't have no L'Oréal.'

Everybody laughs. Not sure it is the kind of laughter that I like. Dr Daley's wearing a dark blue suit and a blue tie with thin black stripes, so I say to him, 'Your sartorial elegance surpassed itself too Dr Daley.' They all laugh again. Dr Daley leans forward and says, 'How are you at the moment, Gloria?'

'OK. I'd like to go home.'

'The nursing staff tell me this has been quite a difficult week for you. You're still not sleeping for more than a couple of hours and you're causing quite a lot of disruption on the ward.'

'What disruption?'

Dr Daley opens a notebook and looks in it for a while. Then he says, 'When you went for the walk the other day, you were very loud and jumping around a lot.'

'I just enjoyed the walk, that's all.'

'And then on Saturday, at the Founder's celebration, you were so excitable and agitated that you had to be sedated.'

It's hard to know how to answer this. Feels like Judgement Day when the Angel of the Lord reads out all the sins you ever committed from his big gold book. I start to protest my innocence but he holds up his hand to silence me. 'Are you saying that these things didn't happen, Gloria?'

'No. They happened. But there is different ways of seeing it, you know.'

'Different ways of seeing it?'

I really hate it when they act like parrots and repeat the words you say. 'Yes. What is excitement to some people is normal behaviour to others, isn't it?'

He smiles, like he has caught me out. 'This is the crux of the matter, Gloria. Your view of what is normal conflicts with that of most other people.'

139

'So how come you're so sure that you are right and I am wrong?'

'I think it's fair to say that your judgement is impaired at present and that is why you need to be here, in this psychiatric unit.'

I start to speak again, but my words get confused. It is the situation and the way all these people that I don't even know sit here in judgement and criticize my clothes.

'Calm down, please Gloria.'

'Don't have to be calm just because you say so. You are not at the right hand of God sat in judgement. You can't fly, don't have no wings. You don't have no right to tell me what is right and wrong. I am not a person.'

I don't mean to say I am not a person. I mean that is how I feel, like they took away the human part of me and put a mental patient in its place.

Dr Daley turns to the other staff in the room and he says, 'Does anyone have any further questions for Gloria?'

Spiky hair just got to have her say. She sits back and crosses her long legs in the miniskirt and asks, 'What kind of progress do you think you've made these past few weeks Gloria?'

That is it. I have had enough of these damn fool people. Before she can shake her head and look sad and disappointed, I run from the room and into the dormitory. Alex has a teddy bear sitting on the end of her bed. I pick it up and take it to the television room. I fling open the door and throw it in the middle of the floor. It lands at the foot of all them stuck-up mental health professionals. 'If you want to ask fucking stupid questions, ask the teddy bear,' I say. Then I run out again, and I make sure I bang the door so hard the whole unit rattles. Can't help but laugh at the look on Dr Daley's face.

Hilary rushes out after me and says, 'It's all right, Gloria.' It's then that it hits me and my whole body starts to shake. They'll never let me leave and go home after that. I've really done it now. Should have played along with them. Should have said the things they wanted to hear. That is my trouble at the moment, you know. I always have to run off my mouth, and I never see the consequence until it is too late.

Chapter Twenty-One

There is a nurse with me all the time now. I know why she's here. As we sit together I keep writing in my notebook. If you repeat the same words often enough they lose the power to confuse.

'Where are your clean clothes?' the nurse says to me.

I don't answer her. I hid my T-shirt in the cistern when they forgot to watch me for a moment. I have to be so careful what I wear.

See the way she comes down the stairs in a skirt that's three or four inches above her knee and a top tight enough to show the curve of her breasts. These are the clothes she's always worn, but her father says they are a temptation to sin. When men look at her, they are filled with forbidden thoughts. Beyond their control. She examines herself in the mirror and becomes aware of the body she has taken for granted until now. She tries to see what her father sees but it remains undetectable to her. She wants to wear the skirt but she's afraid. Perhaps her father's right. She goes upstairs again and puts on a pair of jeans.

*i am captured in the looking mine and theirs
all tangled up*

Her father comes to talk to her. He sits in the chair by her bed. 'You
know how much I love you and your mother,' he says. 'I only want
what's best for you. I missed you so much. You were always with me,
even in my dreams. My one great regret about that time is that I didn't
see you growing up.'

She knows that he is only trying to protect her. She wants to please
him, to be the daughter that he dreamed about.

'What would you like most? I mean, if you could choose any present
in the whole world, what would it be?'

She tries to think. There are so many things, yet nothing that really
matters to her. Perhaps she should say clothes but they will only be a
source of conflict. A music system. Or a dog, she's always wanted one.
She can't decide.

When the compensation comes, he buys her a computer. 'It's to help
you with your school work. You could get top grades.' He's already
mapping out her future. Sixth form college. University. She's slow to
get the hang of it but eventually she learns to type her essays on the
laptop he's provided.

They move again. To a three-bedroom terraced house just off Hackney High Street. They buy it outright. Her father takes a pride in this;
he says he earned the money. They've got a garden again now. She
could have had a dog.

Her father is always there, watching her. He follows her round the
house, telling her what she should be doing and how she should
behave. In the early days of his return, she longed for him to come

143

alive. Now she wishes he'd go back to playing dead again. She needed to be visible to him then but now she wants to be ignored. She feels confused.

the tangle of my thoughts

But sometimes he surprises her. He takes her to a fair. They go when it's dark. The lights glow red and green, bright enough to dazzle. She thinks he'll tell her it's a place of sin, but instead it's as if he's gone back to being the father she knew at four years old. He takes her on the dodgems. He buys her candyfloss. He shoots metal ducks and they all fall flat, pinging as they go. She sees a fish. He wins it for her. Shiny fish in a plastic bag. She feels warm inside. Safe. Wrapped in his love. It's as if the last ten years have been wiped away. They ride on the waltzer, the music vibrating beneath them. Her head is thrown back by the speed of the ride. When they return home she hugs him tight. It is the first real holding. She thinks that the bad times are over now. She thinks they've put it all behind them.

then i spoil it

He sees her with a boy. Benson Miller, he's in her class at school. She's walking down the street with him. They're holding hands, they laugh and shout together. They share a cigarette. When she gets home her father shuts her in her room. He won't let her out. He tells her she's the devil's child. Now he wants to know where she is every minute of the day. He takes her to school in the car and fetches her home again.

He says he wants to meet her friends, but she dares not ask them back. Too many questions. He wants to know more about the boys she spends her time with. What she does with them. Where she does it. She is silent because there's nothing to tell, but he doesn't believe her. He says she's always telling lies.

liar liar pants on fire

She is not allowed to leave the house without him. When she goes to buy new clothes, he makes her get the ones he likes. Neutral colours, nothing much revealed. His voice rings in her ears whenever she goes to dress herself. That T-shirt's too low cut. You can't wear those jeans, they're too tight in the hip. She looks like a tart in the strappy shoes she wears. The earrings she wants to buy make her look cheap.

my outsides been taken away from me

It is as if he wants to worm his way inside her, fill her mind with nothing but his thoughts. He says he has to keep an eye on her. Keep her from sin. She is pert. Insolent. She doesn't do a thing she's told.

Sometimes, she escapes from him. She goes to the library or sits in the park. But no pleasure is innocent to him. He suspects her constantly.

i try to understand i know how hard its been for him.

She pretends compassion is the only feeling that she has towards him.

bad thoughts inside my head

He says she's almost past redeeming. Even at night, he watches her. He sits by her bed in her room to stop her falling into sin.

The nurse sits beside my bed. If she doesn't stay with me, the evil will get out. She takes me for walks, and goes with me to the dining room. When I have a bath, she's watching me. She knows she has to do it, she knows it keeps things safe.

Chapter Twenty-Two

Don't know why you still want to hear me with this tape recorder thing. It's not like you really bother listening to what I have to say. And it's hard to find a place quiet enough to do it. On the last one I recorded, all you got was background noise and the sound of the machine polishing the day room floor.

Dr Raines said if I behaved myself, you'd think about letting me go home. But in the ward round everybody said I misbehaved too much. It seems to me you always move the goal posts. And it's not even true, you know. I done a lot of good things since I come to this unit. For a start, I cheered up Mr Lemmington. I tried to cheer up Mrs Isaac too but this was not a great success. And I also got the new patient to do all kinds of thing she never done before, like talk a bit and watch TV and comb her hair each day and sit down quiet from time to time and just enjoy the peace. It don't seem right, you know, that no one been to see her yet. You sure you done everything you can to find her relatives? And it's time you got her sorted out with proper meals. I can coax her to eat a little bit but not enough. She is going to waste away like Alex if you don't watch out.

Something she could do with is a few more books here on the ward. When we went to the Founder's Day thing, she spent hours looking at the books they had for sale. Think she'd get better quicker if you got her some good books to read. And another thing, the door to the ward should not get locked, you know. This is not a locked ward and you can't just lock the door when you have a mind to. Louise says it's because you feel concern that the new patient might get out, but she don't show no sign of leaving yet and we have the right to an open door, it's part of our human right. That's all I have to say for now. No, hold on, there's something else. I forget what it is . . . How long is this tape? It's going to run out before I'm done. The thing I forgot to say is about the light bulb in the toilet area. You told me you would get it fixed, but everything's still dark. It's dangerous, you know. Why do I have to remind you all the time? You don't have hospital maintenance no more? Or is it cost? Everything has to get done so cheap these days. It's a wonder we don't have to bring in bulbs for lights the day we get admitted. Lots of waste go on in here you know – all the paper you throw out. You not heard about recycling yet?

Oh, I just remembered something. You said I have to talk about my family. What if there is not a lot to say? Family is personal, it's not a public thing. And if I tell you, it's not like you're going to tell me all the things that happened in your own life in return. This is strictly one-way traffic and it don't seem right. That's all I have to say to this tape recorder thing. You hear me now? You get all that?

148

Chapter Twenty-Three

Each morning it's the same old routine; some loud nurse stomps through the ward, yanks open the curtains and switches on the light. I put my head even further down the bedclothes. Morning is hard even when I'm high.

Today it's Louise. She looks so nice and dainty but she clod-hops like the rest of them. 'Morning!' she shouts and when she gets to my bed, she pulls the covers back. 'Come on Gloria, it's time to get up. We can't have you lazing around on a lovely day like this. I don't know how you'll hold down a job when you get out of here if you can't even manage to get out of bed.'

She believes it is laziness. It's not just a race thing. All mental patients are the same to her, stupid shirkers who give up the right to her respect. As the day goes by, the energy starts to spark from me, but when I just wake up, it's like my body's being flattened by a weight. I struggle to move, but my arms and legs are pinned. I do get up, in the end, and it is not so hard as usual. The shower cubicle is empty, don't have no queue, and I brush my teeth in double quick time. They gleam white, twinkling at me in the mirror like a toothpaste ad and getting larger in my mouth. I smile again and my mirror image grows, teeth first, until I am one large grin, Aunt Jemima-sized.

'Wake up, Gloria. I'm tired of telling you.' Thought I was awake. Thought I done the whole wake-up thing. Force my eyes to open, and sure enough it's Lou, she stands by my bed, shaking my shoulders and telling me I have to come and get my medication, even though it's because of the drugs they give me that I keep on thinking I'm awake when really I'm asleep. It's no good stepping out of bed softly-softly when I feel so tired as this, so I fling myself over the edge of the mattress and land upon my knee on the floor. A rude awakening, and the pain in my knee is sharp but it works every time. Pity I couldn't fix it so I land on top of Lou.

Can't find my slippers, so I patter to the duty room with my feet bare. I'm the last in line. I take the little plastic cup and pop the pill inside my mouth, but suddenly I start to slide down the wall. One of the nurses charges towards me and tells me to lie flat. 'You're just a bit faint,' she says, 'you must have got up too fast. Low blood pressure. It's one of the side effects of your medication.'

Now they tell me. I lie without my dignity by the hatch outside the duty room like a beached whale. They all have to step their way around me. One of them gets out a pumping machine and straps it round my arm. Eventually, they allow me to get up again. I go and lie down on top of my bed.

Louise follows me into the dormitory. 'Come on, get dressed,' she says.

Start to explain about the faintness but she cuts me off with an impatient wave of her hand. 'The best thing you can do for yourself is to keep moving. The dizziness will stop if you stay active. You're not an invalid, you know. Come on, hurry up.'

Thought it was the morning caused my slowness, but now I start to realize I feel different today. So quiet inside. Not like calm, a different kind of quiet, a dread quiet, the kind of quiet you get when you are in a mental emptiness. My body don't want to move no more. All the thought and energy that bubbled up inside me has been sucked away. Flat is what I feel. Flat like blotting paper.

Can't believe I'm still the same person. Once I've dressed myself and combed my hair, I go and sit in the day room. *Sit*. It seems like weeks since I sat myself down. Always moved before. Still now, like a tree. Hilary comes and says to me, 'I'm glad to see you're so much better today, Gloria. How about some breakfast?'

Don't want to eat. Don't see the point. Why have they done this? Why is being full of life such a wrong thing? Now I feel like death they tell me I am better. What kind of cock-up world we living in, I ask myself. No energy to put up a decent fight, so I follow Hilary to the dining room. She loads up my plate with scrambled eggs. Puts a fried tomato on the top. I sit and play with it, like Alex. This dread quiet feels strange. Sadness takes me now, such sadness filling up my mind.

I go back to the dormitory and make my bed. Hilary helps me tuck the corner bits. Fold my clothes. Didn't used to fold. Too much movement, no stopping time to fold. Where has all the motion gone? Shock still. Still like death.

'It's time to go down to OT.'

Hilary takes me by the arm. We march towards the woodwork place for occupational therapy. I made a shelf before. She places it in front of me. Can't see it turning out so good no more. Got no need for shelves.

Lots of shelves in the house me and Josie shared. We had a book or two to read, some videos and the ornaments from the holidays we had back home, a palm tree with Jamaica printed up big in the branches. Another one from Blackpool where Josie's mother was born. Is Josie really gone?

Fix up this and fix up that. We always fixed up everything in the house when it went wrong. Fixed the chair we bought from the second-hand shop. Fixed the leaky tap, painted the window red and polished up the brass we bought until it shone. We learnt the fixing out of books. Josie never paid good money out for things that we could fix ourselves. We made some proper shelves, not like this stupid thing laid out down here. Big shelves, the kind that last. Did Emilie take the shelves?

She will let herself in the house while I'm stuck in here. Or did I change the lock before I come to hospital? Think I changed it.

It vexes me to think of all the things we have to lose. It's sad, you know. This life is one big sorry sadness, we weep to think on it so we have to shut it out. That's what I do, speed up inside myself, push out the sadness so I don't have to feel it. Josie and the house and all manner of things affect me now and it is hard to bear.

Time drags by. Used to do so much but now I only have the strength to watch, and all the while the bad feeling in me grows, and all I can think upon is how it was when Josie died. How the sadness hurt me like a cancer in my soul.

*

I hear the news on the radio. Twenty people die for sure. Scores of others suffer injury.

At first, I take it like I take the news every other day; bad things happen all the time. No one is to blame. Just one of them things. And then I start to hear the rest, that it happened at the station on the seven-thirty train. And then it hits me so hard I have to hold on to the side of the sink to keep myself from falling down. Josie was on the train that crashed. It is the one she always catches to her work at the factory. And suddenly I know that she is hurt. I know because I feel it so.

I fly out of the house, fly like my legs have wings. And all of a sudden I realize I am standing on the street half dressed, without the fare to the station. Without awareness of the world around me. So I try to pull myself together because I know that if I go on like this it won't be good for no one. So I go back inside the house, put on my coat and fetch my hat because if you go to a place and need to ask officials what is happening, they always pay you more respect if you are well turned out. I get a taxi for myself. The driver says the route to the station is blocked with all the traffic and the ambulance and things. So I say to him, take me as near as you can and I will walk the rest.

He drops me on the hill. I walk down slow, in a daze. From here, I see the train lying on the track and it is mashed up so bad I can't see how anyone survived. Start to run again, like at the house, and my breath comes quick, so quick I think I am about to have a heart attack. The police have cordoned off the area. Smoke billows in the sky. There is wreckage glinting all about in the morning sun. Shouting round me now. And crying. Crying from the soul. I catch my breath and see a policeman standing at the tape they use to keep us from the area. He looks shook up himself, like he never seen a thing like this before. 'My friend is here,' I say to him.

He looks at me. 'Please stand over there, madam. Someone will come to take your details in a moment. Please stand back. Try to stay calm.'

I'm so calm it frightens me. Still like death.

A policewoman comes and write my details down. 'Is she a relative?'

'No.'

'A friend?'

I nod my head.

I wait. Endless waiting for the news to come. And then they tell me she is still alive and they are taking her to hospital. I get another cab. I arrive at the casualty department but I can't get no further news. Only relatives, they say to me. Should have said I am a relative. They don't have no time to check. They tell you more if you say you are related. Why is it so hard for the world to understand that love is more than just a man and woman thing? When she died, it was almost a day before I heard. No one bothered telling me the news.

This grieving is a funny thing, you know. The hurt is always there but it comes and goes in its intensity. Today as I sit upon the ward, the tears fill up my eyes and spill out from time to time as if I have to cry. Didn't do no crying at the funeral. Don't know why it was but the tears refused to come. Funny thing, this grieving.

Chapter Twenty-Four

One of the nurses says he has to go to pharmacy. He takes me with him. Gloria comes too but she is almost silent and she doesn't really see me any more. She's gone inside herself the way we all have to do sometimes. I miss the singing.

We go through the walkways and then out into the grounds. It is damp but I like the freshness and the cooling breeze. I take Gloria's hand and she gives my fingers a gentle squeeze so I know she is still there even though she doesn't talk. She is carrying her bag, the one she got at the bring-and-buy. She lets me hold it for a while. We pass it back and forth between us.

The nurse walks ahead. I linger, looking at the autumn shrubs. There's going to be a firework party soon, but I doubt if I will be allowed to go. I touch the leaves. I need to be connected. Sometimes it's as if there is nothing beyond the world I carry in my head. The earth smells yellow.

We wait as the nurse collects the tablets in plastic containers that rattle as he walks. They look like sweets but they taste bitter and when I'm made to take them, they burn the inside of my mouth.

The nurse says he is going to visit his mother tomorrow. I like the every-dayness of the things he does. 'What does your mother look like?' I say to him. I want to get a picture.

The nurse thinks for a moment. Then he says, 'She's tall and she always wears smart clothes. She has light brown hair and blue eyes.'

'Do you love her?' I ask.

He laughs uneasily. 'Well yes, I suppose so. She's my mother, isn't she?'

It is as if we give love automatically. When the nurse asks how I feel towards my mother, I don't answer him. My mother was a silent person. She watched a lot of things but she seldom intervened.

Her mother watches as her father sits in the big armchair and hears him tell her she's the devil's child.

I wait for her to contradict him but she doesn't speak. I don't know whether to believe him.

He sees everything she is. He sucks her thoughts away from her. There is no difference between her and him. He is a ventriloquist. She moves her mouth. He speaks.

I want to be with him. We've waited so long to be together.

She wants to escape from him, his crowding of her, the lack of space between them. She tells her mother that she needs to have some time alone, away from him.

156

'It's been so hard for him, all the things he's been through,' my mother replies. 'We lost our family for such a long time, we need each other more than ever now. All he wants is for you to be a good daughter. He only wants to keep you safe.'

My mother has become him too. Always a shadow. She has unlearned to speak with her own voice. She needed him to come home so much and, now that he's here, we must both make up for the 'everything' he lost.

There will be no utterance of disappointment, nor of expectations unfulfilled.

'I have someone else's voice,' I say to the nurse.
'That doesn't make sense,' he replies to me.
'Do you believe in God?' I ask.
'Yes, I do,' he answers.
'Do you believe in the Devil?'
'I believe in evil, I suppose.'
'Do you think that people are ever possessed?'
'No. It's just a kind of superstition.'

She is possessed. He owns every part of her. There are no spaces left. She has to steal away from him in order to spend some time alone. She goes to the park and sits on the roundabout. It's cold and getting dark, so there's no one else there. She savours the quiet of it. She spins round slowly; her feet scuff the grass. Her mother wouldn't listen, she's on her own with it. What will she do? She can't bear the constant presence of him, the overwhelming loss of self.

I arrive back at the house and go upstairs. My room is full of him.

She opens the window. When she turns round again, he's hovering beside her.

'Don't come in my room when I'm not here,' she says.

'I'm your father. I can go where I please in my own house.'

She closes the door on him. She leans against it, but she cannot shut him out.

'Evil is inside of me,' I tell the nurse.

'You're no better and no worse than anyone else,' the nurse replies.

She has no close friends any more. It's the badness in her. And there's too much in her life that she's unable to explain.

I slip away from him. I go to the library and read. I write a little too. When I get back home, I am punished for it.

She likes the sense of being surrounded by words. Her essays are the best in the class.

You can be whatever you want to be when you write things down.

One day, after school, she finds him in her room again. He's read her diaries, they're lying open on the bed; all her thoughts about him, all the secret things. She thought she'd hidden them where nobody could find them. *All the private parts of her are left exposed. He's shouting at her, calling her names. She snatches up the notebooks and stuffs them into a carrier bag which she clasps to her ribs. She'll burn them tomorrow. They are no longer hers.*

'I have no words of my own,' I say to the nurse.
'I don't understand what you mean,' the nurse replies.

One morning, just before six, she goes into the bathroom. The lock no longer works, so she can't shut the door. He slips in quietly and stands there looking at her. She knows he's broken the lock on purpose, to further his invasion of her. She pulls her clothes around herself and in the process, soils them. She needs to clean herself but she doesn't know where to go. There are no spaces left where he can't follow her.

'I have to be left alone,' she says to the nurse.
'When you start getting better,' he replies.

She goes to the park with a sharp kitchen knife. She pushes the blade deep into her wrist, working it in. There is blood, but less than she'd imagined. When she doesn't die, she pulls down her sleeve and buys herself the set of African bangles that she will always wear.

I kick off my shoes and start to run. My feet freeze in the dew-soaked grass but at least I can feel. The nurse runs after me. When he reaches me, he holds me tight.

Sometimes she thinks she will never get away from him.

Chapter Twenty-Five

As we walk back from pharmacy the new patient tries to escape and has to be hauled back by Don. He tells me to go to the ward and get some help because she struggles so. At first, I decide to let him do his own dirty work and I just stand there like I'm too much in a daze to hear what he is saying to me. But then I see how tight he's holding on to her and that it's scaring her half to death, so I go fetch Hilary. Figure she will be more gentle than the rest of them.

After Hilary gets the new patient settled on the ward again, she comes and talks to me. 'How are you feeling today, Gloria?' she asks.

'Not so bad,' I reply. No point in telling her the truth. What them going to do? Fill me with an extra dose of medication or keep me shut up on the ward.

It would have been Josie's birthday today. Fifty-eight years old. No more birthdays to celebrate now. But I will not tell a soul. It is for me alone to think upon. It's like I need to get inside the loss. Can't explain no better. This is my time.

*

Josie's family insist on managing the funeral. Nothing I can do. I have no claim on her, don't count like a relative, and no one is prepared to accept the life we shared. I want to be seen as something special, something that acknowledges the love. When you have a man—woman thing, you get to be called husband or wife. I want a name too. But as I go inside the church, it's clear that no one can find it in their heart to make the acknowledgement. They show me to a pew as close to the back as they can fix it. No condolences exchanged. No word of grief is shared.

There's flowers in the church, and candlelight. I want to feel at peace with myself but my separation from the family fuels my agitation. I know the funeral is part of the goodbye, been to dozens now. At the home, when a resident died, I always tried to attend the funeral, to see them pass from this life to the next. It's sad, but not too much to bear. Old people die, it is the way of things. With Josie, the uncompleteness is the thing I mind the most. I half expect to see her standing there, whispering a joke in my ear. Josie always used to be there through my bad times. This is the first sadness in over thirty years I've had to face alone.

Seventy mourners assemble at the church. Seventy at least for true. I feel a pride that so many gather here to pay their last respects. This is how my father felt when my mother died. All Josie's family is here; brother John leads the service with a self-important air. Twenty years since I seen him. The hair on top of his head is thinner now, and his waist is a little thicker. He has grown a small beard and it makes him look the goat he is. Still the same old John. Can't meet my eye. He tells the world that Josie is at peace. He claims she has the love of God. God showed his love by taking her to him while she was in her prime. It is the same God that John said turned his back on us twenty-five years ago when the family found out we were more than friends. Funny how death brings out the hypocrite in everyone. All the usual marks of passing: hymn singing, reading, and the same old religion stuff. I wait for it to make some kind of impression but nothing is happening for me. Might as well be in the supermarket. I stand there silent now; all this denying me makes me feel small. Emilie goes to the front of the church and speaks of Josie's life, but I can hardly recognize the person she describes. Not the woman I love. The thirty-three years we spent together are wrapped in silence now.

The service comes to an end. Friends and relations move outside. Everyone arranges themselves beside the grave. They leave me standing three or four rows back, unable to see the coffin being lowered. Josie wants me to take my place in front, I know for certain this is what she wants. As the mourners move forward, I push my way through. I tug a handful of grass and leaves and daisies and I throw them on the coffin. Emilie leans forward like she is going to jump inside the grave and take away the one trace of myself that I got to leave with Josie, but she thinks better of it and remains, tottering, on the edge of the pit. Before I know it, I start to shout at her, 'You can't shut me out!' The mourners band together, closing ranks, squeezing my existence out. 'You can't shut me out!' I repeat, louder now, fighting strong, determined to remind them who I am.

Like true Britons, they pretend not to hear. John brings the service to a close, still not letting me within his line of sight. Emilie quivers with anxiety at all the decorum I have breached.

It is over now. I turn to leave. It is a warm day, but the wind disturbs my hat, it slides to the side of my head. I grip it tight. I tried so hard to dress for Josie: I'm wearing my best navy blouse and skirt and my patent high heel shoes. I refuse to wear the colour black. It seems too final to be worn, and not the kind of colour Josie liked. She liked bright-bright clothes, the kind that shine, the kind that give warmth to this cold climate.

Josie's second brother Matthew hurries up the path, but I don't want to speak with him. I quicken up my pace, but he's beside me now. 'Gloria, I'm sorry,' he says to me. 'You know what Emilie's like. I didn't want it to be like this. Do come back to the house with us.'

I look across the grave and see Emilie glaring back at me. I have this sudden urge to run up to her and snatch the hat she's wearing off her smug old head. It's then that I decide to go, refuse them all the comfort of denying me, even though I don't have no energy to fight. Even though all I really want is to go home.

Except it's not home now. Emilie took so many of Josie's things. I watched as she wrapped them up and removed them from me. Why did I allow such a thing to happen? When Emilie came, Josie had been dead for less than a week. Hadn't been able to feel. Had no will to act. Words of protest were caught up in my throat. I stood silently by as Emilie ransacked the house, searching out the things she thought she could lay claim to. Worthless objects, mostly, taken to punish me, as if losing Josie weren't punishment enough. Some hurt goes so deep you think you will drop down dead from it. So I decide to go back for the wake. Decide to make them notice me.

Matthew drives me in the car. 'I expect the family will be vexed now,' I say to him.

'Most probably.'

I smile.

Outside, the house is just the same as I remember it: a little terrace with a tiny front garden and a creaky gate. Emilie lives there with her daughter Charmaine, who is almost twenty-two, the age I was when me and Josie first met up. Emilie used to be a big ward sister before she retired. She believed it was a proud achievement, proof that racism gone from the health service. But if she had been white instead of black, she would have been chief director of nursing for true. Emilie always been easy to satisfy.

Matthew leads me in the room like he wants to protect me from Emilie and her disapproval. There is a moment of silence as they all become aware of me. Matthew leads me up to a comfy chair and then he goes to fetch a cup of tea.

Emilie's made sure there's nothing stronger. All about, people gather round in polite little groups, and talk about the last time they met with Josie. It's like an English funeral, it has no warmth. Wish I'd found the energy to override the family and sort out a funeral for Josie myself. I would have had a party, in memory of a life that was full of loving and enjoyment. There would have been music. Dancing too. I sip my cup of tea, and I try to hold back the urge to celebrate.

Chapter Twenty-Six

She is not allowed to leave the hospital. They keep telling her that she is on a section. She doesn't know what that means. Someone always sits with her. Even when she goes to the toilet, she is made to leave the door open while a nurse waits outside. She is exposed, embarrassed by the scrutiny. She feels ashamed of her body and all the functions it performs while the nursing staff observe. 'I want to go away,' she repeats, over and over again. It's all she will say. She hides on her bed, underneath the counterpane. It is hot and she can barely breathe, but at least they cannot see her there. When she briefly surfaces, she scribbles in her notebook, words they will be unable to decode. She has found another way of being out of reach. Her body has to stay, but she has taken her mind away from them. She should have learnt to do it years ago. Then perhaps she could have remained at home.

'I want to go home.'

The nurse stands over me and says, 'We'll discharge you when you're better, but we need to piece together some kind of case history for you. We know so little about what you did before you were admitted. What sort of work did you do? When did you get married? And what about your parents? Are they still alive? Would you like us to get in touch with them?'

She packs a bag. She leaves a note for her parents but it doesn't say much. She's afraid that her father will awaken. She steals out of the house. She's running now, thinking that he'll follow. She gets on a train. For a moment, he's there beside her. Then he's gone. She travels but sometimes she thinks she'll never get away from him.

She doesn't know if her mother will notice her departure, but her father will be hurt, perhaps for days. She goes over what she put in the note: I have to go away for a while. Don't worry about me, I'll be OK. I'll be in touch soon. If she could have stayed, she would have, but she knows that she is catching her father's blank despair and that soon she too will have to displace it – perhaps with God, perhaps with another form of anaesthesia.

At first, she is lonely, but it is better than the isolation that habitual disappointment brings. She scribbles in her notebook on the train; it helps to pass the time.

She heads for the centre of the city. Here, she will be anonymous. She searches for a selling job in Oxford Street. A whole day on her feet and not one interview. Where will she sleep? A B&B, perhaps.

She finds a cheap room near Victoria. She will only be able to afford a night or two. The vibration of the trains keeps her awake and the chimes of Big Ben disrupt her thoughts. She covers her head with a pillow but morning comes too soon.

Breakfast consists of burnt bacon and a rubber egg. She eats a lot of toast, thickly spread with orange marmalade. The man at the next table eyes her up, taking in her slender legs, and the shape of her breasts. He leans across and speaks to her. She shakes her head and concentrates hard on the tea-stained napkin in her lap.

Another fruitless day; the unspoken barrier of race obstructs the search for work. She tries not to mind too much. She buys sandwiches for lunch which she eats in Soho Square. A woman wearing a coat tied round the waist with string feeds pigeons with a mouldy slice of bread, calling each by name: Jonah; Honey; Sergeant Bilko.

She sighs. At least the weather's warm. She feels the sun on her face and thinks of her parents again. Her mother spent all those years awaiting the return of a man who barely seems to know she's there. And now her daughter's left her too. Perhaps they'll pray.

There's a church nearby. She opens the door carefully and goes inside. The smell of incense causes her to retch. She takes a few deep breaths and allows her eyes to adjust to the dimness. Candles are lit in petition, as if any god has time to notice, let alone care. She kneels at a pew and looks around her. The pure white faces of the saints shine out of the stained glass. Statues of the blessed virgin, blonde and stainless, stare at her. A priest swishes by. She fights the desire to confess to him. It's the familiar she's clinging to.

She gets up to leave. Her feet slide across the polished floor. The heavy door of the church creaks shut behind her. She blinks in the sunlight. Her optimism, such as it was, is starting to fade. She may not find a job. She may end up on the streets, a young black version of the pigeon feeder.

It's almost eight o'clock when she begins the walk back to the hotel. As dusk begins to fall, flocks of starlings rise, their shrieking reminiscent of The Birds. Suddenly unnerved, she starts to run.

As she arrives back at the boarding house, she spots a notice on the gatepost of the neighbouring hotel: chamber maid/waitress required. She repeats the words to herself. There's nothing about experience and no indication of the rates of pay. At nine a.m. next morning, she makes herself go up the hotel steps. She enters the foyer and walks uncertainly to the reception desk. She's told she should have used the tradesmen's entrance. She's put in a small, windowless room and made to fill in forms. She's interviewed by a man in a grey suit. She talks up her interest in people and her willingness to learn. She gets the job. She's given a pink overall and a matching pair of rubber gloves, the tools of the trade for chamber maids. For waitressing, she gets a navy suit, cut way above the knee, and a frilly blouse. She's told to start on Monday, six a.m. sharp.

At the end of the first day, she learns from one of the other waitresses that there's a room to let in the terrace where she lives. A box room in an attic, dark and cramped. It's all she can afford. It reminds her of a book they made her read at school when she was nine: A Little Princess. *She shuts out the peeling paint and the damp that seeps across the walls. The kitchen and the toilet are shared by ten, but it's a place where she can be herself, undisturbed. She asks the landlord to fit a sturdy lock on the door to her room. When he prevaricates, she buys a book on DIY, borrows his tools and fixes it herself. She always fears intrusion.*

The work at the hotel tires her and she's constantly bored. The dirt grinds her down. Hair in sinks and plugholes, soiled toilet seats. Staining on the sheets.

One of the other maids is from the Caribbean too. Her name is Winifred. She's forty-five years old, with a husband and two teenage daughters. She treats her like her own wayward child, chiding her to go back to school so she can get a better job. 'This is not for you, darling,' she keeps telling her. 'You are a clever girl, you know, worth more than this old dump.'

'You're worth more too.'

Winifred laughs. 'No opportunity for me. Didn't get no education. Is different for you. Is breaking my heart to see you in this dead end place. Go back to your family, I'm sure they missing you.'

She hasn't rung home, although she knows she promised. She always puts it off. She doesn't want to hear her father's voice, laden with reproach.

Each day has its own routine. After cleaning in the morning, she goes home and returns to the dining room at five. At first she finds it hard to get used to working like this. Always anxious, she spends her free time worrying. Perhaps she'll oversleep and not get back to work in time. Or once she's there, she'll lay out the wrong forks or spoons, or drop a plate. Her dread of the moment when she has to leave the house devours all her leisure time, leaving her drained each day and wondering how to cope. She never seems to sleep enough. But slowly, she's learning to push her work into the background of her life.

On her days off, she visits some of the sights of London: Trafalgar Square; The National Gallery; Tower Bridge. She grows to love the Thames. And in her attic room, she reads and writes, as if her life depends on it, consigning all she's felt in recent months to paper, where it can be contained. As she writes the past, it starts to reshape itself. Her mother grows younger, stronger, more interested in her, while her father seems less sad. Sometimes she can hear him laugh. She wishes she could have had the life she'd imagined for herself, stayed on at school, gone to university, perhaps. She wants to find a way of getting

169

extra time for the reading and writing that for her are both confinement and escape. Sometimes she blames her parents, but mostly she blames herself. She should have been stronger.

The waitressing is harder than the cleaning. No Winifred. And more contact with the guests. They click their fingers at her when they want attention. One whistles, as if she is a dog. The kitchen is noisy and there's more to learn. She's never been good at carrying things and breakages are deducted from her wages.

The guests are always white, all except one, who arrives late one winter evening and places himself at a window table. She guesses that he's in his early thirties. He wears a suit and tie. She waits on him deftly, nothing slipping through her fingers. She's constantly aware of him, the shine of his shoes, the delicate way he breaks the roll they serve with the soup. She learns from the receptionist that his reservation is for just three days. She'd hoped he'd stay longer. When he eats in the dining room again she tries to make him notice her.

She's almost seventeen, but she's never really been interested in boys. She liked Benson, but only as a friend. She thought she was immune. The other girls at school had crushes, sensations of longing which she hadn't understood till now. The wish for the man to be aware of her is all that she can feel. When he finally smiles, she feels pleasure tinged with trepidation.

As he gets up to leave, he presses a card into her hand. 'I'm opening a Caribbean restaurant in a couple of weeks. I'm looking for staff. Come and see me if you're interested.'

She nods. Late that evening after work, she examines every letter of the card. Clyde Hanson. The Calypso: Fine Caribbean Cuisine. A Kennington address. She doesn't know if he meant it or if it was just a line. She tries to recall the tone of his voice, the expression he wore as he said it. She thought he seemed sincere at the time, but now she is less certain. The inflection was wrong. He might not have looked her in the eye. She's not sure what to do.

She talks to Winifred who says, 'I don't understand what's bothering you.'

'If I go there and he didn't mean it, I'll die of embarrassment.'

'And if you don't go and see him, you'll always wonder what you might have missed. Go for it, girl. What you got to lose?'

She takes the bus to Kennington between her shifts. The restaurant is still in the process of being fitted out. A large red sign lies on its side against the wall. She hovers in the open doorway, trying to see if he's there. One of the workmen stops and calls to her, 'Looking for the boss? He's round the back. I'll give him a shout if you want.'

She nods and slips inside. The walls are being plastered and wires are being fixed. She can tell they won't be open by the end of next week. Clyde comes through. He sees her and a look of irritation crosses his face. 'You here to interview for the waitress job? I said four weeks.'

She doesn't correct him. She hadn't realized he'd expect her to interview. He'd seen her working. She'd hoped the job was hers. 'Sorry,' she replies. 'When do you want me to come back?'

'Look it's OK, I just wasn't expecting you. We can do it now if you want.'

She smiles and follows him into an office in the back. There's a desk and a leather chair, but no other furniture. She remains standing in front of him. 'Everything's taking longer than I expected,' he says to her as he perches on the desk. 'I should have put in a penalty clause but they're old school mates of mine. You don't like pulling rank on your

171

mates, but sometimes you have to, you know?' He's confiding in her. It makes her feel important. She nods knowingly.

'Do you want a coffee?'

'No thanks,' she says. If she holds a cup, he'll see that her hands are shaking. There's a pause. She doesn't know how to fill it. She can tell that he's new to this and trying not to show it, and she's aware that he is staring at her.

After a while he says, 'OK, I suppose I should ask what sort of experience you've got.'

'Just the hotel. Before that I was at school.'

'How old are you then?'

'Seventeen.'

'Why do you want this job?'

They always ask that at interviews. She prepared her answer on the bus. 'I enjoy being a waitress but the hotel's too big. I'd prefer something smaller, with a family atmosphere. I'd also like to have the chance to get to know the customers. There isn't much opportunity for that at the hotel. And I know something about Caribbean food. My mother always cooked it for my father.'

He tells her that she can come and help out with the pre-opening preparations if she likes. Basic wages.

'Yeah, sure,' she says.

He smiles at her obvious delight. They are silent for a moment.

Then he says, 'I built this business up from nothing. I started out with a market stall. I work hard, you know? I like my staff to work hard too. Dispel the myths. You hear what I'm saying? A fair day's work for a fair day's pay. What you find now is that everyone wants something for nothing. You got to give in this world. You understand what I'm saying? You see, I don't support everything the government's done but they're right about one thing: it's business that gets you some-where, always has been. That's why we hold ourselves back as a people. We don't set up in business.'

There's a crash in the adjoining room. He goes outside. 'What you think you're doing, Paul? That wood cost. Why you want to wreck the place? I'm getting sick and tired of you. Pull your finger out, man.'

'Oh come on Clyde, it was just an accident. Hasn't done no harm.'

'Sort it out, man, OK? Tired of carrying you all, you hear? Put some fucking effort in.'

She listens, wondering if his show of authority is being laid on for her. She sees his need to impress. As she leaves, Paul calls after her, 'Clyde's gonna get you a nice little uniform, sister, show that pretty figure off, all right?'

They all laugh, even Clyde. She doesn't mind. She's pleased to think they've noticed her.

The restaurant opens five weeks late. Clyde puts an ad in the local paper and lays on a free meal for local bigwigs and journalists. She waits on them quietly and does her best to be efficient. Her uniform consists of a short green skirt and a red and yellow top with a low, scooped neck. Her bra straps show. Clyde tells her that she doesn't need to wear one, but she keeps it on anyway, concealing the straps by allow-ing them to slide down her shoulders. In her skimpy work clothes she feels exposed, but she doesn't protest. She starts work at five in the evening and finishes at one a.m. The taxi she gets home for safety eats into her wages. But it's better than the hotel. A friendlier place. A *slower pace. And she's surrounded again by people who, like her, were born in a country they can never really see as home.*

The nurse puts down her clipboard. Nothing has been written on it. She says in a weary tone, 'You have to start to help yourself, begin to cooperate. You won't get better otherwise, you know. You have to talk about yourself, give us something to go on so we know how best to help you out of this.'

They want to know everything about her. No part of her is private now.

I look across the room and realize I'm back in the dormitory but I don't remember moving from the side room. When did it happen? Yesterday? I want to ask why there are so many gaps. It's as if my mind is full of holes. Gloria is sitting by the radiator. She still seems different. She is very still. 'Gloria,' I say.

'You see, you can speak to people, can't you, when you want to,' says the nurse.

Open your mouth, you've got a tongue in your head.

Gloria turns, but she has a look which says she isn't really listening.

'I want to go home,' I say. It's like a refrain.

The nurse says, 'When you're well enough.'

It's getting dark, so I go to the window and draw the curtains. I am hidden in the quiet. This is the time I like the most, when I am a shadow, when I am between the darkness and the light.

Chapter Twenty-Seven

I like the dark, the way it covers me, but there are constant interruptions – footsteps, heavy breathing, the cries of other patients. Did Clyde ever love me? I try to work it out between my dreams.

Clyde never praises her work, but he doesn't criticize it either. She's just there, like the candles on the table, decor to draw in custom. Soon she is almost as bored as she was at the hotel, and the squalid romance of her attic room has started to fade. There seems to be no future for her. When she wonders where she'll be in five or ten years' time, she draws a blank.

She's enjoying curry at the corner table just before she's due to start her shift. Clyde feeds the staff for free, it's one of the few perks of the job. She's reading, so at first she doesn't notice that Clyde has sat down opposite. He clears his throat, making her jump. They both laugh. 'Sorry,' he says.

'It's all right, I never notice anything when I'm reading.'

'You must have been a good student at school.'

'I was OK.'

'Why did you leave? Didn't you want to stay on?'

He's never asked personal questions before. She tells him no and is unwilling to say more.

'You don't talk much about yourself.'

'I haven't done very much,' she replies.

'But you must have a family.'

'My parents are dead,' she says. 'My father died years ago when I was four so I was brought up by my mother. She died too, before I started working at the hotel.'

'I'm sorry.'

'It's OK. It wasn't your fault.' She finds it hard to lie; her awkwardness is testament to that. He doesn't go on with the conversation. She can see that he's embarrassed so she says, 'What about your family?'

'Both my parents are still alive, and my grandparents too. You know I have a son?'

It's one of the few things she's found out about him. Marcus, now three. Clyde was divorced two years ago. 'Do you see your boy at all?'

'I have him some weekends. I'll be having him more now this place is up and running.'

'I should start to do the tables.'

'They can wait a minute or two. Look, I want to ask you something.'

She waits, but he doesn't tell her what it is so she has to help him out. 'Go on,' she says.

'I have to attend this dinner. It says to bring a guest. Will you come? It's just a business thing but it could be good for Calypso.'

'When is it?'

'Friday night.'

'I'm rostered on.'

'That can be changed,' he says with a slight smile. 'It's formal. Do you have an evening dress?'

She shakes her head.

'I'll get one for you.'

'You can hire them.'

'No, it's OK, this one's on me. You're a size ten, aren't you?'

'How did you know?'

'I remembered from the time I got the uniforms.'

She doesn't know what else to say to him. She's flattered and surprised by his attentiveness. She wonders why he hasn't asked one of the other waitresses to accompany him.

The dress he brings to work is floor-length silk in chestnut brown, with a long slit up the side. She would never have chosen it for herself, but as she tries it on in the women's toilet, she sees that he's selected it to flatter her narrow hips. She loves the feel of it, the way it swishes when she walks.

She opens the door and stands outside. He doesn't say a word, he just walks slowly round her.

'Is it all right?' she asks. 'Is it what you were expecting?'

'It's fine. Do you have any shoes you can wear with it?'

'Yes, I think so.' She bought a strappy pair of sandals the other week in the sales.

'What about earrings?'

She shakes her head. 'Not dressy ones.'

'You'll need them. I'll get you some.'

'No, it's all right. I'll find some gold ones.'

'Then maybe I'm paying you too much.'

'Not real gold, imitation. They've got some down the market.'

'I'll get you some,' he repeats.

She wants nice things. She wants to believe that she's worth the investment. Yet she feels uncomfortable. 'Maybe I could wear them and after you could take them back.'

'We'll see,' he says.

She pushes her African bangles further down her wrists. 'I can keep these on with it, can't I?'

'If you like,' he answers.

He doesn't give her the earrings until he picks her up outside her house on Friday night. They're in a black velvet box. She opens it and smiles wryly at him. 'This is like Pygmalion.'

'Pygmalion?'

'Yes,' she says, but she doesn't explain. She doesn't want to offend him.

Clyde shrugs. 'I need you to look right, that's all. It's a celebration of black achievement in small businesses. In business, impressions always count.'

She nods and puts the earrings on. They're gold and they dangle almost to her chin.

'Fine,' says Clyde.

'Where are we going?'

'A hotel not far from where you used to work.'

'Why were you staying there that time?' She's often wondered. She doesn't tell him Winifred believed he was having an affair.

'Oh, you know. They took so long to do up the flat. No electricity because of the rewiring. I had to get away from it for a couple of nights.'

She's not sure she believes him. He says it in such a casual way that it doesn't quite ring true. Still, it's up to him how much he tells her. She doesn't want to delve too deep. Once you start enquiring about other people's business, it seems to license them to pry into yours.

'Do you mind if I have a cigarette?' she says. She's feeling nervous as she always does when she has to meet new people. And she's afraid she won't live up to his expectations of her.

'No, don't smoke in the car. You can't get rid of the smell.'

She stuffs the cigarettes back in her bag.

'What's that?' he says.

'What?'

'That bag. You can't take that in. It's too bulky, it won't look right.'

'OK, I'll leave it in the car.' She fumbles for a moment. 'I don't have any pockets. Can you take my tissues? Oh. And these.'

He shakes the plastic container. 'What's in here?'

She feels herself flush. 'Tampons,' she whispers. 'I've got my period.'

He slips them into his pocket without another word.

It's a larger gathering than she anticipated. The tables are set with place names and there are menus too. She tries to converse with the people seated round her, but she's aware of her own awkwardness. Clyde shines. He tells funny stories about setting up the restaurant, and the days when he used to have a market stall.

When it's over, he drives her home. She takes off the earrings and puts them back in the box. 'Keep them,' he says.

'I can't.'

He puts his hand on hers. 'Sure you can.' He pulls up outside her front door. 'See you tomorrow then.'

'Goodnight, Clyde,' she says to him.

She was expecting him to want to come in as part of whatever bargain he thought he'd struck by giving her the earrings. When he drives away, she is surprised (though perhaps he's remembered about her period). She doesn't understand what he wants from her. Not closeness. But then she's also wary of that.

Yet I miss his touch.

She ends up in his bed eventually, of course, the little slut.

As I'm getting out of bed that first morning, Clyde reaches out and grabs my arm. 'What's this?' he says.

He's seen the scar I have. It extends across my wrist. My bangles are beside me on the bedside table. 'It's nothing. Just an accident.'

He lets go of me. 'That wasn't any accident.'

'I got a bit depressed when I was living at home.'

'Before your mother died?'

I nod. It's hard to keep track of the stories I've told him.

Liar liar pants on fire.

'Were you trying to kill yourself?'

'It's hard to talk about it.'

'We don't know much about each other.' It's a statement of fact. It seems to bother him.

'We can get to know each other, can't we? I'm OK now. It was a passing thing, a teenage thing. I don't feel like that any more.'

'Put the bangles on,' he tells me.

He liked the perfection that he thought he saw in me. Now I've let him down. I watch for signs that it's changed the way he feels, but he doesn't mention it again; it remains unspoken between us.

Chapter Twenty-Eight

She sits opposite the door. Throughout the day, she watches all arrivals and departures. Each voice, each look, seeps inside her body, until she is so full of the sights and sounds of other people that her head will burst. She has to keep absorbing. Her survival depends on it.

Her constant presence makes her part of the furniture, so she is privy to private conversations. They circulate round her as if she is invisible. A woman with fair hair and a coarse complexion confesses her hatred for a husband who regularly beats her with his fists and the handle of a broom. Alex, fifteen, whose dark skin is stretched across a fatless body, spits out her loathing of the food they are making her consume. Shouting. Crying. All in the public space that is the unit. Ward C is a confessional. You are required to tell the secrets of your soul so they can be put on file and salivated over in the duty room.

The investigations never seem to cease. There is a fat nurse with red hair and skinny ankles that look as if they'll crack beneath her bulk. She moves briskly though, tip-tapping through the ward. Each day, she brings her breakfast on a tray. The task is to seek out information but it is a slow and inept interrogation. She stares at the nurse mutely, listening each morning to the catalogue of questions, her face impassive. The nurse sits beside her and watches her eat. 'You're doing very well today,' she says.

She mashes her cornflakes into the milk. The nurse doesn't seem to notice that she rarely swallows. And it never seems to matter that she doesn't answer. Her silence seems to meet their expectations.

She tries to scrape the butter off her toast with the knife and napkin but it has already melted in. She can feel fat forming in her arteries. It is clogging up her veins, making her bloat, heart beating bumpily against her chest, fatly swollen. She knows her heart will burst against this feeding. She doesn't want to be fed. She wants to melt into air, her black heart intact, unscrutinized and fading. The nurse says, 'Try to concentrate. You should have eaten up that toast by now.' She pushes it aside.

From the corner of my eye, I can see Gloria. She's turned towards the wall, rocking to and fro in frantic rhythm, heel to toe and back again. She is singing softly; *I say a little prayer for you.* She is singing for my salvation; her prayer will intercede for me. Her hands are waving in the air. Her fingers were once slimmer than they are now; I know this from the tightness of the ring she wears on her wedding finger.

The nurse notices I am watching Gloria so she turns to her and says, 'Are you OK over there?'

Gloria doesn't reply – she has to keep on singing if I am going to be saved. Her voice is getting louder as she soars from one note to another. Now she is moving away from the wall.

I sigh.

The nurse picks up the slice of toast I've left on the corner of my plate. 'Do you want this?' she asks. 'Only I didn't have time for breakfast this morning.'

I watch her as she eats. It is an interesting reversal.

She knows that she is getting better. She can see the world outside herself. The other world was frightening, but she wants to be more fully there again. No decisions to be made. No expectations of her. A kind of oblivion.

Gloria begins to walk towards my bed, smiling broadly. She is singing a song called 'I Will Survive'. She keeps on singing even as she reaches my bed. 'When you going home?' she says.

I hear the message in the question. She's asked it many times before and always in front of the nurses. It's to remind them that we are not fixtures in the place; they should not take our presence here for granted. I don't reply, but I know that Gloria doesn't expect it of me. She has respect for other people's silences, even when she finds it hard to keep her own. 'They can't keep me here, you know, not once the section finish.' Another reminder for the nursing staff. We know it isn't true, of course. They can do most things with us. And to us. The flimsy logic of the outside world doesn't apply in here.

Gloria pauses. My eyelids flicker slightly as I look back at her. The nurse assumes that it's an involuntary gesture, but Gloria knows different. She winks at me and heaves herself up from the bed. She's wearing slippers in the shape of dogs; the movement of her toes causes their ears to flap.

I close my eyes, forgetting for a moment that I have to stay alert. I open them again. Everywhere there is movement, the quick tap-tap of nurses' feet or the heavy shuffle of medicated patients.

I must have slept. I come to sharply, roused by a prod from a nurse. Time lost. An hour, maybe more. Gaps in what I have to know. If I can fill the spaces with my thoughts I might still be safe. I start to summon all the words I must have missed, chanting them inside myself, but the nurse interrupts, scattering the sounds. I push her aside with the flat of my hand, but the nurse continues to stand in front of me and talk.

I have no control over my surroundings. My spaces can be constantly invaded. There are no walls here, no front door that I can lock.

She draws up her knees and rests her head on them, her arms drawn around her tight. Her body is the only barrier she has.

They come to weigh me. Two nurses march through the dormitory bearing a set of scales. They place me on them. The dial spins, then settles.

One of the nurses makes a clicking sound between her teeth. 'She's losing too much weight. She isn't anorexic, is she?'

The other nurse shrugs and says in an audible whisper, 'No, she's definitely psychotic, she hallucinates and everything. She just doesn't seem to want to eat.'

'Oh well. I'd better tell the doctor.'

Later that day, I am summoned to Dr Raines' office at the far end of the corridor. He is sitting at his desk. He motions to the chair placed opposite so I sit down. He obviously expects me to do as I am told.

'Do you know how long you've been here?' he says.

I don't answer him.

She's looking at the bookcase at the side of the room. More words to absorb. Too many now.

'It's been a while since I last saw you. How are you feeling at the moment? Any problems?'

A tiny ball of fluff is forming on the sleeve of her sweater. She starts to roll it. Slowly it begins to grow.

'Do you know why you were brought in here?'

She looks at the wall behind him. His questions are so foolish she can't be bothered answering.

I know that I should try but there isn't anything to say. The phone rings. He tuts his irritation but turns away to pick it up. My attention returns to the bookcase. There is a large blue volume in the centre of one of the shelves. I can discern the word *'Psychotic'*, nothing more.

She knows she should remain in her seat but she has to look at the book.

I edge my way towards it, trying not to be seen. *The Management of Psychotic Disorders*. I slide open the doors and carefully remove it.

'Please don't touch that,' says Dr Raines, still holding the receiver.

I stand with the book clasped tightly to me. Dr Raines winds up his conversation and puts down the phone. Then he says, 'The books are in a particular order. I don't want that disturbed.'

I begin to replace the volume.

She should keep the book. It concerns her. One of the words in the title has been used to describe what she is to them.

Then I think better of it and continue to clasp it to me.

Dr Raines sighs. Then he says, 'Would you like to borrow the book?'

She knows that if she wants it she'll have to answer him.

There is a long silence. Then I say, 'OK, but won't it disturb your order?'

A flash of anger passes across his face. She's said too much. She's undermining him.

For a moment, I think he'll start to shout at me, but instead he says, 'I would like to be able to help you, but for that to happen, it's going to take a lot of cooperation from you.'

She doesn't need his help. What help does he have that will be of use to her? He's got into her mind. He'd like to get inside her body too. She has to protect herself.

'I don't need help.'
'There's no shame in it. Everyone needs some kind of support at one time or another. You don't have to do this alone.'

She doesn't understand what he means. Of course she has to do it alone. There isn't any other way.

'I think deep down you know you need help, and that frightens you.'
I run my fingers across the title of the book. 'What does it mean?' I say to him.
'What does what mean?'

He is talking in riddles.

'I'm not sure what you want from me,' he says, after a pause. 'I feel rather sad that you seem so unable to respond to us at the moment.'
'It's not real.'
'What isn't?'

She was referring to his sadness.

I say, 'Nothing is.'
'You're real. Your feelings are real. You have to give us a

chance, start sharing some of this burden with us. Right from the word go you've been determined not to accept our help. You came to the unit full of anger and resentment.'

'I don't want to be here,' I say softly.

'What? I'm sorry, I didn't hear you.' He waits for a moment, wondering if I will repeat it. Then he adds, 'I'm a little concerned about your eating. It appears that you've hardly eaten anything since your admission and you are losing weight. You must try to eat. Otherwise, we may have to ensure that you get the correct nourishment. Do you understand me?'

I don't answer him.

'There are some things I'd like to be clearer about. You've said to some of the nurses that there are voices in your head. How often do you hear them?'

'I don't know.'

'But you do hear voices?'

He's asked her before. Another trick question.

'Is there just one, or is there more than one?'

She remains silent.

'Are they talking to you now? Try to answer me. We only want to help, you know, check that you're on the right medication.'

I don't know how to reply to him. There are things inside me that I can't explain.

'When were you first aware of them?'

'I don't know.'

'What do they say to you? Do they say nice things or nasty things?'

'Both,' I answer.

With one word, she's already said too much. She must fold her body again, to shut him out.

'OK, that's probably enough for today.' He goes to the door and summons a nurse to escort me, even though the dormitory is only a few yards down the corridor. Gloria is singing again, but much louder than before. Her voice bounces across the walls. She sits beside me. She would have sung the baby to sleep. I open my mouth to let out the high notes, but all that comes out is an eerie kind of wailing.

Chapter Twenty-Nine

It's the nights I mind the most. The time between supper and going to bed drags so slow. This is the time you start to brood on things you never going to change. Like Josie. Like how they said I can't have no compensation for the accident because we're not kith and kin. It's not the money. What use is money when the only thing you really care about is gone? No, it's the feeling I am left with – what Josie and me had don't count. It's not counting in the system. It's being thought of as a piece of nothing.

Got someone legal to sort it out for me. He said straight away it was a hard case to prove. If compensation's going anywhere, it's going to Emilie. She is recognized. They can see her. Suddenly I was invisible.

But I am not invisible now. In the ward round the other day, I made them notice me. I stood up and shouted about everything. They can't hold me back. They can't say I don't exist and I am not important. Every day, I make sure everybody knows that I am here.

Funny, it's like I'm a different person. When Josie was alive, we never really drew attention to ourselves, we went about our business in a softly-softly way. We never held hands except when we were alone in the house and after Emilie found out, and the people from the church, we moved away, and never told anyone we were more than friends. When you have to keep up a pretence, you don't mix that much. Too much holding back. We never got to know too many people. We shared a house and each had a separate bedroom for appearance sake.

Sometimes I wish we could have been born at a later time. These days, prejudice still here but it don't run quite so deep.

It's a little after nine, and the dormitory is quiet. Everyone is getting dopey now. Soon it will be time for night medication. I feel tired in my body, but not in my mind. Everything is running on, all the time, all the thoughts I ever had rolling round my head in an order that don't make a lot of sense. Think this is what it must be like for the new patient, except there's even less order in her head. She sits on her bed and stares at everything. There's talk of putting her on the locked ward but so far nothing's come of it.

Don is on nights. He's glad about this because he don't have to do so much. When I go to fetch a hot drink, I see him sitting by himself in the television room watching a repeat of *Morse*. You get paid for watching television now? Nice work if you can get it.

So I go in and sit beside him, and I say, in my innocent mental patient voice, 'That is the murderer, the one in the car. He committed the murder and tried to frame the other guy.'

Don bangs down his cup of coffee and he says, 'What are you doing in here, Gloria? Why aren't you getting ready for bed?'

Don't answer. I just pick up the remote control and turn to the news. Nothing good happened in the world again today. Every kind of disaster. Compared to that, my life looks full of bliss and joy.

Don gets up and walks away, and I consider my work done. The weather for tomorrow's not so good. Snow in the north, on the Pennine hills and freezing fog in the middle bits. The weather man says this in a regretful tone of voice, like he has personal responsibility for the way the days turn out. At times like this I wish we never come to Britain.

When I was young, people always asked me why we come to this country in the first place if we don't like the weather or the laws or the government. It's always like we're unwelcome guests. And it was not until I read some books and understood the history we have that I worked out how to answer them. Never got much chance to learn before, you see.

This is why I get fed up with Alex. She has so much opportunity and here she is, all the life thinning out of her. She could go to Oxford or Cambridge, you know. Her father said she got ten A grades for her exams. That is some achievement. So what is she doing here, this is what I would like to know. Girl like that should be living the good life. I switch off the television and see her in the corridor. She don't do nothing much, just jumps up and down. She believes that if she moves about all the time, the pounds she's put on these past few weeks will start to drop away from her.

'It's not going to work, you know,' I say to her.

'What isn't?'

'You won't lose much weight from doing that.'

'How do you know?' she says breathlessly. 'Are you some kind of expert on thinness? Because if so, you'd better look to yourself and stop bothering me.'

Always seem to rub the child up the wrong way. Don't mean to do it, it just sort of happens whenever I see her. But you know, I'm starting to feel sorry for her now. She is so young, and it must be hard living up to all them top grades and having to make sure you go to the best university to satisfy your father. I don't say nothing more, I just go back in the dormitory and open up my drawer. Lots of chocolate in there. That's the last thing she wants. I break off a piece and pop it in my mouth. Now let me see. Must be something I can find for her. My hand settles on a brooch. It glitters in the strip light of the dormitory but I can see that it is not her style. It has red in it and green and blue and the youth prefer dull colours, all this black and brown. Then I see I have a card still in its wrapper that caught my eye in Woolworths the last time I was there. I bought it because it had a sunrise on it and that seemed to stand for the future. Must have been in an optimistic frame of mind. Pity it don't last. Still, the card has its use. I write in it, taking care to get the spelling right. She's the sort of girl who sets a lot of store by proper spelling. I put her name on it and leave it on her pillow. Hope she'll understand – it's a peace offering I want to give to her. Something that says we're all in the same boat.

The nurses give the call for medication. I go stand in the queue. Then I go and find my clean pyjamas.

Always find it hard, being in a dormitory, especially if I'm feeling low. And it seem as if the highs are quickly followed by the lows. There are six of us in here and the beds are pushed close together. Each one has a bedside cabinet and a fibreboard partition but it still don't make for privacy. And sound don't pay no mind to fibreboard – every noise penetrates all through the night. I undress quick, before Don comes in. He is supposed to ask if everyone is decent before he opens up the door, but he never bothers doing that, he just comes straight on through. If I was young, or in another place, maybe I wouldn't mind them seeing all my flesh, but here it's like your body's not your own. I have an old bra which I have to wear for comfort's sake but the elastic's frayed a bit and it has a yellow look from too much time spent in the wash. The lace edging got a little torn in parts, but I sewed it up and it looks almost like new. Could pay for new bras but I have to break them in and I hate that tight-up feeling that you get when your clothes start to pinch. Anyway I have no need to put on decent underwear. No need to allure. I'm past all that now.

Funny thing, I don't miss sex so much. Just being close, and holding Josie in my arms. And tenderness. I miss the tenderness. My body is changing every day. Perhaps I have an allergy to hospital. My breasts droop and the skin around my thighs is starting to get lumps. Or maybe I just notice more these days. A body is a private thing unless you're with the one you love. And then it's two bodies that exist together in an equal way. There is nothing equal here. Don sees my belly and my flabby neck, but I don't get to see his wobbly bits, though I have to say, I shudder at the thought.

I put on my dressing gown and go to the washing cubicles. Someone has left a mess of hair in the plughole of the sink. Hope it is hair from the head I am fishing out.

I get in my bed just as Don turns out the lights. 'Goodnight, ladies,' he says, and then he adds, 'Or is ladies not PC these days?' He closes the door. I'm the last. Everybody else is in bed already. 'Gloria?' Alex whispers to me.

'Yes?' I whisper back.

'Thanks for the card.'

'No problem,' I say to her. I snuggle down in the sheets and wish I didn't ache so much. The doctor says it's arthritis in my knees. Should have lost some weight. It's always a toss up between thinness and chocolate. Most of the time, chocolate wins out.

'You eat for comfort, Gloria,' Louise said to me the other day. They make something out of every little thing we do.

Wish I could just fall asleep. Everybody else has dropped off now and I can hear them breathing heavy in the dark. Someone starts to snore. That's all I need. I sit up and try to trace the sound. Could be Alex, could be Mrs Isaac, can't be sure. Why is it that every noise sounds ten times louder in the dark? And every ache feels deeper than it feels in the day and every bit of loneliness just magnifies? But there is no sense dwelling on the misery of life. When I can't sleep, I sometimes think of all the nice things I done. Sailing on a boat across the river. The picnic me and Josie had just after we first met. The day I bought a stereo for Christmas. And I run the pictures over in my head like an old video film, and I freeze frame every now and then and pick up on the detail: the bobbing of the boat upon the water; the tree that sparkled with the coloured lights; the pattern of the beads on Josie's purple dress.

Chapter Thirty

It is hard to tell where day ends and night begins. Once, it was clear, but now they merge with a greyness that stands for both. The moon shines visible, its roundness outlined on the flimsy fabric of the curtains. She listens to the murmured conversation of the night staff beyond the door and the buzzing of the night light that shines above her head. The bed is too soft; her body curves into the mattress achingly. She aches. Hungers. Longs for comfort. Quiet. An end to the unceasing sounds. When did she forget who she is, where she came from, what she wants to be? The darkness of her skin is heightened by the whiteness of the pillow slip.

She still doesn't dare to sleep, but often she can't help herself; her eyes close and she ceases to be vigilant. It is then that the evil escapes from her, twisting through the air, melting everything around her. She is aware of nothingness, of things destroyed. She's aware of the greatness of the magic that has been conferred on her, the awesome power of it. She can kill with a look, burn with a touch.

Don't look. Don't touch.

See the crack of light that shines through the door? Searing light. It blinds. It's getting wider now. Someone's coming in. Sit up and see if you can tell who it is.

A man.

He's got nothing on. Look at him, white-paper skin, blue veins protruding through skinny thighs. Do you want him? Can you feel him thrust his way inside you?

no

Say it again.

no

She means yes when she says no, you can tell by the way her eyes widen and her lips part into a narrow grin. He moves towards her, silently, and pulls back the bedclothes. He knows what he wants. He will take it from her.

no

She's going to let him do it. Look at her now, lying there, like a lump of wood, pretending that she doesn't feel. The little slut. A whimper eases from her throat. He thinks he's pleasing her. His small white arse moves up and down, hollow in the moonlight.

No.

The word is said aloud; it judders through the dormitory. Her body comes alive; her arms flail, her legs kick out.

Feet pounding on the floor. Faces blinking in the surge of light. There is blood on the sheet where I'm scratching him and a small tear in the counterpane.

I use my body like a weapon and I make him stop.

He shrinks as I claw at him.

Stop.

He can't force his way inside of me.

Stop.

'Merle!'

I jump as Gloria sounds my name. Over and over again, she repeats the flat rhythm of it, her noise and mine enough to wake the dead.

She's beside me now. She hauls him off, holds him by the arms, pins them to the back of his pale, flaccid body.

She is shaking uncontrollably.

Not from fear.

Passion then.

From rage. All the feelings bubbling up inside.

Don surveys the scene. 'What do you think this is, a fucking knocking shop? Come on Jim, get back in your own bloody bed.'

He doesn't look at me. Why can't he look?

She is insignificant.

No.

Silent.

No.

She hasn't got a voice.

I am screaming suddenly; the pitch of it cracks glass, splinters the rotten wood that frames the door. And all the while, Gloria is holding me, rocking me, telling me that everything is going to be all right.

She is my Orisha, African angel of light. Did I choose her or did she choose me? She walks with me, guiding me steadily out of the dark.

Chapter Thirty-One

This tape is almost full up now, so I'm not going to talk for long. But it seems to me you need to tighten up security. How come you let all that stuff happen with Merle the other night? Where was the night staff? It's all very well Don acting like the cavalry, but he arrived too late. You're always talking about how the patients on the ward get traumatized by one thing and another, but you don't do nothing to stop a whole new set of traumas getting added to the list.

And while we're on the subject, the big trauma I have right now is thinking about more weeks spent on Ward C. I talked to Dr Raines and he said if I stay calm for another two or three weeks, you'll let me get discharged. I'm telling you this so you know and try your best not to make it hard for me to be in a good frame of mind. This ward's not the best place for keeping calm. Too much going on, too many people in distress. So I think that if you let me off the ward some more, I'll be able to hold myself in a whole lot better.

One thing I'd like to do is go for walks by myself. And I'd also like to go home for a day real soon. In other words, it's time I got a free pass and can roam around without getting stopped every two or three minutes. This is not too much to ask. And along with that, you can cut down on my medication so I have the energy to do all these things. How am I going to live a normal life when I get out of here if all I want to do is sleep? You never had to take lithium, so you don't know how it acts when it gets inside the body. You think that as long as my mood don't get too extreme, everything is going fine for me. You forget that there is more to life than this. And I also want you to know that Merle is still having fits before she goes to sleep at night. I know from when I worked at the home this is not a good thing and you have to give it some attention. Otherwise, what's the point? You make her well in the mind but sick in the body. This don't make a lot of sense to me. That's all I have to say for now. If you give me a free pass, I'll try to behave better, OK?

Chapter Thirty-Two

Something has come alive in me. It is still night – another night,
I think. I've lost track. It hurts to be alive. I am aware of all the
gaps that I can never fill. Like the baby. Whenever I think of the
child that we lost, I tremble violently, as if the thought alone is a
kind of assault. I bury my face in the pillow, trying to stifle the
sounds of aching, the depth of the pain inside me. And then I
remember the flowers. I creep out of bed and open the wardrobe
door. I find them buried beneath my clothes. They are coated
with dust. I blow it gently away. Roses, red, the sign of love.
There is incense too, wrapped in tissue paper. Orange and blue. I
didn't want white; too clean and clinical. The colour of sterility.
I search in my drawer for the matches and then I remember
they've been taken from me. Can't trust a mental patient. I might
set fire to the place. Whenever I want to smoke, I must ask permission from the nurses. I have no means of doing the things I
need to do. I will do this though, this important thing. I will do
it without the gaze of my father or the gaze of the nursing staff. I
will do it beyond the gaze of Clyde.

I creep into the corridor at the back of the dormitory trying not to wake the nurses. I have timed it well. It is a little after three. Don seldom does his rounds and never after two. I open the bathroom door. The quiet of the place unnerves me for a moment. I am so used to sound.

What is she going to do? See her hesitate. She doesn't really know. She is moving in a dream, walking in the in-between, trying to find the sense of self that bled away from her. She wants to pray. Not to God, she has no faith. To herself, perhaps; she needs to find the soul of her, the essence of the things she lost.

I place the flowers round the bath, one by one. The plastic thorns gently prick my finger tips. I wish I could light the incense. I need the glow in me. I kneel by the bath and turn on the tap. Water rushes through my open fingers. I want to feel. I want to bury everything that hurts, not the way I've always buried things, not just inside me, no. I want to bury the baby here, in imagined earth, safe in remembered spaces, safe in the soul of me.

She speaks. Unlinked words, sentences severed from their meaning. She is tired of seeking meanings, the endless, fruitless search. She likes the chaos that she activates; it sits better with her now than the order she once tried to cultivate. She wants to swim. She wishes she'd been born a fish.

I skim the water with my child, circling endlessly, the baby crying in my arms, the sound rising and falling; we are weightless now, the weight lifted from us. Bobbing up. Then diving deep into the waves, down and down again, gliding through the water. We see a fish. It multiplies. Multi-coloured fish, fins sparkling in the light. The baby's crying ceases and she laughs.

The door opens. Gloria is standing there. She produces matches from her pocket. We strike them, two or three at a time. They spark and then they flare. Brightness, dazzling in the dark. Gloria Mundi, light of the world. She too has burials to perform. Mother, sister, father. And a lover who is too much part of her.

When does the grieving cease? Even angels sigh and whisper in the dark, remembering the end of things. We stand side by side, aware of all the endings and beginnings. We see that it's the finding then the losing that hurts each of us the most.

Chapter Thirty-Three

I hear a sound in the dark and strain my eyes to see. Merle is creeping round, her body bent in two, as if she's trying to cradle herself from all the hurt she feels. I get up too, my body bowed in image of the way she's carrying herself. She don't hear me though, she's too far down inside her sadness. I try to straighten up but something pulls at the soul of me and holds me close to the ground.

She opens up the door to the wardrobe and takes her incense out. She rummages in her drawer and I guess she needs a match. Not much chance of that. The nurses take them from the sicker ones in case they do themselves a damage. She has some flowers too, wrapped in cellophane. I wonder how they stay so fresh – and then I remember that she never bought the real kind, she got the plastic ones, the ones that always keep.

Wish I had a pair of wings like proper angels have. My body aches, and I could use a little flight. Even putting one foot down in front of the other pains me so I just want to crawl back in my bed again. But I can tell by the way Merle looks that something is troubling her deep and I should stay close. I hear her go into the bathroom and shut the door. She puts the water on, it runs through the pipe. I pause in case the nurses come, but Don's on again tonight, and he don't hear a thing.

I know from the way she's behaving that Merle could use some time alone, so I leave her for a while. Then I remember Mrs Isaac smokes when she thinks no one can see, and she has a box of matches stashed away. I creep across and pull open the drawer of her bedside cabinet and feel around a little. Sure enough, my hand rests upon the matches. I'll borrow them and give them back to her tomorrow. I'm sure she won't mind, it's in a good cause.

There is silence in the bathroom now, except for words spoken soft. I open up the door. Merle is kneeling by the bath. She smiles at me. She takes my hand and she whispers something about a baby. I give her the matches and she smiles again. We light the incense up.

We stand and watch it smoking in the semi-dark, sweet scent filling up the room, and I know this is a time of setting things to rest. I remember when me and Josie had incense in the house. It was the first time we touched.

I'm twenty-two years old and I have always hidden from the touching side of things, told myself I have no need of another human body next to mine. Fear takes hold of me. I want Josie's touch so bad it triggers panic in my bones and makes me want to run. Wanting and not having. Being scared to have. And Josie pulls me back towards her and she is soft as dark brown silk, so warm the heat rises up in me and I ache from need of her. And then I feel her touch on me, the gentle stroking of my cheek, my mouth, my belly. Fingers probing every part of me, all the hidden parts, making me draw in breath, making me shiver, making me want with every fibre of my being. And I feel a closeness so sweet it makes me cry out, and the sensation in my body and the ease in my mind come together in the moment of her touch and all thought of sin is gone, all thought of all the things that we could lose, the family and friends who will turn their backs on us, and all I feel is happiness wound around me tight.

And then I open up my eyes and I feel the sadness of things ending, the closing off that comes with parting, the ending of the time when all I needed could be given to me, the time when I could give and all my giving was returned ten-fold. And I am standing in the bathroom and I see the flowers strewn around the bath. Red roses, the colour of loving.

Chapter Thirty-Four

I follow Louise to the doctor's room. He's sitting in an armchair. He leans forward as I enter, nodding a greeting. It's then that I see Clyde.

A few weeks before, his presence would have prompted a whole range of feelings: fear and anger, relief and joy. But the medication has pushed feeling so far down inside me that mostly I can only remember these sensations, and try, hopelessly, to summon them. I never imagined I would want to be afraid, but any emotion is better than this flatness. It stifles me.

Clyde isn't meant to be here. I thought he was installed in a new block of flats, with his first wife and Marcus, watching television – a flat-screen version, with satellite channels and digital sound. I touch my hair. It is matted and coarse. My eyebrows haven't been plucked in weeks, and a fine down of hair is covering my upper lip. It is as if every bit of woman-ness has been removed from me. It's as if they've brought me in here bare and unprotected.

See her nakedness.

'Darling, it's me.'

Terms of endearment, even though he's been absent for so long. I shield my face with my hands and sit by the door, away from the doctor and away from Clyde. In the moment that I looked at him I was aware that he seemed different too – shrunken and older, his presence diminished by the largeness of Dr Raines. We barely recognize each other.

I'd imagined seeing him again, but not like this. I get up and open the door, but my path is blocked by the nurse who has delivered me. 'Go back in and sit down,' she says.

'All right, Nurse,' says Dr Raines. 'I'll let you know when I'm ready for you to escort her back to the ward.'

Clyde pats the seat of the chair beside him. 'Come back in and sit with me. It's all right, darling, it's OK.'

I uncover my face and look at him again. He is smiling at me sheepishly, as if the weeks without him have been just a day or two.

'How have you been?' he asks.

I feel in my pocket for my cigarettes and the matches I've managed to hide from the nurses. How does he think I've been?

She's been such a bad little girl.

'Please don't smoke in here,' the doctor says.

I light up anyway. What can he do to me that hasn't been done already?

Dr Raines says, with an edge to his voice, 'She's been having trouble cooperating with us, haven't you?'

'Cooperating with what?' asks Clyde.

The doctor sits back in his chair and gazes into space, recalling every misdemeanour. 'She's not too happy with the medication. She avoids group meetings. She doesn't really socialize with the other patients and she's fought with the staff who've tried to keep her on the ward.'

Bad girl. Naughty girl.

I shrug. He believes it to be true. What does it matter whether I agree or not? Clyde looks . . . troubled, as if he doesn't know how to reply. He is out of his depth.

'Sit down, please,' Clyde says again.

I sit, but not because they've told me to.

'How long have you been like this?' asks Clyde.

Like what? 'Not long,' I say. 'I don't really know.'

'She's very much better than she was. She's on a section – that means, as I said to you earlier, that there are certain restrictions on her and she can't discharge herself. This ends in a few days' time, and if she'll agree to stay as a voluntary patient we won't need to think about extending it. It's in her own best interests. She's had a complete psychotic breakdown. Obviously, we must ensure that she's fit enough to leave before discharging her.'

Clyde turns to the doctor. 'OK, she isn't well, I can see that. What are you doing for her?'

'Well, as I've tried to indicate, we've put her on some medication. It has helped to reduce the symptoms. Generally, a little rest and some medication tend to do the trick in these cases. We think she's on the mend and, as I've already said, she is considerably better than she was when we admitted her.'

'What's she shaking for?'

'It's nothing to worry about, it's just a side effect of the medication. We wanted to put her on something to counteract this, but she refused to take it.'

I don't want more drugs. They'll be giving me pills to counteract the side effects of the pills they've given me to counteract the side effects . . .

'Look at her. How can you say she's better?'

'As I understand it, you were away for some time prior to her admission. You are therefore not in a position to know how she was when she arrived here.'

'She can't have been worse than this.'

'Your wife's been very ill, Mr Hanson. I do understand how hard this must be for you. It's often a shock to relatives to see the condition of the patient.'

'I am not an idiot, Dr Raines. Don't treat me like a fool,' he says, then falls silent. He gets up and goes to the window.

'Mr Hanson, I assure you, I have no intention of doing anything of the sort. Would you like a cup of tea? Or coffee perhaps? I'm sure one of the nurses would get one for you.'

'Coffee,' he says. He's taking the offer as a sign that the doctor is prepared to treat him with respect and he comes and sits down again. The doctor goes to the door and summons a nurse, who is sent to fetch refreshments. No one bothers asking me if I am thirsty, even though the medication dries up my mouth.

'So how much longer are you going to keep her here?' asks Clyde, his tone amicable, conciliatory even.

'Well, it's hard to say at this point, Mr Hanson. It depends on her.'

Clyde looks at me. 'Do you want to stay in here?'

I look away from him. It depends on so many things. I don't want to be back home – alone except for the devils and angels in my head.

'Don't you know?' he says in a gentle tone.

'I think it's difficult for her to make any kind of decision at the moment, which is why we'd like to keep her here.'

But I don't want to remain on the ward either, shut in half the time, losing all sense of myself. I want Clyde to say that he'll stay with me, and to show that he cares about what's happening to me, but instead he is taking coffee from a nurse and looking pleased with himself.

After a while, the doctor says, 'Mr Hanson, we asked you here because we want to try to build some kind of profile of her, a full case history. She's said very little since her admission and if it wasn't for her notebook, we really wouldn't have very much about her background at all. We're hoping you can fill in some of the detail.'

'Sure, if it helps.'

'What do you know about her parents?'

'Only that they're dead. Her father died when she was four, and her mother shortly before I met her. That would have been . . . seven years ago now.'

The doctor taps the cover of my notebook, which sits on his desk — irrefutable evidence that there is something wrong with me. Then he says, 'There are indications here that sexual abuse occurred in her childhood.'

Slut. Whore.

Clyde looks uncomfortable. He shifts in his seat.

'She writes a lot about her father. Has she ever said anything to you about things that were done to her?'

She won't speak. She won't defend him. She'll let them think he did it.

'What are you saying?' Clyde asks in bewilderment.

'Sexual abuse is quite common, Mr Hanson. We just want to know if you can confirm it.'

Clyde shakes his head. 'She never said anything about him interfering with her. Nothing.'

'But there must have been something to suggest this in your marital relations.'

'Well, at first she was a bit . . .'

'A bit what?'

Clyde blows air through his mouth. 'Look, is this really necessary? Why do you want to know all this?'

'We just want to build some kind of picture so that we can help your wife. Anything you can tell us will be useful.'

'Well, she was . . . nervous, you know? Scared. She didn't seem to like being touched.'

'She didn't like being touched?'

'She was nervous,' he repeats.

'And she's continued to be like this throughout your marriage?'

'No, not exactly. I think she got used to it.'

How was it for you?

He invites her back to his flat. She knows she's going for sex. She wears her satin knickers and a flimsy little bra. She's hot for him.

Clyde no longer lives above the restaurant. He has a new flat on Brixton Hill. He arranges to pick me up at eight. He's always prompt. It's one of the things I like most about him, his reliability. I get into the car. I think I'm ready, but I can't be sure.

Ever ready. Turned on. Like a bitch on heat.

I need him but it's not a sexual need. I want to be like other women, loved and cherished. I want to feel that I belong again, to somebody. In his flat, the living room surfaces are polished to a shine.

He will see the dirt on her.

He switches on an Ice T tape and pours us each a drink. I don't like rum and coke but I don't want to tell him, so I slowly sip and wait for the effect. The music is loud.

He puts down his glass and kisses her, his tongue probing her mouth. She's sucking him, wanting to fuck. Her body is taut, she's his

215

little black whore. Look at her now. Look at what she wants to do with him. Teasing him, loving every fuck-full minute.

I try to love him back, but I know that I can't do it right. He pushes me back so my head is resting on the arm of the leather sofa.

He cups his hand across her breast. She feels a pulse of pleasure.

A single beat, a moment, but it quickly fades. I want to love him but I'm not sure that I can. Touching and being touched is a necessary stage in our relationship. 'I need to go to the bathroom,' I say to him.

He sighs. 'First door on your left.'

The tiles are black and white. The bathroom suite is gleaming porcelain. I lock the door and lean against it, stealing a moment to think.

She's out of her depth.

'Do you need anything?' he calls to me, after a while.

'No, it's OK,' I say from behind the door.

There are things that I should tell him, and questions I should ask. I don't know how to phrase them.

He might have a disease. A dirty disease for a dirty little girl. Has he got a condom in his pocket? Has he got one just for you?

I flush the toilet and return to the living room.

216

'Come here,' he says.

I walk towards him, conscious only of my body and the awkward way I move.

Thick thighs. Fat arse. Flesh that wobbles as she walks towards his touch. A wetness deep inside her.

He draws me to him and buries his face just below my breasts. I stroke his hair, but it feels contrived. 'I'm not on the pill,' I say. 'It's OK, I'll take care of it.'

Is it condoms he's talking about? I can tell by his tone that I should know exactly what he means, so I can't ask him to explain.

She knows what he means. Don't play the innocent, you're as practised as a £10 whore.

He kisses me again.

Tonguing deep inside her mouth, tasting the staleness of her, scenting every whiff of foulness that she carries.

I expect him to take me into the bedroom, but he seems to want to do it there, in the living room.

He'll fuck you on the floor, he doesn't care.

He lifts my T-shirt and places his hand inside my bra, touching my breast again.

217

Tingly shivers. Sweat. Wet between her thighs.

He puts his mouth to me. What should I do now? Should I touch him back? I don't know what to do.

Such a knowing little girl.

'I don't know if I can do this,' I say to him, trying to keep the panic from my voice.

'It's OK, just relax.'

I can't convey to him the measure of my fear; it's impossible to name. It's to do with intimacy. It's locked in my dread of losing myself. And it's in my sense of sin.

She quivers with her longing for a fuck. Shakes with it. Desperate to feel him inside her.

Clyde withdraws his hand and sits back on the sofa. 'You're shaking. What's the matter? Look, you won't get pregnant, I promise you. I'll take care of it. I've got the stuff.' He pats his trouser pocket.

I shake my head.

'What then? Are you still a virgin? Is that what it is?'

The thought hasn't occurred to him before. I wonder why he has assumed so much about me. 'In a way,' I say to him.

'Either you are or you aren't.'

'I don't know what counts,' I say to him.

Clyde laughs. 'Come and sit here,' he says, patting the sofa. 'We can go more slowly if it helps. Look, I'll just kiss you, OK?

And I won't do anything unless you say I can. Men aren't monsters, you know. I'd never do anything to a woman that she didn't want me to do. And it's good that you're with me. The first time, you need someone experienced. I can help you to enjoy it. Come on, just relax.'

I am disappearing inside myself. Clyde fades into the distance until I can no longer hear him. I don't feel. I shut my eyes, shielding them with my arms.

'Oh for God's sake,' says Clyde. Then he laughs again, though it sounds forced. 'Do you want to go home?'

'Yes,' I whisper.

Yes, yes, oh yes.

'OK. I'll drive you back.'

'I can get a taxi.'

'No I'll drive you. It's all right.'

Dr Raines leans towards Clyde. 'So you're saying she began by being frightened but after a while you were able to have a full sexual relationship?'

'Yeah.' Clyde traces a circle on the knee of his trousers.

Penetration. Ejaculation.

I'm afraid I'll lose my job. I don't see how I can work with him now. Every time I see him I'm embarrassed. I try to avoid him in the coming days but he's always there. He treats me briskly and there's little warmth. I wish I could have been the things he wanted me to be. I wish he could have liked me. And then, early one evening, before we open up, he sits down beside me and he says, 'Do you want to come out for a meal one night? We could start again. I rushed things, I guess.'

We eat at an expensive restaurant in China Town, watching the waiters with a professional eye, gauging the efficiency of their service. I especially like the pancakes and crispy duck. I've been grown up for years, had to be, but I haven't felt it until now. There are many more nights out: *Porgy and Bess* performed in Hammersmith, a club in Wardour Street. I learn to wear the right clothes, the kind he likes to see me in. I buy them cheaply from the market. I know that he cares about me when he lets me be with him the weekend he has Marcus. We do the Sunday father thing and go to the zoo. I've always got on well with children. I know how to play, and I make Marcus laugh uncontrollably. Yet all the while, I wonder what his mother's like.

I allow him to touch me again after that.

Gagging for it.

I'm slowly starting to feel safe with him. It's hard to respond, and I'm still afraid, but not so much that he can't enter me.

She loves the feel of him. She loves it when he enters her.

That's what it feels like. Being entered. My whole self is suddenly penetrated and exposed to him. Yet there is pleasure too.

Pleasure in the way he touches her. Pleasure as she's sucking him.

And as I become accustomed to the closeness, the terror diminishes and becomes entwined with yearning. We are lying side by side. He's asleep. I find it hard to share a bed. To me it seems more intimate than sex. Eventually, I will get used to it.

Dr Raines says, 'I know these questions must seem intrusive, but they are necessary if we're going to be able to give your wife the help she needs.'

'And you think she was interfered with? As a child?'

'Everything seems to point to that.'

'And that's what made her ill? What her father did to her? Hold on, she was four. She was *four* when he died. You really think . . . ?'

Her evil's in the lying that she does. Tell them that it wasn't that, are you listening? Tell them now.

'It's a strong possibility. She'll probably tell us when she's ready. Obviously, we don't want to push too much while she's still in such a fragile state.'

'And what he did . . . that's caused all this?'

'No, you misunderstand. I wouldn't say that. The thing about the kind of psychotic illness your wife is exhibiting, Mr Hanson, is that it occurs regardless of a person's history. There are genetic factors. It's part of her make-up, if you like.'

'Then why do you want to know about this abuse thing if it didn't make her sick?'

'Well, it helps us to understand her, to find ways of supporting her.'

Clyde sucks his teeth. It's the only indication that there might be scepticism.

'We know this must be difficult for you. We do understand.'

Clyde nods. He looks at me for a minute, then he looks away. I am dirty to him now.

Soiled.

'Don't do that,' Clyde says to me. He takes hold of my hands to stop them pulling at my hair. 'Why is she like this?'

'She has a severe mental illness, Mr Hanson. Your wife's very ill.'

'I went away. Could that have caused it?'

'No. As I've already said, it is a genetic disorder. That means it's something she's inherited.'

'I know what genetic means. Who did she inherit it from?'

'Well, these things are very complex. There isn't a direct line of inheritance. It's part of a broader genetic pattern.'

'You done tests?'

'We've talked to her extensively.'

'No, I mean, have you done physical tests? Examined her brain? Found some sort of chemical in her?'

'Measuring psychotic illness is still at a relatively early stage. There are no conclusive physical tests of the kind you're suggesting.'

'Then how can you know it's genetic?'

'The symptoms she's exhibiting: hallucinations, aural and visual. Confusion. Thought disorder. There's evidence of delusions.'

'But you say she doesn't talk to you.'

'I wouldn't say that. She doesn't communicate much, but it's clear in the little she articulates that these things are happening. And confusion's very evident in her notebook too.'

'What is this notebook thing?'

'We've managed to persuade our patients to write things down, keep a record of their thoughts and feelings. We've been utilizing these journals in all kinds of different therapeutic activities and it has helped us to learn more about the patients. We've also found that we've been able to relieve some of their anxieties by getting them to write their fears and to articulate their problems. It's been an interesting experiment.'

'Experiment?'

'By that I mean it's been an interesting way of testing what is helpful to them in learning to manage their illness.'

'Can I see the journal – her journal, I mean?'

I shake my head. Not Clyde. He won't understand. The doctor sees my look and says, 'Not without your wife's permission. It's a question of confidentiality. Give her a little time and I'm sure it's another thing that will happen when she's ready.'

Dr Raines goes to the door and opens it. He shouts for a nurse. Louise eventually arrives, looking breathless.

'You can take her back now,' he says.

Take me back? I'm not ready to go.

Dr Raines pats my shoulder. His hand burns through my

cotton shirt. 'If you like, I'll send your husband along to talk to you for a while once we've settled one or two things. Perhaps you'd like him to take you out for an hour or so this afternoon? I know the two of you must have quite a lot to discuss.'

'But . . .'

The doctor looks at me quizzically. I want to tell him that I have to stay, hear the things they're planning for me, contribute perhaps, but he turns back to Clyde and Louise escorts me from the room. Halfway up the corridor, I run back. I go in again without knocking. They look surprised to see me.

'Please,' I say.

'What is it?' asks Clyde.

I can't answer him. I want so many things that I don't know where to begin.

'Come on, stop being silly,' says Louise, and she leads me back to the dormitory.

Chapter Thirty-Five

OK, you say you're getting tired of listening to the tapes because they don't say much about the way I feel. Think you need to sharpen up your ears. And I know I don't say a lot about the future but it's because the future don't interest me no more, OK? The future is cancelled as of now.

And before you say it, I am not angry. I'm not an angry person. Anger gets you nowhere, so I don't bother feeling it. All the energy people use up getting angry is a waste of time. If I'm going to get a feeling, it will be for something useful, something that will carry me into this future I don't have.

This is why I like happy. It seems to me that happy is a useful feeling. So why are you so keen to kick it out of me? Why you so determined to make me flat like the rest of you? Seems to me that everything I want is wrong and everything you want is right. Something wrong with that.

The feeling I have in plentiful supply is boredom. This is because there's nothing to do on the ward except make shelves in occupational therapy and tell the nurses all the problems you got.

This is a recipe for people sitting down and moaning about life instead of getting on and living it, OK?

And another thing, ages ago now, on that first tape I done for you, I told you to hurry up and let me go back home on a visit like you promised. And what has happened since? Sweet FA. And sweet FA just about sums up this bloody place. When you going to let me go back home for good? What use is it to keep me here? I am a hopeless case. You keep on saying how lucky we are to be in this place with all this caring sharing nursing and all the kindness you bestow. Some poor people hammering on the door, trying to be let into a place like this, you say. Well, I don't mind giving up my bed for some poor soul that would appreciate it more. Seems to me you get it all wrong. You keep the ones that don't want to be here and shut out the ones that are trying to get in. Some strange logic, that.

I know in advance that you're not going to be pleased with what I put on this tape. But I never asked to do it you know. And it seems to me you can't complain if it don't turn out the way you expect. Foolish thing, expectation. This life is always one big disappointment.

Chapter Thirty-Six

Clyde has a new car; a company car. It's shiny silver and the engine purrs. I get in carefully, trying to measure the distance between seat and windscreen. The world appears to me through a refracting lens.

'How long can we be out?' The words come slowly; I have to force them from me.

'Dr Raines said we could have the whole afternoon if you wanted it.'

Do you want it? Do you?

'I get tired.'
'Yeah, OK. See how it goes.'
'Where are we going?'
'I thought we could take a trip into town.'
'What for?'
'For lunch. Shopping, if you want.'

He wants something from her. What can it be? Can she work it out?
She's getting slower all the time.

'It's the medication.'

'What is?' asks Clyde.

'Why I'm slow.'

The traffic is heavy so they barely move. Clyde asks too many questions, it's hard to know what he's hoping to hear. 'That stuff the doctor said. Was it true?'

'Which part?'

'Your father. What he said he did to you.'

'No, it wasn't true,' I reply, but I say nothing more. I want to keep the truth inside myself where only I can see it. Private spaces. Private thoughts. Why should I tell everything? I want to protect myself.

'Are you losing weight? You seem thinner. Don't they feed you right?'

'The food's OK. It's just hard to eat. To swallow. Big throat.'

Deep throat.

'Deep throat,' I say aloud. Shouldn't do that. The inside and outside spaces will get mixed up.

Clyde turns his head sharply. 'Don't say things like that,' he says to me. He is embarrassed. He overtakes the car in front and picks up speed. 'Dr Raines thinks you'll be coming home quite soon. What do you think about it?'

'I don't know.'

'I came back, you know. The house was a mess, I mean really filthy. Stuff on the floor. What were you doing? What was going on inside your head?'

'I don't know.'

'You can tell me. I know it was just because you were ill. I know you're not like that. You've always been . . . nice. It wasn't you, I know that. I just want you to be ready when they discharge you. The new job's good, but it's long hours. Do you think you'll be able to cope on your own in the house?'

I don't answer. I look out the window. Children in a park. Climbing flowers. Dark brown sun spreading violet light.

'My colours are wrong,' I say to him.

'What?'

'My colours are wrong. I can't make them go right.'

'How do you mean?'

'I can't see things in the right way.'

'Did you tell Dr Raines?'

'Yes,' I answer.

Little liar.

'Don't worry about it then. He said a lot of the stuff that's going on with you now is a side effect of the medication, like the slowness you talked about.' Clyde keeps one hand on the steering wheel and unwraps a mint with the other. He puts it in his mouth.

'My body's gone. They took it away from me.'

Clyde sighs. I fall silent and look out at the ultraviolet light. I need suntan lotion.

'They let me see the consultant, you know. He came in specially to talk to me. He said that if you continue to take the medication you should be almost well in two or three weeks.'

'The consultant?'

'Dr . . . God, what was the guy's name? The one with the long grey hair. Soft spoken. Very polite. He said you hear voices. But that's not true either, is it?'

'No, it isn't true.'

Liar, liar, pants on fire.

'Then why did you tell them that you did? He said you told them.'

I remember the consultant then. Dr God. I've only ever spoken to him once, shortly after my arrival. They called it a ward round. I sat in a room with him and his twelve apostles and answered questions about how I felt and why I behaved the way I did. I don't remember what I said. I don't think I said anything. I sat in silence, mostly, trying not to cry.

'I didn't tell him. I don't think I did.' It is all in fragments, everything. Shards of memory.

'Do you think you'll be OK, eating out in a restaurant? You won't feel strange or get in a state?'

'I'll be OK.'

He's afraid she'll say something bad. A dirty word. An unclean thought bubbling aloud from her head. Such a dirty little girl.

'I'm not dirty,' I say to him.

'No, I know you're not,' he answers but I don't believe him.

The restaurant he's chosen stands by the river. She gets out of the car when he tells her to and goes to look at the water. Dark and dirty. Trying to see a fish. Peering over the parapet, bottom raised. She thinks that if she sees a fish, nothing bad will touch her today.

Clyde takes my arm and leads me into the restaurant. He hasn't made a reservation but he knows the manager. They smile and nod at one another. At least we get a corner table. I'm wearing a top that stretches tight across my breasts and reveals the protruding outline of my stomach. Curved and full. Fat while the rest of me is thin. I look as if I'm pregnant.

One of life's little ironies. She's infertile, incapable of reproduction. But her belly's constantly inflated. They must have known she'd never have children when they examined her after the miscarriage, but no one thought to tell her.

They said they did. They said they told me at the hospital.

In her stupidity, she failed to understand.

They told me like I should have known what they were saying. I didn't like to ask them what they meant.

She didn't have the sense to ask them to explain.

I didn't know that they were telling me anything important. All that mattered to me then was the baby I'd lost. I couldn't think about the future, couldn't take it in.

She puts a hand across her barrenness. Tries to hide the bulge of it.

'Look at the menu,' Clyde instructs.
I pick it up. The words are blurred. I can't decide.
The waiter comes. 'Are you ready to order, sir?'
Clyde looks at me. I shake my head. 'Can you give us another couple of minutes?' The waiter goes to the furthest corner of the room. Clyde says, 'I'll order something for you. Something that you'll like.'

How does he know what pleases her? Is he inside her head?

'I'll do it,' she says. 'Just let me think.'

Thinking is the thing she cannot do.

When the waiter comes back again, Clyde orders pork for himself and lamb for me. Meat lies heavy on my stomach.
We begin with prawns.
'I can't eat these,' I say to him.
'Why not?'
'They kill them while they're still alive.'
'That doesn't make sense.'
'You know what I mean. We used to do it at the restaurant.'

'You didn't mind it then.'

She didn't mind a lot of things once upon a time. She minds them now.

'Pass them to me then. I'll eat your share. Do you know how much it costs to have a meal in here?'

'Can we afford it, Clyde?'

'I've got a new job, remember?'

He likes to spend it while he's got it. Remember when the restaurant folded?

That was the recession.

He's all image and no substance. Doesn't she know that by now?

I watch while he eats. 'How's Marcus?' I say to him.

'Fine.'

I want to ask him where he went after he left me in the house, but if he was with his other wife, I don't want to hear it. I'm quiet for a while but eventually I say, 'Have you come home for good now?'

'Look, forever's a long time. Let's take it slow for a while, see how things go. The doctor thinks that's the best way to handle things.'

'And what do you think?'

'Let's just wait and see.'

'Why did you go away?'

'You know why.'

'No I don't.'

'You do. You know you do.'

'Tell me.'

He hesitates. Then he says, 'You weren't behaving right.'

It's the same conversation. We had it the day he left and I ran after him. I could ask what I do wrong but I know that he won't answer me.

The waiter brings the second course. Clyde helps himself to vegetables.

'Tell me about the new job.'

'It's a chain of restaurants. The Piper group. I got the area manager's job. It's temporary, but they might make me permanent if it works out.'

'That's good. How long have you been working there?'

'About five weeks. First pay cheque last Tuesday.'

'How long before you know if it's permanent?'

'They didn't say. It depends.'

'What if it doesn't work out? Do you know what you're going to do?'

He bangs down his knife and fork. 'Why do you always have to see the worst side of things?'

'I'm sorry, I didn't mean anything.'

'Our lives are just starting to get back together again and all you can see is problems.'

'No . . . I didn't mean that.'

'Eat your food. It's going cold.'

'Have you seen your mother lately?'

'Haven't had time.'

'I expect she's been missing you then.'

'She phones.'

'Don't be angry with me, Clyde.'

'I'm not angry.'

'What then?' Someone smashes a plate. I jump and drop my glass; water floods the tablecloth.

'For God's sake!' says Clyde.

I start to mop it up with the corner of my napkin but the water still spreads.

'Never mind, just leave it. The waiter will sort it out.'

'He hasn't seen.'

Clyde laughs grimly. 'Everybody's seen. For heaven's sake, just leave it. Let the waiter do it. That's what they're paying him for.' Clyde signals to him and he hurries over.

'My hands were shaking,' I explain.

Clyde puts his hand on my knee to silence me. I shrink from his touch.

'Would you like me to replace the tablecloth?' the waiter asks.

Clyde shakes his head. 'It's all right. We'll be leaving soon.'

The waiter lets the worst of the water soak into a sponge. Then he disappears again.

'Clyde . . .'

She can't talk to him any more. She doesn't know what to say. Has she ever felt at ease with him? Strange to live with someone, yet feel so foreign in their presence.

Foreign. That's what I am. A foreigner.

It's her fault.

I was eighteen when I married him.

It's her fault they are strange to one another. She keeps herself to herself. Hides things deep. Doesn't know how to share.

'I'm sorry,' I say to him.
'It doesn't matter, it was only water. It will dry.'
'No, I didn't mean that.'
'What then?'
'I don't know.'

See? She doesn't talk to him. Doesn't know how. She twists her tongue around the words she wants to say, but she never manages to string them all together.

He doesn't talk to me.

They don't talk to each other. Might as well be living far apart.

'What will happen when I leave the hospital?'
'What do you mean?'
'What will we do?'
'It will be all right,' he says. 'We'll do the same as we've always done.'

That's what she's afraid of.

236

Chapter Thirty-Seven

Gloria is leaving the ward. She's creeping through the door as the last nurse on the early shift reports for duty. I put my purse in my pocket and I follow her.

She moves stealthily, looking out for signs of pursuit. She sees me but there's no acknowledgement; she's too intent on getting out. She goes down some steps and takes a hidden corridor, one that winds along the basement. We pass yards of piping and the clanking drowns the tapping of our feet. It's hot down here and the musty air catches in my throat. No sign of anyone but us. In the furthest corner, barely visible, there is another staircase. We climb and surface. Through the last exit. Out.

We are dazzled by the winter sun. Blinking, breathless, we stand still for just a moment. Then Gloria moves on. I pick up speed and soon we are walking side by side. Now we are behind the hospital. The red brick building towers round us. They're demolishing the walkways. Swinging demolition balls. Cranes. The crash of rubble as it tumbles round us. Dust, thickly rising. I begin to cough.

Gloria raises a hand to silence me. We must be careful not to draw attention to ourselves. It is as if our craziness is visible, as if the world can tell with just a look.

Past the building work there's a fence to climb. My legs and back are agile but my skewed sense of distance slows me down. I miss my footing, grazing my elbow on a post. Gloria stoops and cups her hand. I place my foot in the stirrup that it forms, haul myself up and drop on the other side, losing my balance moment-arily on landing. Gloria is taller than me and has less far to reach and fall but age impedes her and she struggles. I catch her arm and worry that we will land together in a messy heap but she pulls herself up, then down and starts to laugh. 'Lucky I put my baggy pants on,' she says as she dusts herself down.

I don't ask where we're going. Gloria hurries on, no longer pausing for breath. 'You still on a section?' she asks after a moment or two.

'Only for another day or two, Dr Raines says.'

'They'll still call the police.'

I nod.

'I just want a little bit of time away from the ward, that's all I want.'

'Me too,' I say to her.

'All right,' she concedes, with a sigh. 'They won't give me a free pass, you know. Should have brought a coat.'

She's wearing a large jacket, so she must mean me, but I'm too excited to be cold.

'Maybe you don't feel it now but it'll hit you later on.' She sheds the jacket quickly to reveal a cardigan which she takes off. 'Wear this,' she says. It's in rainbow wool, little flecks of colour, reds and blues and greens.

'No, it's all right,' I say to her.

'Come on, I'm not going to miss it. Take it, Merle.'

I put it on. 'Are we going to get a bus?'

'In a while. Once the heat dies down.'

We are Bonnie and Clyde, Butch and Sundance, Thelma and Louise all rolled into one. 'Are they searching for us then?'

'Maybe. Can't take the risk.'

'Then what are we going to do?'

'Stay here a while, behind the bins. I done it before. It always works, don't worry.'

We crouch behind the containers. They reek of stale cabbage leaves and rotting fish. Gloria puffs a little.

'Are you OK?' I ask.

'Just a little rheumatism in my knee,' she says. 'It'll be all right.'

We fall silent. I look down at the cardigan. It still glows red and green and blue. Proper colours now.

'You got a watch?' asks Gloria after a while.

I shake my head.

'What time you think it is?'

I can't even guess.

'Never mind, don't matter all that much. Just want to make sure we don't run into the OT team coming on duty.'

She knows everything about the workings of the unit. Every coming and going, all accurately measured. I give a nod of respect for her observation skills. 'How long do we have to wait here?'

'Not that long. Just enough time to let them look for us outside and then go back.'

'Is that what they'll be doing now?'

Gloria nods. 'Both on a section so that's what they'll do.'

I feel in my pocket. 'Do you want a cigarette?'

'Don't smoke. I prefer my food: chocolate. Ice cream. Ginger pudding.'

'Will they see my smoke?'

'No, it'll be OK.'

Gloria knows everything. I nod and try not to mind that I am sitting in a patch of damp.

I have two cigarettes before Gloria decides it's safe to emerge. We wander through the back streets, past the high street shops and across the supermarket car park. Here, we catch a bus, the first one that comes along.

'How much is the fare?' I say to her.

Gloria doesn't answer, she just asks the driver what it costs to go to the end of the route. She pays for both of us. I try to give her some money but she waves it aside. 'Hold on to it for now. Maybe we will need it later on,' she says to me.

We go upstairs and slide into the front seat. I am on the inside. I feel a little squashed. The bus starts the slow trek out.

'Where are we going?' I ask.

Gloria shrugs.

'Go on, tell me,' I say to her.

'Don't know where we're going. Just wherever it takes us.'

'No plan?'

'No plan,' she replies.

I hope it's somewhere nice. The end of the route sounds a long way off.

'If they don't know where we're going, they won't know where to find us,' Gloria states.

I see the logic of it and light another cigarette.

'You're not supposed to smoke on here,' says Gloria, but her tone sends a message of approval.

'What time is it?' she asks again.

I pull back the sleeve of the cardigan to reveal the empty space where a watch should be.

'I forgot,' she says. 'You cold yet?'

I touch the front of the cardigan. 'Warm colours,' I reply.

She laughs. The sound reverberates around the bus.

It is a long journey. 'Should have bought some chocolate before we set off,' she says to me. 'Got a can of orange sparkle?'

'Like a rabbit out of a hat,' I reply. Where would I be keeping a can of orange drink?

She shakes her head slowly to let me know I've failed her and kicks the boards beneath the front window with her toe. I watch the scuff marks form. A middle-aged vandal. It's a novelty.

'All change,' the driver says. We are the only two passengers left on the bus. We hurry down the stairs. 'Where are we?' Gloria asks the man as we get off.

'Asda,' he says and he turns the bus around and drives away.

'Asda?' I look at Gloria.

'Place named after supermarkets now?' she says.

We are standing on a wasteground with nothing in sight but a high-rise housing estate and the Asda store. All around us are signs of things half finished. Holes dug and fenced in. Table-sized tree stumps. But nothing being built.

'Might as well get some chocolate,' says Gloria.

We eat it as we sit on a wall and wait for another bus. 'There's water down there,' I say to her. I'm looking across the landscape beyond the tower blocks. I see the sun reflecting off the mud-banked river. 'Come on,' I say to Gloria.

'Wait,' she calls to me, but all I want to do is reach the riverside and see a fish. I scramble down the hillside and try to forge a path as the crow flies but within minutes I am blocked by no-through roads and fences. I peer through the wire mesh, searching for a route, but all I can see are washing lines, stretched loosely over balconies.

I run back to the bus stop where Gloria's still waiting. 'Did we miss it?'

'No, not yet.'

I take my seat beside her again. She hands back the half-drunk can of orangeade that she's been guarding for me.

'Are we going back to the hospital?' I ask.

'Eventually.'

'But what in the meantime?'

'What do you want to do?'

'I don't know,' I say quickly, trying to ward off the fear that decision-making strikes in me. It's been so long since there were choices.

'Think of something,' Gloria persists.

'Well, we're going to catch the bus.'

'After that. What do you want to do? What would be good?'

'Find a fish.'

Gloria laughs. 'What sort of fish? A battered fish with chips?'

'A swimming fish.'

'OK, if that's what you want.'

The bus comes. The driver is from the Caribbean too. I feel relieved. It's a good sign, like the fish would be if we could find one. Boys in leather jackets run up to the top deck and grab the front seats so we sit at the back and watch the Asda store recede.

'Is this the same number bus we got before?'

Gloria shrugs. 'Don't know. But it goes to the river. The driver's nice. He said he'll put us off when we reach there.'

I'm feeling tired and my head is starting to ache, but I don't tell Gloria. I don't want to spoil things. 'We missed our medication,' I say to her.

'You feel all right?'

'Not so bad,' I answer, but I am scared inside. Dr Raines said if I fail to take the tablets, he won't answer for the consequences. What does it mean? Perhaps my hair will fall out or my head will mutate into something twice the size. 'What will happen?' I ask Gloria.

'About what?'

'Missing the medication.'

'Maybe you're going to feel a little funny but most likely skipping one or two doses won't make no difference.'

'Do you feel OK?'

'I feel fine, darling,' she answers with a smile.

'Yo, upstairs! This is the stop you want,' the driver shouts, so we hurry down.

'What's the name of this place?' asks Gloria, phrasing her question in a way that's likely to get us a proper answer.

'Greenwich,' he says.

'Greenwich,' Gloria repeats. 'You sure?'

I nudge her. Of course he's sure, he probably drives the route every day. But he only grins at Gloria and winks at me before he pulls away.

'Must be time for dinner,' Gloria says.

'We've just had the chocolate.'

'It's not the same.' So we buy fish and chips and sit in the park.

'You sure this is not the kind of fish you want?' says Gloria. 'Save us a lot of looking.'

'I'm sure,' I answer, as I stuff chips in my mouth.

'Your appetite's come back.'

'Sometimes it's easy for me to eat.'

'All the time for me,' she answers sadly.

'Can we climb the hill?'

'What for?'

'The view.'

'It's a long way up.'

'But worth it, Gloria.'

'If you say so, Merle.'

For the first time, I feel like I have energy inside me. I scramble up quickly, barely feeling the climb. But Gloria is slow; she pauses frequently and fights for breath.

'You can wait here if you want,' I call to her, before we're half-way up.

'No, I'll follow you. I'll just take it slow.'

It's a cold day and although I'm warmed by the climb, my fingers are numb. I put my hands in the pockets of the cardigan and they start to tingle, sharp and prickly beneath my skin. I like the feeling. It's been so long since I've been able to recognize and name the ordinary things.

I reach the Observatory and spread below is the river and all the sights of London ranged behind: the flashing concrete of Canary Wharf and way beyond, the smoke-grey roundness of St Paul's. The metal spines of the Millennium Dome stand up like the prickles of a porcupine and glisten in the sun and way below, tiny cranes sway, reach up and fall again.

The Maritime Museum suddenly stands out. I remember being taken there while I was still at school. I saw submarines and sailing boats in miniature but there was not a slave ship anywhere in sight. I look at the horizon and I know that I will always be a tourist here. The vastness of it overwhelms me. I've lost all sense of place. As I stare across the Thames, every speck of detail leaps towards me: background, foreground, sky and river all assume the same proportions; birds and buildings are identical in scale. All sound stops. It's as if I am suspended in a single moment, mesmerized and motionless.

'I can't see,' I say aloud.

'It's all right,' answers Gloria. She puts her arm around me and we walk away. I don't dare to look back.

'We must find a fish,' she says.

We go to the pier. Boats carry tourists to the Tower even in the winter months. I stare at the timetable pinned to the board, trying to work out how long the journey takes.

'Do you want to go for a ride?'

'No,' I say to her. 'I just like looking.'

We stroll along the walkway and take the steps down to the shore. I know without looking that there will be no fish. The water is grey. Mud-filled. Chocked. Nothing swimming here.

'It's all right, it doesn't matter.'

'Don't hurt to have a look,' says Gloria.

We walk towards the edge, but before our feet can touch the water, a pink fish with yellow fins skies towards us, weaving in and out of the clouds. I point upwards, but it has already gone. 'Did you see?' I ask.

She shakes her head. 'What?' she says.

'Nothing, it's OK,' I answer her.

We catch another bus. It is empty but for us. Gloria leans back and shuts her eyes. I think she is asleep. Then suddenly she turns to me and says, 'We never going to get out of that damn place you know, if we don't start acting normal.'

She doesn't know what normal is.

'No voices?'

'No voices.'

I rest my head against her shoulder. It feels nice. 'No skipping,' I say to her.

'Eating up your greens.'

'Acting like a grown up,' I add.

'Not biting the nurses.'

'Toeing the line.'

'Being happy.'

'But not too happy, Gloria. Happiness in moderation.'

'No singing?'

'No singing.'

'It's going to be hard.'

I sigh. 'I don't think I can do it just like that. The voices won't just go away and I can't control the other things . . . the things I see that other people don't.'

'No one knows what things you see or hear unless you tell them. Can't see inside your head.'

The idea is new to me, and a little frightening. 'I'll have to think about it.'

'True. It's going to need a lot of thought.'

The hospital looms into view. Gloria takes me by the hand. I am warm in the multi-colour cardigan. She starts to sing. 'One last time,' she says.

I don't know the words but as we walk up the steps, I hum, loudly, soaring with her to the high notes.

Chapter Thirty-Eight

Get a lecture from the nurses. Have to go to the duty room and stand in front of Don and Lou. They give me all this talk about responsibility, how I took another patient off the unit and threatened her recovery. They say I let them down, and behaved like an eight-year-old. Funny thing, they think I care. But I remember the talk I had with Merle and I twist my face until it has a look of penitence. I even let the word sorry slip past my lips.

I decide I need a bath. The only privacy I get in this damn place is in the bathtub with the door shut tight and locked. There's no colour here, just cold white tiles and a little stool with cork fixed on the top. The window is frosted glass so no one can see in but it's so thick you don't get no feel of sunlight. I like to bath in the afternoon when everybody else is watching television or painting pictures that are supposed to show your life. Some of the other patients make soft toys in the occupational therapy room but I don't see no point in it. Stuffing kapok up the backside of a dog don't do much for my mental health. Louise never lets me bath this time of day so I don't bother asking her, but Hilary don't mind. She says it keeps me off the streets. It irks me, you know, that I have to ask permission for every little thing I want to do.

The water is almost cold now but it don't bother me. The bubbles have gone flat too, so I imagine I'm a film star in a bath in Hollywood where the foam's so thick and deep you never see a trace of nakedness.

There is a crack in the ceiling that stretches from corner to corner and spreads out in thin lines like a spider web. Nothing to do in here but contemplate. I stretch out my foot and wince at the pain that shoots through my knee. Never thought I'd start to get decrepit. Pity you can't trade in an old body for a brand new style. I would get another one in black but it would have long legs and a smaller arse.

It's quiet in here and you don't get interruption unless you stay too long. If they don't see your face for a while they start to get jumpy in case you drowned or hanged yourself. Never been a suicidal person though, not even when I'm low. This life is for living. Fat chance I got of living stuck in here.

Have to haul myself out of here real soon or Louise will be bursting in to give me artificial respiration. They never get the towels white in here, you know, they only have a yellow shade of grey. In my bathroom at home I have matching towels in dark pink that tone against the sky blue walls. Josie chose the style. I would have gone for red but you don't often see red towels, it's not a bathroom colour Josie said. She was pretty big on convention some of the time. She rubbed my corners off. Seems like my corners got stuck back on again once she was gone.

A knock at the door makes me jump. Don't get any peace in here, that's for sure. 'Are you in there, Gloria?'

It's Hilary. Perhaps she thinks I've fallen down the plughole. 'Yes,' I answer in a weary tone.

'You've got a visitor.'

'A visitor? You sure?'

'Quite sure. Hurry up, she's waiting for you in the day room.'

It's a mistake, it has to be, but I towel myself so quick the clothes I put on my back cling tight. I let the water out but don't bother wiping round the bath. I had to wipe it round before it was fit to use, so I don't see why I have to do it twice. I try to think who the visitor could be, but no one knows I spend my time in here. When they asked about next of kin, I told them there was no one they could contact for me.

I hurry to the day room and for a moment, I think that it's Josie sitting there. It's like the time I thought she was in the gym on the day of the bring-and-buy. But the visitor rises to greet me and I see that it is Emilie.

This is the first time I have ever noticed a family likeness. She and Josie are sisters for true. The eyes are the same, and the nose, and the way the wrinkles gather on the forehead.

'Hello Gloria,' she says to me, but I am tongue-tied and I just stare at her.

Eventually I ask, 'Who told you I am in this place?'

'I went round to your house. One of your neighbours told me you got put in here for making a nuisance of yourself. It was in the local paper, apparently. And the incident at the shopping centre.'

Never occurred to me that I got my fifteen minutes of fame out of them old ladies' hats. Pity I never thought to get the paper for myself. Could have had a scrapbook and everything. Yet I feel embarrassed too that Emilie should hear the news.

'Do you want a cup of tea?' I say to her.

'You can get tea here?'

'They let us make it in the kitchen.'

'Don't go to any trouble.'

'No trouble,' I say to her. 'You can come if you want.'

She follows me through the kitchen door. 'It doesn't seem too bad here, I suppose, though this ward could do with some upgrading.'

'It's OK.'

'How are they treating you?'

'OK.'

'Do you know when they'll be discharging you?'

'Soon,' I say to her. 'Very soon now.'

'Do you have a date?'

'Any day now, it's bound to be.'

She gives me this look which says she knows they have locked the door and thrown away the key. Emilie always did see the gloomy side of things.

I boil up the tea and put it in a clean cup that don't have no ring around it. Emilie is very particular about that kind of thing. I get myself a cup of juice and we walk back to the day room. We get the window seats. Outside, a man tidies up the lawn, gathering the leaves and putting them in a burner. It smells sweet. Even though the sun has gone, I wish I was outside. Didn't value fresh air so much when I always had it.

'Why have you come here?' I say to Emilie.

She takes a deep breath and then she says, 'I don't know. For Josie, I suppose.'

'What do you mean?'

She hesitates and then she says, 'You remember the day I came to the house and took away those things?'

I don't speak, just nod my head.

'Perhaps I shouldn't have done that.' She's silent for a moment, then she says, 'You know, grief takes people in different ways. I wanted to have something of Josie. Do you understand?'

'You only had to ask.'

'I was angry, about you and her, and the way you'd taken her away from us.'

'I never took her away. We just couldn't stay, not after the way everybody treated us.'

'You took her away, Gloria. She left her family.'

'You drove her out.'

'This is getting us nowhere. I didn't come here to fall out with you again.'

'Then why?'

'Because when I went through the things Josie had, I saw how much she cared for you.'

I remember what she took from me: personal things from the drawers; letters, cards, mementos. Photographs.

'I've brought them back. They're not really mine.' She unzips the large bag at her side and puts the contents on the table. All the things I was afraid I'd lost.

'She made a will, you know.'

'A will? Josie made a will? She never told me this.'

'There's a letter for you from her solicitor. He said he posted it to you.'

'Must still be at the house – haven't been there in a while.'

'She had some money from my parents when they died. You know about that?'

I nod. Her share of the proceeds from the sale of their house. Several thousand pounds.

'She left it to you. Everything. It's all legal, they tell me.'

Thought I would lose our house. Now that I am on my own, I am struggling with the payment on the mortgage. All my savings already been eaten up. Thought everything would get taken away from me. 'She made a will?' I say again.

Emilie gives this sigh, like it hurts her to repeat it. 'Yes, there was a will. Josie was always organized and she didn't leave things to chance.'

Not like me. I leave things to chance every opportunity I get. I'm not a planning person. This was a bone of contention with the two of us. Once she left me for it, but she still came back. She said she'd got too used to me over the years just to give up on everything. 'And this is what you come here to say to me?'

Emilie nods.

For a while, I don't get it. Then suddenly I see she's feeling guilty now. She's feeling guilty about how she treated the two of us and for stealing Josie's things. And about me ending up in this damn place. She's feeling guilty about everything.

And for a moment, I want to make her suffer for all the grief she's caused. But I'm tired of aggravation, all the fretting and the misery. Emilie's not so important any more.

'OK,' I say to her, and I get up. 'Thank you for coming to see me.'

'I was glad to. It's what Josie would have wanted.'

I take her cup from her and put it on the table. 'I'll see you out,' I say, as if I'm in my own home. 'The weather has been good these last few days,' I observe as we walk down the corridor.

'Yes, it has been good for the time of year.'

We continue this politeness right to the door. And as I open it to let her leave, I snatch the hat off the top of her head and run with it, I run and run, can't help myself, and I'm laughing all the way.

Chapter Thirty-Nine

They let me spend a weekend with Clyde. It's part of my rehabili-
tation. Hilary sits beside me on my bed. 'We'll give your
medication to Clyde when he comes. That way, you won't have
to worry about whether you've taken it or not.'

'I can remember.'

'Well, maybe you can, but it isn't really worth the risk, is it? If
Clyde's got it you can just relax and concentrate on having a good
weekend.'

'I'm not stupid.'

'No, of course you're not. It's just that you're recovering from
a very serious illness and we want to ensure that everything goes
smoothly. Now, you know you can come straight back here if
being away seems too much for you?'

I nod. I'm going home for one night. From lunchtime on Saturday until teatime on Sunday. I walked and talked and kept
myself in order before coming here so I think I can manage it
again – it's only been a few weeks. 'I'll be OK,' I say to Hilary.
'I'm not on a section any more.'

'No, you've done really well. As I think Dr Raines has said to you, we feel that as long as you're prepared to stay as a voluntary patient until you're fit to be discharged, there's no need for the section to be extended.'

I put a book inside my weekend bag. When is a voluntary patient not a voluntary patient? I ask myself. Perhaps there's no such thing.

'Don't forget, if you start to feel bad, you can ring the ward.'

'I'll be OK. I can do a lot more than I was able to do even a few days ago. I can concentrate to read now, like I used to. I'm almost all right again.'

'Yes, but you must remember that it might seem strange to you at first, being away from the ward.'

It does seem strange. Clyde takes my arm and leads me from the car up to the house. He lets us both in. I watch as he deactivates the alarm. The numbers that he punches in are unfamiliar. 'Did you change it?' I say to him.

'No.'

'It was five-two-eight-one. Remember?'

'I must have changed it then. Does it matter?'

'What if I'd come home? I would have set it off.'

'You wouldn't have come home without me knowing.'

'I might have done. I might have wanted a break from being at the unit.'

'The doctors said you weren't allowed to leave the ward so I knew you wouldn't be here. What's the matter? You know the new number now.'

'Only because I looked. You didn't tell me. How will I remember it?'

'I'll write it down for you, OK? Don't get so agitated, it's no big deal. I wasn't trying to keep you out or anything. Just sit down, I'll make us both some coffee. I got some of those biscuits you like.' He's protective, solicitous. Feeling guilty, perhaps, about everything that's happened. I look around once he's gone into the kitchen. The house seems smaller than it was when I left. My sense of scale keeps shifting. I get up and walk round the front room, trying to locate myself. Am I really home? It seems unfamiliar.

The bookcase that stood against the far wall has been shifted to a space beside the door. And the sofa is closer to the fireplace. 'Why have things been moved?' I call to Clyde, trying to keep my voice steady.

Clyde comes back into the room carrying a tray. 'No reason,' he says. 'I just felt like a change.'

He is taking away the sameness of things, the patterns I have built for myself. Tearing them down. I can't survive when the outside is unfamiliar. He is making things strange because he wants to be rid of me so he can have his other wife. 'You should have kept it all the same,' I say to him.

'I'll move it back if you want.' He looks at me critically, as if there's something wrong with me.

'No, it's all right,' I answer. I stare at the sofa, hoping that there's no further meaning in its new positioning. I can't decipher the patterns now. I don't know how to understand what's happening. My legs begin to shake, so I sit down again and cross them tightly at the ankles. Clyde sits down beside me. He passes me some strawberry creams. They lie thickly on the plate. I try to see messages in the way they are arranged but the significance of it slips away from me. Clyde removes one just as I am starting to see the shape of it. I can't tell him to put it back. He won't replace it exactly as it was. I have no control over anything here. It is as if I'm a visitor in my own house. I want to walk around again, go upstairs perhaps, but it doesn't feel as if I can without his permission.

'Well, at least you're home,' he says.

Does that mean he's glad I'm here? I don't know how to interpret what he tells me any more.

'What do you want to do? We could go out this afternoon if you feel up to it.'

'No, I just want to stay here.' If we go out, there will be more things to understand. System overload.

'I need to get someone to check out the car on Monday. Did you hear that noise it was making? The garage was meant to fix it last time round.'

I didn't hear it. Why didn't I pick it out? Why is it that some sounds get through to me and others don't? 'Can't we do something together?' I say to him.

'Like what? I said we could go out but you said no.'

'I mean do something here.'

He looks exasperated, as if I can't make up my mind. 'All right,' he says, 'if that's what you want. What sort of thing?'

'I don't know. Talk for a while.'

'We could listen to some music.' He gets up and puts on a CD:

Ice T. He always plays it. The words circle in my head: bitches; whores; dirty little girls who need to be kept in line. How many times must I have heard it? It seeps inside me.

'Turn it off,' I say.

'What?'

'Turn it off, Clyde. I don't want to listen to that.'

'Why not? You always listen.'

'I don't like the words.'

'The words don't mean anything. It's the sound. The rhythm.'

'Please turn it off.'

He looks at me as if I'm crazy but he changes the CD. The sound of Shabba Ranks fills the house.

'I didn't get any food for dinner time. I thought you'd want to go out.'

'It's OK, I'm not really hungry.'

'We'd better have sandwiches.'

'If you want.'

'Then you can have your tablets. The doctor said they should be taken before meals.'

'It doesn't really matter when I take them.'

'Look, why don't we go out? You'll feel better, it'll take you out of yourself.'

'No, I don't want to.'

'Come on Merle. How are you going to get better if you just mope around all the time? Let's go for a drive somewhere, get a bite to eat, catch a film or something later.'

'No, I don't want to see a film. Can't we just stay here?'

'Going out will do you more good than stopping in. Why don't you get changed? Dress yourself up a bit. You'll feel better for it. Wear your brown top and skirt, the one with the blue in it. You always look good in that. Your boots are in the cupboard.'

'Can't I stay in what I'm wearing now?'

He looks me up and down with a steady eye, appraising my jeans and my purple T-shirt. He doesn't like me to wear trousers; he says they make me look too thin, like a boy. He likes me to look feminine.

'I think you should get changed. That T-shirt needs a wash.'

I try to keep clean, but in hospital it's hard. At first I didn't bother, but now I do, it seems important. Sometimes, though, I don't remember to put my clothes in the washing machine and I have to wear the same thing twice. I'm ashamed of my dirtiness. I go upstairs. The brown and blue skirt with matching top are laid out on the bed. He knew exactly how he wanted me to look before he'd even got me home. I change into them slowly. I am not me in these clothes. I am his other wife.

He takes us to a café on the outskirts of town. No one knows us here. At first, I am relieved but then I start to realize he's ashamed of me. He hands me my tablets under the table and watches as I slip them surreptitiously into my mouth. He puts his hand on mine to stop me shaking as I cut my meat. He tells me to wipe the food from the side of my face in an anxious whisper, as if he can no longer bear the sight of me.

We walk round the market on our way home but he keeps his distance from me. I try to catch up, but each time he quickens his stride and I lose him again. He only seems aware of me when I make a mistake. When I touch the fabric on the stall to feel the colours in it, he pulls me away; when I drop my money as I buy some fish he scrambles to pick it up before anyone can see what I've done. It's hard to understand what's happening. He's treating me as if I'm made of broken glass, pieces missing, scattered. This doesn't feel like being home. Or maybe I've forgotten how it used to be.

When we get back, he watches television for a while. I curl up on the sofa and try to read a book. The words don't get through. Why are there so many barriers, so much that doesn't reach me? I look at Clyde. He's leaning back in the chair, his feet on the coffee table. The remote control remains in his hand. He zaps from one channel to another restlessly. Am I the source of his anxiety? What is it that he wants from me? He's ordered a takeaway. He's chosen chicken korma and pilau rice for me and he has beef madras with naan bread and popadoms. He eats his rapidly, while I pick at mine. I wanted to cook the fish but he said it would be too much for me and I'd end up spoiling it.

I put off going to bed, even though my eyes are closing. I don't want to sleep alone; I've become accustomed to the sounds of the dormitory, the steady breathing in and out that constantly surrounds me. But I also fear the closeness of lying in a bed beside another person, feeling the warmth of their body, the softness of it, the joy and terror of being held. Clyde begins to end the day; he draws the curtains, bolts the door, tells me to go up and get undressed while he sets the alarm. I get into bed and lie still, my body wrapped inside the covers. I am losing myself. Everything that's me is being sucked away.

She has to learn to keep herself.

The words force themselves inside my head. It's been quiet for days but now the sounds are back again.

She doesn't have to do everything he wants her to.

He gives me structure, tells me what is happening. With Clyde, I know what to do. Yet when he comes to bed, I keep myself in my own small space and stop him touching me. And in the morning, when we rise, I put on my purple T-shirt and my jeans.

Chapter Forty

I flick open the exercise book they gave me. The paper is the cheap, absorbent kind that makes the ink spread. I haven't noticed this before. The ruled lines are too narrow for my long style of writing. It's a wonder anyone's been able to read it. I suck the end of my pen and try to concentrate. What should I tell them? What do they want to hear? I look over previous entries in this diary. Ramblings, mostly. They seem incriminating now, evidence of scrambled thoughts. How can I put my mind in order? Once, I didn't need to think about it, order happened of its own volition.

There are too many possibilities and yet at the same time, nothing I want to say. I picture the staff in the duty room, poring over my words, trying to get inside my head. And what will I learn about them in the process? Yet there is a part of me that wants to convey something of myself to somebody. My isolation makes me safe but it is my prison too.

Gloria asks if I want to play cards. I join her for a while in a game of rummy but it's difficult to keep my mind on it. When will my concentration be back to normal? Is it the medication or is it something else?

'Weekends are too quiet,' says Gloria.

'But at least we don't get made to do things all the time.' I get bored with cards after a while, so we switch to Scrabble. Gloria tries to cheat – she hides most of the As beneath the cardboard box and uses them whenever she needs one.

I want to spell out cracker so I say to her, 'Pass me one of those As you've got down there, will you?'

She bursts out laughing and she says, 'A week or two ago you'd never have noticed. It's good, you know. You getting more . . . you know.'

We never use words like sick or well. It's part of a tacit agreement between us. I look across to my bed. There's a new patient and she's got hold of my notebook. She's torn out some of the pages and she's crumpling them into little balls. I feel obliged to go and salvage them, though I think she has the right idea.

I rub my fist across the rescued pages. I hate creases. Clyde once bought me a linen suit which crumpled as soon as I put it on. The creases were such a source of irritation that I could hardly bear the sight of it. Neatness was important to me then. Still is, I suppose. It is the outward sign of an order that constantly eludes me. I gaze at the blank pages pressed out in front of me and wish again that I could order my thoughts, really order them, give them form and structure. Maybe the staff would see this as a sign of wellness. But how do I begin to give shape to the chaos that is bumping round my head? I suck my pen again and try to concentrate.

Food eaten today. I underline it. They want me to keep a list of everything I eat the way that Alex does. I think it is meant to be proof that I'm able to look after myself. Food eaten today. Perhaps I should give it capitals – it is a kind of title. Food Eaten Today. Sugar puffs with milk. Toast and Marmalade. Tea.

I remember talking to Alex about food words and the way they look and sound. She said that milkshake was an upper case word when she saw it in her head. MILKSHAKE. She said there were all kinds of fat words. Bowl. That was fat. *Bulbous*. B words make you think of size. Crisp is a skinny word. I'm losing concentration again. That's the trouble with being in hospital. Once, I could have polished off a task like this in a few short minutes. Now, even the simplest thing is taking all the energy I have. What else did I eat? Fish pie for lunch. Followed by fruit tart with custard, except that I never eat custard, not even when I'm in a really good frame of mind, so I left it. Will they see this as a sign that I'm not prepared to eat enough? Perhaps I should write it down anyway, as if I did eat it. Who's to know? Then in the afternoon there was tea and a biscuit. This evening I had some kind of casserole with rice. And an apple afterwards. That sounds healthy. Responsible.

Louise comes in and peers over my shoulder. 'How's it going?' she says.

'Look.' I show her the list.

'This isn't what you're meant to be doing.'

'You said to write about what I've eaten.'

'That was one possible option. And I didn't mean you to list every item. I was using the idea as an example, you were meant to write about how you feel right now, and about what's happening to you and how you view your time on the unit.'

'Oh. Nothing about food then? I thought I was supposed to do the same as Alex.'

'She shouldn't be writing lists, that's not what this is about.'

'What is it about?'

'It's about communication. It's intended to help you to express yourself.'

'I am expressing myself.'

'No, you're not. There are no feelings here. We want to know what goes on inside you.' Louise gets up to go. 'Try to listen more carefully to what's said to you. Then maybe you'll really begin to get better.'

Why do they have to make everything so complicated? I open the notebook again. What do I feel?

I begin to write: *I can't seem to understand what you want from me*. Then I cross it out. They don't like you to use can't. They're always saying there's no such thing as can't and that we have to take responsibility for our actions. *I don't understand*. That sounds better. Then I cross that out too and put: *You're always confusing me*. But that sounds hostile, defiant. They don't like defiance. How about: *I wish I understood what I'm supposed to do* . . . No, that's wrong as well. It sounds whining. And it makes it seem as if the fault is mine alone. I go back to 'can't'. I ought to be able to have any words I want. This is meant to be my notebook.

What else? I know what I want to say but it is hard to think it, let alone to write it down. But I want them to know, and this is easier than saying it. I don't want to go home to Clyde. The words jump out of the page. I have to go back there. What other home do I have? I cross it out and write: If I go home to Clyde I will lose myself again. No, I can't put that. It doesn't sound right. They'll say I'm not sounding well again. How can I phrase it? I think it would be better for me if I lived on my own for a while, not with Clyde. Yes, that's OK, it sounds as if I'm taking responsibility, not blaming anyone. Is this the sort of thing they want me to write? No feelings in it yet. I hate all the stuff you make me do. I didn't mean to write that. They'll say I'm feeling aggressive. And the hate bit sounds childish. They'll just go on and on about how angry I am, the way they do with all of us. OK, start again. When I first came into hospital, I thought you would help me. No. When I first came into hospital, it seemed as if it was possible for me to be helped. Yes, they'll like that better. No blame attached. Now it doesn't seem possible because... It's hard to decide about this. Because...we're not on the same wavelength. What I want is different from what you want. Not too confrontational. They'll want to know where the difference lies. Do I want to tell them? I need more space to be me, things need to be done differently, although I'm not sure how. Perhaps if I was treated more like an adult...

No, it's getting an edge to it now. Keep it neutral or they won't listen. I read over what I've written. No, it's wrong. Scrub it all and start again. This is taking forever.

Gloria taps me on the back. 'Do you want anything from the shops?'

'Where are you going?'

'Just the Late Shop.'

'Will they let you?'

'They let me do a bit more now. Been behaving myself.' We grin at one another. 'Still doing the notebook?'

'I don't know what to say to them. Everything I write sounds wrong, as if there's something wrong with me.'

'I don't want to do the tape no more, but I suppose I have to keep on doing it.'

'Why?'

'Because if I stop, they're just going to tell me I'm avoiding something.'

We sigh.

'I'm trying to explain that I have to leave Clyde.' I say it quickly, forcing the words out before it seems impossible again. Then I add, 'I can't find the right way of saying it.'

Gloria sits beside me. 'You sure this is what you want? Leaving him, I mean.'

'I think so. I think I'm sure. I've lived on automatic pilot for so long that it's hard for me to know what I really want. And yet for months I've had this sense of being stifled, choked. I need to get away. I've been hiding it inside myself, too scared, if I'm honest, to really see it until now.'

'If you're sure, just write it down. *I want to leave Clyde*. No one can stop you. No one can tell you how to run your life.'

'I know. I know they can't,' I answer. Gloria stands up. She checks in her pocket for her purse. 'Can you get me a can of coke?' I ask.

'Sure,' she says.

I try to give her the money but she tells me it's her treat.

I glance through the pages I've already written. Nothing salvageable. I tear them out.

I wish I could choose who has access to this. Hilary's OK, but I don't want to show myself to any of the others. I could say no one except Hilary is meant to see it, but it doesn't work like that; confidentiality only means that things can't be made known outside the hospital. Within it, everything about me is open to everyone. But I'm determined to say the things I need to say. Always, in the past, I've fumbled for words, been unable to convey the important things. But as I write once more, the words begin to bubble up the way they did when I was telling Gloria.

I put in the bit about leaving Clyde. I have to say this sooner or later. Writing it down almost makes me think it's possible for me to lead my life without him.

Chapter Forty-One

Dr Raines says he wants to talk to me. He leads me into his room. I take the seat closest to the door. The room is hot and I'm aware that sweat is running down my nose. I hope he won't mistake it for nervousness – I want to show him that I'm stronger now. I'm wearing my smart blue skirt and I've put some make-up on. These are signs of recovery and they are valued on Ward C. I cross my legs at the knees and remember to look him in the eye. I smile a lot.

'I've brought back your book,' I say to him, placing it on the low table that stands between us.

'What did you make of it?'

'It was interesting,' I answer him though I've barely read it. I tried to look at the outline of psychotic illness but I couldn't recognize myself.

'What interested you most?'

I feel as if he's testing me on what I've read. My answers won't be satisfactory. I try to tell him what I think he wants to hear. 'I understand my illness better now.'

'Can you say more about that?'

'It's difficult to put it into words.' I need to change the subject so I ask, 'What did you want to see me about?'

'I've been looking through the most recent entries in your notebook. I see that you're thinking of leaving your husband.'

I knew Dr Raines would want me to talk about this so I've been practising the things I need to say. I'm almost word perfect now. I take a deep breath. 'I think it would be easier for me to get my life back together again if we separate for a while.'

'But you have been apart and it resulted in complete collapse.'

'Not exactly.'

'Not exactly?'

'I don't think being apart from Clyde was the cause. Not really. It was other things.'

'If your husband had been with you, we might have been able to treat you earlier, ensure that you took your medication. You were trying to cope on your own and it was impossible for you.'

'It was difficult but it would have been hard with him too.'

'It seems to me that you're not really in the right frame of mind for making major decisions. You're trying to recover from a serious mental illness. It's not the right time to be making big changes in your life.'

I try to speak calmly. 'It may not seem like the right time, but I know it's what I need to do. When I went for the meal with him, and even more when I stayed with him for a weekend, I saw all kinds of things that I've sort of been aware of but at the same time not aware of, if you know what I mean. It was as if I needed to be apart from him in order to uncover the relationship, see it as it really is.'

'That's the point I'm making. You're not able to see things as they really are at present. Your judgement has been impaired by your illness. It happens to patients who've had this kind of experience. You need to give yourself more time.'

Everything I say and do is nothing but a sign of illness to him. What right has he to tell me his way of seeing is more real than mine? I look at him steadily and say, 'You don't understand. I went into the marriage without really knowing what was right for me. I wanted someone to look after me I think. I was seventeen when I met Clyde and we got married in less than a year. I'd had no experience of anything and he'd already been through a marriage. He even had a child. I just drifted into it. And I never really thought about that until now.'

'It's not a good idea to make hasty decisions that will affect your entire future at this particular juncture. You may be one of the lucky ones who recovers completely and never experiences this type of illness again, but on the other hand, and this is the more likely scenario, you may be subject to psychotic breakdowns periodically and need regular treatment. If this is the case, you will need a great deal of support from family and friends. You can't afford to sever relationships now. Rather, you need to be building on them, really trying to make them work, as a way of safeguarding your future.'

'If I stay with Clyde, I may not have a future. We're swallowing each other up.'

'What does that mean?'

I can't keep the anger from my voice. 'It means we're not OK together any more, and I can't see us ever being OK. I could go back to him but what would be the point? I'd start to lose myself again.'

'Lose yourself?'

'That's what it feels like. I can't go back to him.'

'Where will you go?'

'I don't know.'

Dr Raines sits back in his chair in a gesture of exasperation. 'We can't discharge you if you have nothing to go back to. You must see that.'

'No, not really. I'll be OK.' I'm trying to sound calm again. He'll only see anger as another sign that I shouldn't be allowed to control my life.

'What about the practicalities? Money? A roof over your head?'

'It won't be easy, but I'll find something. Get a job.'

'Millions are unemployed. It's very hard to find work when you've had, in lay terms, a mental breakdown.'

'Yes, but it shouldn't be impossible. And who's to know if I don't tell them?'

'Do you think you're well enough to hold down a job?'

'I don't know. I'll have to wait and see.'

'My opinion is that you are not. I'm not suggesting that you'll never be ready, but you're not ready now.'

'That's your opinion.'

'It's an informed opinion, and I'm not prepared to discharge you unless you have somewhere to live. Could you stay with friends? Family?'

'No. There isn't anyone. You know that.'

'Then you must go home, at least for the time being. I have to think about what's best for you.'

'I really don't want to go home.'

'I'm sorry, but I do believe that's the best thing for you at present.'

'Please don't do this.'

'It really is for your own benefit, Merle, nothing else.'

She thinks she's strong, but she's weak as water. She's losing faith in herself; starting to believe what he's saying to her. She'll never amount to anything, she'll never do anything with her life. She should stay with Clyde, let him look after her. She'll never be able to take care of herself.

I get up to leave. There's no point in talking to him.

'Sit down, Merle.'

'No. I don't want to hear any more.'

'You're showing me that you still don't have the maturity to manage by yourself.'

Proving his point. That's all she'll ever do.

'I'm not just a patient.'

Not human. Outside everything.

'Sit down, come on,' he says again.

I stand there, unwilling to do as I am told, but afraid to leave in case it gives them grounds to keep me here. I'm aware that I'm crying. Tears of frustration. Anger beyond words.

'Try to calm down,' says Dr Raines.

I compose myself, sit down again, and smooth my smart skirt across my knee with the flat of my hand.

'That's better. You do see, don't you, that this isn't the time to be making decisions?'

I nod.

'Good. I'll talk to Clyde if you like, tell him you're a bit anxious about going home. It's understandable. This is a big step but it's the next stage in your recuperation.'

I nod again.

'I think we'll keep your medication at the same level for the time being. It seems to be having the right effect. We might think about reducing it when you're more stable.'

'I don't have the job at the café any more. They wrote and told me they couldn't keep me on after such a long absence. I didn't let them know that I was ill, you see, not until a week or two ago, so I'll be at home all day, with nothing to do.'

'You'll find that just keeping on top of things around the house will take all your energy for a while, but after a few weeks perhaps you could do some voluntary work, something that won't make too many demands on you.'

'I don't want to be in the house by myself.'

'Exactly. That's why you shouldn't be considering a separation from your husband right now.'

'That's different.'

'How?'

I can't explain it to him.

'Being back at home will seem strange initially, but you'll get used to it. And one of the community psychiatric nurses will be keeping an eye on you. If you really start to struggle, we might be able to find you a place at a day centre. Let's see how it goes.'

I feel myself dismissed. I go to the door.

'And let me say, Merle, what excellent progress you've made in this past week or two . . .'

I click the door shut, curtailing the rest of his speech.

I walk out of the main door and into the grounds. The hospital building stands tall behind me. Dull red brick. The branches of trees reflect in panes of glass and make me think of bars. I remember my father. What separates me from him? Looking back over these past weeks, I am struck by the similarities between us. I begin to understand how he needed to shape a space for himself where he was powerful and loved.

It's starting to sleet. Perhaps it will snow for Christmas. I imagine spending my first Christmas alone. I wait for the fear to start, but I feel a tinge of excitement. No turkey dinner. None of Clyde's siblings to face. No screaming children, vying for attention. I imagine the end of the year and for a fleeting moment, I see a future for myself.

Chapter Forty-Two

Don't see why you can't let me go home today now you finally decide. Why you make me wait another week? What you think it's going to prove? And why must I carry on with this tape recorder thing? You don't get tired of hearing me yet?

I took such good care of it, but the volume control got a little stuck. This is not my fault. Would have happened no matter who been using it. And the scratch on the side was there before I got it.

Looking forward to going home, you know. And I know it's better not to sing, so I'm not about to cause more trouble with the neighbours. So you can see I learnt how to behave myself from being on Ward C. As for the future, think I'll try to get myself another job. This is a good way of keeping out of trouble.

Now that I'm going, it all seems a little strange. The problem with this place is it becomes more real to you than the outside world. I know you think you'll see me back in here from time to time, but I can tell you now, I don't have no intention of getting caught in that revolving door I hear about. The only door I intend to use will set me on a straight line out of here. And it's the same for Merle. Don't assume you'll be seeing her in here again. The woman has more sense than you people give her credit for.

Chapter Forty-Three

I get up early and don't have no trouble knowing if I'm asleep or awake. Can't hardly control my excitement. Today is the day I leave the hospital.

Merle's up early too. We chat to each other as we're getting dressed. She seems a bit subdued, but even so, she manages to hold a conversation like the last few weeks don't exist for her. She puts on her best blue skirt for the outside world, the one that looks so smart and nice. I put on my red and purple dress but then I take it off again. Don't want them to look at my brightness and decide to keep me here. I change into the dress I bought the other day in honour of freedom approaching. It's a sensible shade of green, the colour Josie liked.

For once it's hard for me to get my breakfast down. Feeling all buoyed up at the thought of seeing my house again and being back in my own bed. But I force myself to stay still and try to look as if I'm feeling calm. It would make Louise's day if she had to keep me here because I don't behave myself.

Have to go to pharmacy with one of the nurses to collect my

medication. Seems to be part of the discharge ritual. Seen Mr Lemmington go through it, and Mrs Isaac too.

Merle and I follow Don through the corridors. Know every inch of this damn place by heart. It's funny, you know, but you can get so used to a place that even when you hate the sight of it a little part of you is sad to leave. Never thought to hear myself say such a thing. It just goes to show, you have to take real good care with institutions. They have cunning ways to get you every time.

Don picks up the tablets and gives me and Merle the stupid-patient lecture. 'It's vital that you keep taking these in order to stay well. And you should take them at the same time each day to get the maximum benefit. Your GP will continue to prescribe them for you. Don't think that because you've been discharged you can afford to cut down. You must keep to the required dose. Never take more than you're supposed to. As you know, there are side effects. And if you're in any doubt at all about any of this, remember, you can ring the ward.'

Me and Merle nod in unison like a pair of puppets from a children's television show. We go back to the ward to collect our belongings. Been packed since the day before yesterday. Merle don't have much, just a small bag. Wish I learnt the art of travelling light. Everybody gathers as we leave the ward and wishes us good luck. I give Alex a little cuddle. She has more meat on her now but I can still feel her bones through her fluffy sweater.

Don walks us to the main gate. 'Somebody should be collecting you, Merle.'

'Clyde's only just started a new job. He can't afford to take time off just yet. He's sending a taxi for me.'

'And what about you, Gloria?'

'Think I'm going to catch the bus.'

He hovers beside us, like he can't bear to see us get away.

'It's OK, Don,' I say to him.

He glances at his watch. Almost time for a tea break. 'All right, if you're both sure you're OK. Take care of yourselves and don't hurry back.'

We grin at him, like it's a good joke, and we watch him disappear into the hospital building. Merle breathes a sigh, as if a weight's been lifted from her. 'It's good to be out,' she says.

'Least we're not stuck in there for Christmas.'

Merle smiles. She's been doing that a lot these past few days. Makes her look a different person. 'Have you got any plans for the New Year?' she says.

'Maybe go back to Jamaica for a while. I have a little money now. Or maybe just stay here and be glad we survived. What you going to do?'

'I don't know. Perhaps I'll be with Clyde. Or with my parents. Or on my own. I just don't know.'

'Thought your parents died a long time back.'

'No, they're still alive, or at least I think they are. But no one else knows that.'

'No one's business but yours.'

'Things happened . . .'

'Don't need to tell me, you're not in group therapy no more.'

'I hope things will work out. It's odd, being out of there. Daunting.'

'This thing is over. It's *over*, Merle.'

The taxi arrives. I touch Merle's hand. 'Going to miss you,' I say to her.

I say goodbye to my Orisha and I get into the taxi to begin the journey home. They've decorated the high street. Christmas lights twinkle in the daylight. Suddenly, I lean forward. 'I want to go to Hackney,' I tell the driver. Going home can wait; there are other things to settle. The taxi pulls into a driveway and turns. Now we are in the back streets I used to know so well. I picture my mother. She'll look different. Will I recognize her? I try to make her fatter and give her greying hair but in my mind's eye, she remains the same. My father is taller, softer than he was. His fingers have lost the nervousness that made them twitch even as he slept.

The house is not the same as I remember. Not even the shrubs remain. I pay the taxi and hurry up the steps to the front door. I hesitate. Do I look different too? Will they be pleased to see me? I ring the bell.

I don't recognize the man who comes to the door. He's never heard of my father. He doesn't have a forwarding address. No happy reunion then. Perhaps it couldn't have existed outside my imagination.

I walk through the streets, trying to find something I recognize. None of the shops are the same; there's a bank where the bookshop used to be.

Stupid to have imagined that everything would be the same as when I left it. Seven years in suspended animation, my father and mother waiting for me at the door as if I'd just slipped out to buy a paper.

My father probably wouldn't have forgiven me for deserting them. Or perhaps I would have been the prodigal daughter. I don't think I'd have told them where I've been these past few weeks but perhaps I would have let them know I understand a little better. Or maybe the old feelings would have resurfaced, flooding out the new.

Where to now? I suppose I must go home to Clyde. I stop a passing taxi. It's only as I speak my destination that I realize I could go anywhere. Who is here to stop me now? Not Louise, nor Don. Not Dr Raines. Not Clyde.

The driver drops me off outside the mainline station. I'm going to catch a train. I don't know where I'll finish up. Perhaps I'll see a fish.

I watch Merle's taxi disappear from sight. I'm on my own again. It's a strange thing, going back to an empty house. But there is no sense in feeling dread about the future. It's coming anyway. And if on New Year's Eve, I have to get dead drunk to deal with it, then that's what I intend to do. Free to do it now. The curfew's come to an end.

I go over all the promises I made myself. Be your age. Watch what you say. Don't talk too loud. Never skip. Act ladylike. And I walk down the street, full of decorum. The rain feels good against my skin. Never thought I could enjoy getting wet. And, all the while, I feel the sounds in my throat: sounds of living, sounds of joy, like Josie's still beside me. And then I can't help myself; I open up my mouth and I just sing and sing.

Acknowledgements

I would like to thank the following former colleagues at Manchester Metropolitan University for their support during the writing of this book: Caroline Ukoumunne, Maria Delgado and Kate McGowan.

I would also like to thank John Thieme, Lyn Innes and Lynette Hunter for their support and encouragement in the early stages of my writing career.

Special thanks are also due to Anna Pollard, Helen Ketchell and the late Victoria McKenzie. My wonderful agent, Milly Reilly from the Jo Unwin Literary Agency, has provided invaluable assistance and advice during the republication of this novel, and Pauline Edwards has, as always, kept me going with her humour and friendship.

BLACK BRITAIN: WRITING BACK
Curated and introduced by Bernardine Evaristo

MINTY ALLEY / C. L. R. JAMES

It is the 1920s in the Trinidadian capital, and Haynes's world has been upended. His mother has passed away, and his carefully mapped-out future of gleaming opportunity has disappeared with her.

Unable to afford his former life, he finds himself moving into Minty Alley – a bustling barrack yard teeming with life and a spectacular cast of characters. In this sliver of West Indian working-class society, outrageous love affairs and passionate arguments are a daily fixture, and Haynes begins to slip from curious observer to the heart of the action.

Minty Alley is a gloriously observed portrayal of class, community and the ways in which we are all inherently connected. An undisputed modern classic, this is an exceptional story told by one of the twentieth century's greatest Caribbean thinkers.

WITHOUT PREJUDICE / NICOLA WILLIAMS

Lee Mitchell is a thirty-year-old barrister from a working-class Caribbean background: in the cut-throat environment of the courtroom, everything is stacked against her.

After she takes on the high-profile case of notorious millionaire playboy Clive Omartian – arrested along with his father and stepbrother for eye-wateringly exorbitant fraud – the line between her personal and professional life becomes dangerously blurred.

Spiralling further into Clive's trail of debauchery and corruption, she finds herself in alarmingly deep waters.

Can she survive her case, let alone win it?

BLACK BRITAIN: WRITING BACK
Curated and introduced by Bernardine Evaristo

THE FAT LADY SINGS / JACQUELINE ROY

'That is the glory of being a mental patient, nothing is impossible.'

It is the 1990s, and Gloria is living in a London psychiatric ward. She is unapologetically loud, audacious and eternally on the brink of bursting into song. After several months of uninterrupted routine, she is joined by another young black woman – Merle – who is full of silences and fear.

Unable to confide in their doctors, they agree to journal their pasts. Whispered into tape recorders and scrawled ferociously at night, the remarkable stories of their lives are revealed.

In this tender, deeply moving depiction of mental health, Roy creates a striking portrait of two women finding strength in their shared vulnerability, as they navigate a system that fails to protect them. Life-affirming and fearlessly hopeful, this is an unforgettable story.

BERNARD AND THE CLOTH MONKEY / JUDITH BRYAN

When Anita finally returns to London after a long absence, everything has changed.

Her father is dead, her mother has disappeared and she and her sister Beth are alone together for the first time in years.

They share a house. They share a family. They share a past.

Tentatively, they reach out to each other for connection, but the house echoes with words unspoken. Can they confront the pain of the past together?

Dazzling and heart-breaking, *Bernard and the Cloth Monkey* is a shattering portrait of family, a rebellion against silence and a testament to the human capacity for survival.